FOOLS

A LICKING THICKET NOVEL

LUCY LENNOX

MAY ARCHER

Cover Art: Cate Ashwood Designs

Editing: One Love Editing

Beta Reading: Leslie Copeland

1

TUCKER

2-DOWN: Fallacy; hallucination (8 letters)

"Doc Wright?" my office manager called. "Hey, Tuck, ya got a visitor! Where'd you get to?"

I froze, pencil in my hand and crossword book on my knee, glasses sliding down my nose, half an unchewed mint Milano cookie between my teeth, a thirty-six-year-old picture of guilt.

I reached up and flipped off the light on my headlamp.

Vienna Goodley had one of those voices that carried — as in, through the walls of my medical practice on the ground floor of the old Victorian and up the stairs to my apartment, down Walnut Street and over the highway, southwest as far as Nashville, and east to the Smokies. She was lovely and kind and terrifyingly efficient, but the way she yelled made vases tremble and cracks appear in the enamel of my teeth.

Still, I couldn't exactly fire her. For one thing, I genuinely liked her most of the time. For another thing, I hadn't ever really *hired* her. I'd just sort of inherited her when I bought the practice from Doc Thorne before he and his wife retired to Cape Coral a couple of years back, and I'd found it easier not to question things.

My first morning in the house, I'd stepped out of the shower dressed only in a towel and found her coming out of the utility room off the kitchen in my private living area carrying an enormous wrench.

"Mornin', Tuck! I'm Vienna Goodley, your office manager," she'd said cheerily, once I'd peeled my testicles off the ceiling and finished screaming. "I remember you from when you were a little boy. Noticed the hot water pressure was a little wonky, so I fixed it for ya."

I hadn't known it then, but this was Vienna's MO: she identified a problem, and she solved it, by God. And she preferred to ask for forgiveness rather than permission.

Most of the time, this was a wonderful thing. She'd managed my bookkeeping and dealt with insurance hassles. She'd enforced a flawless scheduling system for patient appointments, working with my receptionist, Annie, that helped me run more efficiently *and* guarded my personal time for fishing and volunteering. She gave practical advice, and always made extra roast beef on Sundays so I could have her leftovers.

But there were also times when her take-charge attitude was less wonderful. Like the time she'd cleared my pantry of refined sugar (an incident I privately referred to as the Great Cookie Massacre of 2017), or the many times she'd leaned over my shoulder to provide unsolicited feedback on my crossword puzzles (if a man *happened* to spelled sassafras with the extra *s* in the wrong spot, that was his own damn business and nobody else's), and most recently, after what I could only assume was a pumpkin pie–fueled Hallmark movie marathon, her insistence on overhauling my lackluster love life by inviting prescreened "gentleman callers" to the office for me to "interview" as potential lovers.

One guy had brought a list of references.

Not kidding.

I'd tried talking to Vienna about this a whole bunch of times, but she never seemed to get the message, and to be honest, that was probably my fault. I was shit at setting boundaries with people who cared about me.

Strangers and acquaintances, colleagues and patients? I could lay down the law without a problem. But how did you enforce a boundary when someone genuinely had your best interest at heart? How were you supposed to tell someone they weren't loving you the way you needed, you know?

I'd found the easier thing to do was to simply avoid the situation entirely. Vienna couldn't get me to agree to a date if she couldn't find me.

"Doc Wright? You in here?" Vienna knocked on my office door before pushing it open with a squeak. "Well, I just don't know where he could've gone! I'd swear I didn't hear the door." I could picture her in her fall wardrobe of black turtleneck and khaki pants, hands propped on her hips, peeking under my desk in case I'd somehow gotten stuck there and needed an assist. I heard her cross to the window and pictured her peering out at the leaf-strewn backyard, wondering if I'd made a break for it.

My mouth started to go cottony around my cookie, and I felt the urge to cough.

"No worries, Ms. Vienna," a familiar, deep voice reassured her. "I'll just sit right here, put my feet up —" I heard a squeak as my best friend settled his large, muscular frame into my chair and no doubt tilted himself backward with his hands stacked behind his head, like my ultra-ergonomic desk chair was the old, plaid recliner in his fishing cabin. "—and wait for Tuck to show up."

The voice rumbled with hidden laughter I liked to think only I could hear. It made my heart squeeze and an answering smile hover on my lips. Dunn Johnson always, always found something in life to smile over. It was one of the things I loved best about him.

"Alright, then. Suit yourself, Dunn." Vienna sighed. "Though I have to say, I don't know what's gotten into the man lately, disappearing all the time the way he has been. It's not like him. You don't suppose he got his heart broke by that Parrish Partridge, do ya?"

I rolled my eyes at this. I'd gone on exactly one date with Licking Thicket's newest resident a couple of months back. *One.* And, okay, if I were being honest, there *had* been a minute in that sunny apple orchard at the Lickin' Pickin' when Parrish had kissed me and maybe we'd both wondered if there could be something real between us.

A minute later, though, both of us had gotten an irrefutable reminder of what "real" looked like when Dunn Johnson—*straight* Dunn Johnson—had kissed me (platonically, of course) and Parrish had kissed Diesel Church (not-so-platonically). Our potential relationship had ended before it began with no hard feelings on either side, and since Parrish was now happily married to Diesel—a man twice my size and all kinds of possessive—that was all for the best.

"His heart? Tucker?" More of Dunn's hidden laughter. "No. Parrish Partridge is nice enough, but he wasn't half good enough for our Tuck. For one thing, the man doesn't fish a'tall. Doesn't know his bass from his bowfin. Who'd help Tucker tie his clinch knots? Nah, Tuck could never take him seriously… even if I thought so for a minute there," he added darkly.

Of course it was all about tying clinch knots.

I sighed silently around my cookie.

"And for another…" Dunn lowered his voice. "You know Tuck's family owns Pete's Pork Pavillion, right? And Parrish's family owns Partridge Pit? Massive barbecue rivalry," he lied. "Sworn enemies."

"Really?" Vienna asked. "But I didn't think Doc Wright was close to his family."

"It's true, he's not. But you know how those barbecue folks are. If Tuck and Parrish had gotten serious, it still might've turned into a whole Romeo and Romeo situation, pitting all us Thicketeers against each other. Imagine, sword fight duels all up and down Walnut Street, all of us snapping our fingers like the Jets in *West Side Story*…"

Dunn demonstrated, and my heart squeezed again. That man was the smartest fool who'd ever walked the streets of the Thicket, I'd swear to it.

"Snapping? What the heck would we do that for?" literal Vienna demanded.

True fact, some people were not as taken with Dunn's quick wit as I was.

Dunn laughed, because of course he did. "Tuck and Parrish woulda been a tragedy, Ms. Vienna," he said. "Trust me. Not good."

"If you say so. I s'pose you'd know, since y'all are friends."

"Not just friends, *best* best friends," Dunn corrected. "Tucker Wright is the finest human on the planet, and he deserves nothing but love and happiness in this life. Parrish wasn't right for him, but some lucky guy will be, and I'm gonna personally ensure Tuck ends up with him. I won't let him settle for less than pure, head-over-heels love."

Aaaand there went my foolish heart again. *Squeeze, squeeze, squeeze*, like Dunn Johnson's personal stress toy, just the way it had since I'd moved back to the Thicket. Didn't matter that I was eight years older than Dunn, or that I'd vaguely remembered him having been my little brother's goofy friend in high school, or that he was four billion light-years hotter and more interesting than me, or that I was six hopeless notches on the Kinsey scale gayer than him.

Even though my logical, science-loving brain knew that all those things meant we would *never* be more than friends —friendship wasn't the same as love, no matter how many "bests" Dunn threw in there—my foolish heart kept hoping.

I was starting to think it always would.

"Speaking of love," Vienna said coyly. "I heard a *certain someone* might have some news to share, Dunn?"

"Who, me?" Dunn sounded so shocked I nearly laughed out loud and gave myself away.

As his "*best* best friend," I happened to know that his on-again, off-again thing-that-wasn't-a-thing with Jenn Shipley was firmly in the off position and had been since the Pickin' weeks and weeks ago.

Gossip at the Wisteria Cafe said Jenn had been really put out when Dunn kissed me that day, even though it had been super platonic, and totally inconsequential, and a Thicket tradition... sort of.

Funnily enough, even though it had been all of those things, I'd still added it to my mental playlist of Tucker's All-Time Favorite Moments. Dunn's sun-warm body, his soft green eyes, and his smiling lips on mine had been better than any of my many, many fantasies.

So I waited for Dunn to say something a little snarky to Vienna about how he wasn't settling down anytime soon, or how Jenn's low-key homophobia was unwelcome and disgusting, or how Jenn had particularly hirsute toes and laughed like a donkey doing Lamaze breathing. Any of those things would have been acceptable, really.

Instead, Dunn swallowed audibly. One might even say *nervously*. "Where'd you hear that?"

"Aw, honey. You remember you're in Licking Thicket, right? Where folks know your business before you do?" She sounded sympathetic. "So then a few of us asked your mama to confirm —"

"Oh, Lord."

"And she said she'd already talked to you about it, and *you'd* said —"

Dunn swore under his breath, and the chair creaked like he was sitting forward again. "The things my mother and I talked about were... were... were *hypothetical*, Ms. Vienna. Not something I need the Thicket gossiping about just yet. Or ever." He cleared his throat and said faintly, "This would change everything. My whole... identity. The most fundamental parts of who I am."

I frowned and pushed my glasses up. What the heck was he talking about?

"Sweetie, don't you think you're being a bit dramatic? It wouldn't change *everything*. It's just one part of who you are, after all. Every living person changes and redefines themselves, sometimes daily."

"But not like this! This isn't like changing your *socks*, Ms. Vienna. This is a big deal. It's a fork in the road. You don't get to backtrack."

"Now, that's not true at all. Look at your brother! He and Ava were the closest thing to engaged, and now he and Malachi are planning their wedding."

I froze in place. I'd been starting medical school around the time Dunn's big brother graduated high school, but Thicket legend said Brooks had been the Bovines' quarterback and all-around golden boy, even down to dating the head cheerleader, until he'd outed himself publicly at the Lickin' eleven and a bit years ago and left town the next day. Now he was back in the Thicket and planning a dream wedding.

To a man.

Did that mean Dunn was thinking he also might be — ?

"Brooks was still a kid then, though, and I'm not. When I decide, I've gotta decide for good." There was a sound of rustling fabric, like Dunn was rubbing his palms on his thighs — a rare but unmistakable sign he was anxious. "And I'm not saying I'm not gonna, you know, be open and honest about it, if it feels right to me. I'm just saying I'm not in a hurry to slap a label on things. Labels don't change the way a person feels about another person."

My jaw dropped, and the spit-soggy Milano cookie landed on my sweater.

"I'm gonna think on it," Dunn continued. It sounded like he was trying to convince himself as much as anybody. "And I'm gonna talk to Tuck, obviously — "

Vienna sighed. "Tucker's got enough on his plate, honey. You don't need to drag the poor man into your love life when it's got nothing to do with him."

"No, ma'am, it's got *everything* to do with him!"

"It does?"

It did?

"Sure! Tucker and me… We're not just friends, you know? What we have is special. I can't be happy unless Tuck is happy too."

My heart beat fast.

Too fast.

Concerningly fast.

See-your-cardiologist fast.

Dunn was considering changing his identity? The most fundamental parts of who he was? He was worried about labels? A-and… he couldn't be happy unless I was happy too, because we were *not just friends*?

It almost sounded like—though it wasn't and couldn't be, *obviously*, since Dunn had never shared a homosexual thought with me, and to be frank, I wasn't that lucky— Dunn was conflicted about his sexuality?

My brain flipped and flopped around, trying to figure out what the heck else he could mean, but I couldn't land on a single thing. I needed more data, more clues to cross-reference. I listened impatiently.

"But, Dunn," Vienna began hesitantly. "You've gotta be careful with Tucker. You know he—"

"Will be coming back any minute?" Dunn interrupted politely. "Yes, he will."

"But—"

"Ms. Vienna, you know I always want what's best for him, right? You and I have that in common. You can trust me."

Vienna sighed again, which was unusual. She wasn't normally the sighing sort. "Alright, Dunn. I'll just go keep an eye out for Doc and let him know you're here when he gets back."

"'Preciate it."

The door shut behind her with a click, and the chair squeaked as Dunn sat back once again.

"You can come out now," he said softly, the laughter back in his voice. "The coast is clear."

I stowed my cookies and crosswords, put my glasses in my shirt pocket, brushed the crumbs off my sweater, and prayed my cheeks were not as red as they felt. Then I reached for the latch and pushed open the secret storage area, blinking against the brightness of the office.

Like my office manager, this secret storage area hadn't been my idea, but it had come with the house. Also like Vienna, it had proven very, very useful.

"I left you some books, son," Doc Thorne had said as he

shook my hand at the closing. He'd given me a broad wink. "You might find Jules Verne *real* interesting."

To be truthful, I was a little slow on the uptake, and also a little overwhelmed at taking over the practice. It had taken me a solid three months before I'd bothered looking at the books he'd left behind and found the hidden catch under *Around the World in 180 Days*, along with the bottle of bourbon and the note he'd left me on the shelf inside. "Welcome to my secret thinking spot, Dr. Wright! A secret's only a secret if you don't tell anyone, so not a soul in the world knows about this spot except you and me and the bootlegger who designed it. Use it well."

Of course, I'd told Dunn Johnson about it almost immediately, since he didn't count. What good was a secret hideout if your favorite person didn't know about it?

"There he is." Dunn grinned as he watched me emerge, a little sweaty and a lot disheveled. Late-afternoon sunlight glinted off his golden-brown hair and clung to the hard muscles of his jean-clad thighs and broad shoulders. "Nice headlamp."

I snatched the band off my head, threw it on the bookcase, and ran a hand through my hair, desperately wishing I could be suave. "Uh. Hey. How's it going?"

"Better now." Dunn's grin widened. "Rough day at the office, honey?"

I rolled my eyes. "You have no idea." I tried to motion Dunn out of my desk chair, but he tilted his head and blinked like he didn't understand even though he absolutely did. I rolled my eyes again and propped myself against the edge of my desk so my thigh almost touched his knee. "Two words: Gavin. Mundheit."

"Gesundheit to you too."

"Har har." I rolled my eyes. "Gavin Mundheit was Vienna's man of the week. According to his dossier, he's a sixty-three-year-old organic dog treat baker from over in Turkey Perch. And apparently, November is the busiest time of year for making them because he needs to 'fit me in' between batches if I want a piece of his action. Spoiler alert: I don't."

Dunn pushed his leg against mine in a comforting gesture. "Pause your rant. I'm still back on *dossier*."

"Mmm. Dossier's a seven-letter word for 'folder full of documents.'" I tiredly rubbed at the back of my neck, which was tight after being in the cubby for over an hour.

He snorted. "Dossier is a seven-letter word for 'your office manager is one loose screw shy of a public health violation.'" He pushed to his feet and motioned for me to spin around, then dug his thumbs into my traps. They loosened obediently beneath his fingers, as always. "Is Vienna in the CIA now?"

"I know, I know, it's getting more ridiculous every day. I'm not even sure how she's finding these guys." I blew out a breath. "I need to talk to her, I know I do, but…" I'd rather cut off my own pinkie than be confrontational. Than risk hurting someone I loved.

"Leave it to me," Dunn said confidently. His fingertips coasted up my skin and made me shiver. "I'll talk to her. You won't be needing her help anymore."

"I won't?" I blinked over my shoulder at him. "I mean, obviously I won't. I never did. But *why* won't I?"

"Well." Dunn hesitated. "I'm guessing you overheard everything I said while you were in your secret clubhouse, huh? About me making some big, life-altering decisions?"

I nodded solemnly. "I was getting ready to ask for details."

Dunn's fingers redirected my head to face forward again so he could continue his massage. "I'll bet you were, but you're gonna have to wait. I have a whole script, see?"

"You do?" I glanced back at him. "Hang on, I'll have to wait for what?"

"For tonight." He righted my head again. "You don't have plans, do you? It's Wednesday. Not one of your volunteer nights for Rainbows Over Tennessee."

Did I have plans? In light of new information, my previous agenda of more Milanos and the *New York Times* seemed utterly missable. "No, I'm free."

"Good, 'cause I have a bunch of things I want to talk to you about. Some stuff about me, and some stuff about you… or some stuff I wanna do with you, I guess is a more accurate way of saying it —"

My breath left my lungs in a little wheeze that I turned into a cough, and I waved at the bookcase. "Sorry, sorry. Dusty in there. Go on." *Please go on. Please tell me in great detail exactly what you'd like to do with me, because I will let you do any damn thing, Dunn Johnson.*

"Well, that's just it, I don't wanna talk about this here. Doesn't feel right, you know? This is kind of an important convo. I figure I might have to do some convincing. So I made us a reservation."

I turned around fully at that and stared at him like he was speaking gibberish, because he kinda was. "A reservation?" I repeated. "For us? Are you kidding?"

"Not kidding." Dunn grinned. "Decided to go all out. Table for two at the Steak 'n Bait, seven o'clock."

In a town the size of Licking Thicket, there wasn't much need of fine dining. Birthdays and anniversaries, retirements and new babies meant popping into the Tavern with some friends, or heading over to the cute Indian place, or getting takeout pizza, or frequenting a half dozen other restaurants around town that had hardly any wait and no dress code.

But if you wanted a really special experience and

weren't afraid to pay for it—the first date to impress all first dates, or an apology to end all apologies, or a place to propose to your sweetheart—there was only one candlelit, fine-linen, wear-your-clean-boots establishment in the area that had been the scene of so many proposals they kept a tally of "Yesses" on the giant sign out front: Licking Thicket's own Steak 'n Bait.

I'd been there after each of my graduations, and again for my grandmother's ninetieth birthday. I knew Dunn had been there when he made the All-State baseball team and again when his sister, Gracie, got engaged.

We had never, ever gone there together. I'd never dreamed we would.

Except now suddenly we were, and I was so excited I stopped breathing for a minute or so.

This was highly irresponsible of me, as a medical professional and whatnot, but holy crap, what were you supposed to do when the man you loved wanted to have a candlelit dinner for two to discuss some life-changing revelations involving the both of you?

Dunn grabbed my shoulders in his two hands and shook me lightly.

"Tuck?" he demanded, his face so close to mine that I could see gold constellations in his green eyes. "Y'okay?"

I sucked in a breath and nodded... and then *kept* nodding like a skipping record on Meemaw Wright's old record player. "No. Yeah. I'm totally okay. I'm... I'm great. The greatest." I was floating. Flying. Soaring. "I'll be ready at six-thirty."

––––––––

WHEN DUNN PICKED ME UP, I'd almost talked myself all the way down from excitement to steady caution.

"He's straight," I'd told myself as I'd chosen my favorite outfit—a chunky white sweater that made me look "glowy," according to Ava Siegel, who I trusted to know such things.

"So straight," I'd told the mirror, after I'd gotten out of a fresh shower and styled my hair perfectly.

"Super-duper straight," I'd whispered into the chilly air as I'd waited for Dunn on my front porch after Vienna had left and I'd locked the place up tight. "And that's *fine*. I wouldn't want to change him! I just want him to be happy."

But then the man had shown up in a forest-green button-down shirt I hadn't seen him wear since the Lickin' Dinner Dance last summer, and a pair of navy pants that cupped his ass like they were in love with him too, and when he'd looked across the cab of his truck at me and said, "You know I'd never do anything to jeopardize our friendship, right, Tuck?" I'd lost my grip on the helium balloon of my emotions again, and my heart had squeezed so painfully I'd lost my breath.

Fact: We were at a date restaurant.

Fact: He was sure as heck dressed like this was a date, with no muck boots or fishing vest in sight.

Fact: He kept darting me glances across the table and acting all squirrelly and uncomfortable, which had *never* happened between us before. And while this would normally not be a good thing, it was yet more evidence that somehow, improbably, impossibly, Dunn Johnson had asked me on a date.

Sweet Jesus, Meemaw had been right all those years ago. Miracles really did happen.

"I think we should have a bottle of prosecco," I told the server impulsively when she came to take our drink orders after dropping off water and warm rolls. "What do you think, Dunn?"

"Oh, uh. Yeah," he agreed, tapping his fingers on the

snowy-white tablecloth. "Good idea. Anything you like. And I'll have a shot of Jameson. Neat."

Uh… okay. That was sobering. Dunn wasn't a big drinker any more than I was. Also worrying was the way his gaze ping-ponged around the restaurant, like he was too nervous to look at anything too long, especially me.

"Dunn, you know you can talk to me, right? You can tell me… anything. Literally anything. And I'd never judge you. Or push you," I added, thinking that maybe fear of the unknown was tripping him up. "I can be patient, you know?"

Dunn's eyes came to rest on my face, and he smiled. "'Course I know that, Tuck."

"Then tell me what all this is about." I reached into the basket to grab a roll, then twirled my hand in the air to indicate the beautiful restaurant and the *reservation*. "Spill your guts, please." *Before I lose my mind.*

"Well." Dunn swallowed. Cleared his throat. "I invited you here to talk about… love."

I dropped my roll.

"Wow. Is it warm in here?" Dunn tugged at his collar. "Because I'm really feeling warm. Am I feverish? Or am I having an allergic reaction to discussing emotions? One time Mal said that Brooks used to be allergic to discussing emotions, but I thought he was being sarcastic. Now I'm thinking it's real and maybe… genetic?"

"You're not having an allergic reaction," I whispered. "What about love?"

"Well, it's like this, Tuck… You've given me so much over the years. You've been the best friend I could ever have—going ice fishing in the dead of winter when I *know* you'd rather have been home drinking cocoa, helping my family navigate all the medical stuff when my dad had his heart issues last year, stepping up as a legal guardian to

Bernadette, even though you said you weren't sure you wanted kids…"

"Dunn," I said, squeezing my roll very tightly as I stabbed it with butter, while also trying to be patient like I'd promised. "I still don't have kids. Bernadette is your pet pig—"

"Pfft. *Pet*. I'm a farmer, Tucker. Farmers don't have pets, we have livestock." He sipped his water. "Bernie just so happens to be livestock with special needs."

Needs like extensive ear scritches. And a nightly bedtime story. And a legal guardian to manage her inheritance should Dunn pass away. But I wasn't here to confront Dunn over his porcine pipe dreams.

"Keep going," I suggested patiently and supportively.

Dunn's eyes flicked to the butter knife clenched in my fist.

"Right. So, I want you to know that I see all you've done for me, all the support you've given me. The love you've given me. And I want to do the same for you. I want—"

Holy shit.

Holy shit it was happening.

I took a deep breath. I set down my knife and roll. I attempted to memorize the moment as best I could—the slight smoke tang from the restaurant's wood-burning fireplace, the way the candlelight danced in Dunn's eyes as he smiled at me with honest affection.

Breathe, Tucker, breathe…

"I want to find you a boyfriend."

I blinked, confident I'd heard him wrong. I replayed the words in my head and blinked some more. I waited for him to apologize, to say he misspoke, but instead, he tilted his head like a puppy, confused by my confusion.

"Is this… are you blinking at me in code? Shit, Tuck,

you know I'm not great with puzzles. Um. Are you spelling out 'Thank you'?"

I closed my eyes very tightly and breathed through my nose. We'd learned in medical school about this phenomenon called phantom pain, the pain an amputee feels in a missing limb. I wondered if the pain I was feeling at that moment, like my heart was simultaneously breaking and missing from my chest entirely, was anything close.

"Tuck?" Dunn continued quickly. "I don't just mean *a* boyfriend, okay?" He snorted at the very idea. "I mean *the* boyfriend. The one. The... the guy you're meant to be with. 'Cause nobody knows you better than me, right? Nobody, not even you yourself! So I figured, who better to make sure you get exactly the guy you deserve than the guy who loves you best?"

I waited for my heart to squeeze excitedly, but it didn't. Maybe I'd finally been cured.

Yay?

The waitress came with our drinks, and I belted Dunn's whiskey back before he could reach for it, only shuddering slightly at the burn.

"Another, sir?"

"Better make it two," I said with a polite smile.

When she left, I turned that same smile on Dunn. "So you planned this whole evening, this reservation and everything, just to tell me that you wanted to find me a boyfriend?"

Dunn grinned broadly. "Yep. Cool, right? 'Cause you're important to me, and I know it's not gonna be easy to convince you to let me set you up." He laid his hand over mine on the tabletop, casually affectionate as ever. "I know you hate Ms. Vienna interfering. But it wouldn't be like that with you and me, 'cause I know you. Like I said."

I nodded slowly and drew my hand away. "And all that

nonsense back in my office, when Vienna was giving you the third degree and you were going on about changing your life, and redefining yourself, and whatnot?"

"Oh, that." Dunn waved a hand negligently. "Jenn's getting antsy again. You know how she can be. 'When are we gonna get serious, Dunn? You gotta fish or cut bait.'" His face twisted up, and I knew it was because he hated that expression with a passion. "She went out on a couple dates with Kevin Barker—Monster from the Devoted Dogs?—and it didn't work out, so now she's telling her friends it was just so I'd get jealous and wanna commit, when anyone who knows me knows I've never been jealous over a woman a day in my life, and the only person I'm committed to is you." He grinned. "Buuuut my mom caught wind of it, so I had to sit through one of those 'Dunn Johnson, I love you, but you drive me crazy' speeches of hers—"

I felt a sudden, painful kinship with Cindy Ann Johnson.

"—where she talked about the beauty of partnership and respect, and opening my eyes to what was right in front of me before it all passed me by, and blah blah, which I could only assume was her way of saying she wanted me to lock Jenn down." He shrugged. "I hate to disappoint her, but in the end I told her I wasn't ready to make any commitments, and if Jenn wanted to find someone who'd offer her that, I understood." His green eyes clouded over with genuine worry. "But I don't get what's so wrong with keeping things just as they are. I'm not hurting anyone, am I, Tuck?"

I rolled my lips together. Was he?

The deep ache in my chest suggested *yes*.

But I felt pretty confident answering this one for me *and* for Jenn. Life hurt. Circumstances hurt. Silly, senseless hearts that insisted on hoping for things hurt. People who rejected you because of who you were, like I'd seen with some of the LGBTQ folks I volunteered with, hurt. People who didn't love you back the way you wished they did hurt.

None of that was Dunn's fault.

"No. As long as you're being honest with yourself and everyone involved, you're good." I forced myself to smile and add lightly, "But hear me now, Dunn Johnson: there is no way on this earth I'm letting you find me a date, you understand?"

That would be beyond humiliating.

It wasn't Dunn's fault he couldn't love me the way I wanted him to. I needed to accept that we'd never be anything more than friends, because allowing myself to think otherwise was a recipe for disaster.

And for my own sanity, it was time I learned to draw some healthy boundaries between us.

How hard could it be?

2

DUNN

13-Down: A person who is not very bright (4 letters)

"Now hear me out," I said to my brother, who I could tell was giving me some serious side-eye. I couldn't blame him. This situation of me trying to find Tuck a man had been going on for months now.

"This sounds like the setup of a plucky sitcom from the eighties. Except gay," Brooks said before tossing his line in the water with a soft plunk.

I reached over and grabbed my insulated coffee mug before leaning back in my chair. The weather was warming up on a particularly sunny March day, and I was happy to see the first signs of spring. Daffodils sprouted up here and there under the trees at the edges of the lake, and the warm light of sunrise glowed on the water. It was a gorgeous morning that would have been downright perfect if not for Tucker's last-minute cancellation on account of his moody ass being pissed at me.

"I made a list, and did you know there are twenty-six

eligible gay or bisexual bachelors in the Licking Thicket area?" I pondered the number, trying to decide why it sounded so large all of a sudden. "Here and I thought you were the only one."

"Obviously not," he said in a dry voice. "Seeing as how I live with one, had lunch with two others only yesterday, and—"

I held up a hand to shut him up. "Fine. That's not what I meant, and you know it. I only meant, growing up it seemed like nobody was gay, and now it seems like everyone is. Not that I have a problem with it, because I don't. I hope you know that."

Brooks rolled his eyes out at the water. "I know. Your best friend is gay, your brother is gay. Your soon-to-be brother-in-law is gay too, and you agreed to be my best man at the wedding. I'm pretty sure I already know you're okay with gay dudes."

"Have I thanked you again recently for asking me?" I hadn't been expecting that honor when I knew Brooks had a lot of friends who would have stepped up to the plate instead.

Brooks's eyes went soft for a second. "Of course, Dunn. You're my brother and I love you. Now, get back to whatever ridiculousness you were spouting. And, can I just say, how Tucker Wright still puts up with your dumb ass after all this time is beyond me."

I sighed. Sometimes I wondered that too. "It's just that I've already ripped through eight of them trying to find Tucker's soul mate, and I can't make this dog hunt. What am I doing wrong?"

Brooks looked straight up to the sky as if to ask the clouds for help in dealing with his doofus of a brother. It was a sky-daddy plea I was very familiar with.

"Dunn, has it ever occurred to you that the only thing

Tucker has in common with Hubbard Weaver is the fact they both like dick?"

"Don't be crass!" I snapped. Nobody needed to be talking about Tucker's man parts, especially in my presence. Besides, our mama taught us better than that.

"You're going about this all wrong," Brooks suggested.

I leaned forward when I felt a tug on the line. "I don't think so. It's just that apparently leading the horse to water does not, in fact, result in a hydrated equine. And, as I have a particular affinity for and talent with animal husbandry—"

"You're a dairy farmer," Brooks added in a tone that might as well have said "shit shoveler" which was, I guess, *technically* true.

"Like I said," I continued, "I should be able to noodle this situation to a mutually beneficial result. I know how to manage stubborn beasts. It's a matter of taking charge and showing them who's the boss."

"Now we're back to the eighties sitcoms again," Brooks muttered under his breath.

I finally reeled in my line to discover I'd hooked a small decrepit twig instead of the trout I'd been hoping for. "Motherfucker," I said with a sigh, tossing the twig into the woods behind us. "Nothing's fucking biting today."

"Well, now I know you're frustrated. You usually don't bandy about the f-word with quite such abandon. What's really bothering you about this situation with Tucker? Why do you care so much?"

He lifted that ridiculously judgy Brooks eyebrow at me. The one that said he already knew the answer but was asking "for the sake of argument." I hated that shit.

"He's my best friend. I want him to be happy. Duh."

"And you don't trust him to find his own happiness, why?"

I baited my line and cast again before sitting back. "He's shit at it. There, I said it. The man doesn't know how to find himself a love… love… lov*er* to save his life." The word felt icky on my tongue, like I'd accidentally licked a dirty cattle brush. The idea of Tucker with another man always made me feel low-key nauseated. At first, I'd thought maybe I was homophobic, but then I'd rationalized it away. Naw, I just wanted my guy to have the best. He deserved it more than anyone I knew.

"And you do?" Brooks asked. "Based on the number of successful *lovers* you've managed to pin down?"

I took a sip of coffee and sniffed. "I've had lovers. And… I mean… I have Jenn." There was the dirty cattle brush feeling again. Maybe I just had a bad batch of coffee.

"Pfft. Jenn is a hunter. She's out for big game, and you're a buck with a big-ass rack."

I thought of my squishy pecs compared to Jen's perfectly adequate rack. "But—"

He cut me off. "Listen, you need an expert in all things matchmaker. I think it's time you asked Mom for help."

My next sip of coffee sputtered all over the splintered wood slats of the dock. "Are you insane? Do you not remember her trying to set you up with Ava? *Female* Ava? Or trying to set Pervy Wilcox up with Olivia 'Battle-ax' Reynolds despite their contentious history from the cannonball competition at the pool last summer? Or the time Mama tried setting Phil Kingsley up with Mrs. Bridger even when Mr. Bridger was standing right there?"

Brooks nodded. "I get your point."

I sighed and tossed my empty coffee mug back on the shore next to my coat. Once the sun had risen, the air had warmed up enough for me to be plenty comfortable in my flannel shirt and jeans. I loved early spring mornings like these. If only Tucker were there to enjoy it too.

"So, what am I missing? How can I get him to give these guys a real chance? I'm setting him up with Leon Morton next week, but gah. At this rate, poor Leon's gonna get his head chewed off before Tucker even sits down at the restaurant table."

Brooks contemplated the water in front of him as if truly giving my problem due consideration. "What do they have in common? Tucker and Leon, I mean?"

I opened my mouth, but nothing came out. Not for the first time, I wondered why brains didn't come with a return policy. Sometimes mine seemed plenty enough defective to qualify for one.

"Right," Brooks said with a long-suffering sigh. "My point exactly."

"They're both hella smart!" Finally, the brain spat out a fourth-quarter Hail Mary.

"True. If you can call letting Dunn Johnson set you up smart."

"Wait!" I snapped my fingers. "They both like those little chocolate mint things they give you with your bill at the Olive Garden. I took Gracie one time for her birthday lunch and saw Leon steal one from the next table over when his coworker wasn't looking."

"A match made in suburban heaven," Brooks muttered. "Like kismet, if kismet was a store in a strip mall across the street from Mattress Firm."

"Fine," I admitted. "Maybe I don't know much about Leon, but I know a lot about Tuck. And Tucker Wright deserves to feast from a smorgasbord of manly delights. Maybe Leon is just one of them... amused booths. A little taster before the main course."

Brooks appealed to the clouds again before suddenly standing up and reeling in his line. "That's it. Let's go. I can't take any more of this. It's time we bring in the big guns."

"Mama?"

"No," he said, pointing his laser eyeballs right on me. "Malachi. If anyone can find the best available gay man in a hundred-mile radius, it's Mal. Clearly."

He wasn't wrong. Cocky maybe, but not wrong. Mal had a good eye for horseflesh, manflesh, and rusty old junk. Maybe he could help us.

"He's kidding, right?" Mal murmured to Brooks under his breath when we got to my parents' house for Sunday lunch.

"Just go with it, m'kay?" Brooks leaned in and kissed his fiancé before pulling him into a full-body hug. I envied what they had. No matter what happened or what kind of bickering fight they ever got into, my brother and his man always seemed to find comfort and happiness in each other's arms.

I didn't feel like that with Jenn. I wondered sometimes if it was a gay thing, but then I'd catch my sister, Gracie, and her husband sharing an inside joke or a simple foot rub after a long day and realize, no, it wasn't a gay thing. Just a "right person" thing. And I had the right person already. He just happened to be my best friend instead of my... whatever the word was.

"Hey, boys," Mama said, stepping away from the kitchen sink long enough to press a kiss to my cheek and take the coffee thermos out of my hands. "Catch anything good?"

"Attitude," I muttered.

"A gorgeous sunrise," Brooks added a little too happily.

Mama craned her neck to see behind me. I turned to look but only saw the same old photo of a cow dressed as Carol Burnett. One of the ladies in the Beautification Corps had given it to Mama years ago as a joke, and it had hung in our kitchen for as long as I could remember.

"Where's Tucker?" she asked with a frown.

"Um… I don't know?" I said, feeling wrong-footed since Tucker normally joined us for Sunday lunch. "Maybe… at home doing his crosswords? How'm I supposed to know?"

She put her hands on her hips and narrowed her eyes at me. "What'd you do?"

My sister, Gracie, looked up from wiping my niece's sticky hands and snickered. I narrowed my eyes at her.

"Nothing, gah. Why you asking me that?"

Just then, Tucker sauntered in like it was a regular Sunday and he hadn't been giving me the silent treatment for three whole months. Okay, fine. Three whole days, but still. It *felt* like three months because he'd skipped out on our Thursday night trivia at the Tavern, and one of the questions was about bile ducts or some such. When our team had no clue, they all stared holes in me like it was my fault our resident brainiac hadn't shown.

"There he is!" My mom made a fool out of herself by shimmying over to Tuck and smacking a great big kiss on his cheek. "Can't have lunch without all my boys."

Once he'd finished loving on Mama, Tuck made his way over to Gracie and took the baby from her to coo all over. He was good with kids, but it would have been nice if he'd given me the time of day at all.

I sighed and moved away from them. I had better things to do anyway. "Hey, Dad, you said you had a loose shutter that needed fixing?"

Dad looked up from setting the table in the dining

room. "What? Oh, no. Tucker swung by yesterday and knocked it out. At least *somebody* cares about not abandoning me and my stents."

"Your stents?" I looked to my mother for an explanation. "What's the matter with your stents?"

Since my dad had had some heart troubles a year or so before, we'd all taken his health a lot more seriously.

"Not a thing," Mama soothed. "But your daddy's cardiologist is taking a sabbatical—"

"Don't know what anyone needs to see the pyramids of Giza for when we've got plenty of wonders right here in the Thicket," Dad grumbled.

"—and a new cardiologist came in to take his place temporarily all the way from Nashville."

"A doctor with a big ol' toothpaste smile, who looks like a model. A *teenaged* model. If Dr. Rogers spends that much time in the gym, how much could he know about hearts?"

"Rogers?" Tucker narrowed his eyes. "Carter Rogers?"

"That's him," Mama agreed. "You know him?"

Tucker nodded. "We haven't spoken in a while, but I went to med school with him. He... I..." He cleared his throat. "Anyway. I knew him and his family real well. His dad was a respected cardiologist up in Nashville, and Carter followed in his footsteps. He was whip-smart and dedicated. Even spent some time each year working for Doctors Without Borders." He clapped my dad on the shoulder. "I promise, sir, I wouldn't leave you in his hands if I didn't think he was highly qualified."

"Aw. Thank you, Tucker." Dad ruffled his hair, like Tuck was five instead of thirty-five. "That's why you're my favorite son. Along with Malachi, who made the town sign. My other two sons, meanwhile..." He winked.

I felt my teeth grind as Brooks let out a snort of laughter.

"Need help with the grill?" I tried again.

Dad shook his head. "Paul's out there already. Said Ava likes her meat just so."

"I'll bet she does," I muttered, turning back around to face the music in the kitchen. Tucker was smiling big like we weren't in the middle of the biggest fight since the 2017 mustard or mayo fiasco, which had not been my fault, damn it. We'd barely known each other then. How was I to know the man had such a deep aversion to mayo?

He had a good smile. The kind that made my heart feel a little janky. It reminded me of the time he'd been awarded a big grant for the charity he ran and you'd have thought he'd won front-row tickets to see Old Dominion. The man knew how to freaking smile.

Brooks shouldered past me back into the kitchen. "Mom, Dunn had something he wanted to ask you about."

I lifted my boot and nailed him in the keister. "Do not."

Tuck blinked at me, and his smile lost some of its light. "Hey."

I shoved my hands in my jean pockets. "Hey."

"Jesus," Brooks muttered under his breath.

Mama gave Brooks a secretive look and spoke almost too softly for me to hear. "I thought you were going to talk to him?"

I forced myself to meet Tuck's eyes. "Thanks for, uh… fixing the shutter."

Brooks spoke to Mama out of the corner of his mouth. "Nah, this is too fun."

Gracie snickered again under her breath. She was getting good at that.

Tucker swallowed. "Yeah. It's no problem. I was out this way to take your dad's blood pressure anyway."

Mal finished pouring potato chips in Mama's big plastic

bowl and leaned in to put a chip in Brooks's mouth. "This isn't fun. It's downright painful."

"Will you three shut the hell up?" I snapped, waving my arms through the air. "We're going through something, okay? Tucker's mad at me for no good reason. He's throwing a dag-blammed hissy fit."

My mama didn't take kindly to folks taking the Lord's name in vain in her house. Sometimes you had to get creative.

"No good reason?" Tuck asked through gritted teeth. "That right? You call setting me up on a date with Methuselah no good reason?" His voice got louder as he built up a head of steam.

"Oh Lord. Here we go," Ava said, appearing out of nowhere. "Who has the popcorn?"

I ignored her. "He's no Methuse-whatever. Hubbard Weaver is a good man. He's... well, he's a Licking Thicket icon!"

My dad wandered into the kitchen and took a handful of chips out of the bowl. "Hubbard Weaver? I thought he died in the tornadoes we had back in... when was it? Late nineties?"

I squeezed my eyes closed and pinched the bridge of my nose.

Tucker let out a soft snort of laughter, so I kinda opened one eye just a little to see it. I never liked to miss seeing Tucker Wright happy. He had a really good laugh that was not to be missed for love or money.

A warm hand landed on my arm. Tucker was trying to meet my eyes again. "Dunn. He had to take out his teeth to eat soup. *Soup*. Also, he got us the senior citizens' discount, and it wasn't even an early bird thing. Roxie Winslow said if Hubbard was out this late, he deserved the discount regardless."

I felt a laugh bubble up, but I refused to let it out. "He's a stand-up guy," I insisted.

Tucker nodded sagely. "You're right. In fact, I believe he helped save many women and children on the *Titanic*."

I opened my eyes fully and shoved his smug ass. "Shut up. Fine. You win. I'll do better next time. Okay? I promise."

Tucker's laugh died. "No. We're done with the setups. You have to stop this, D. Promise me."

Mal shrugged. "I hope you at least took advantage of those smooth gums before the night was over."

My mother's eyebrows furrowed, my father's face paled, and Ava damned near hyperventilated.

I didn't get it.

"You already have dinner planned with Leon," I reminded him.

"Leon Morton?" Dad asked, getting some color back. "Now, that's interesting."

I held out my hand to display my father's grand wisdom. "See?"

Dad continued. "I thought he was in jail. Wasn't he the one who stole the franking machine from the post office?"

"That was his mother," I explained testily. "And she had about a gazillion postcards that needed postage on them for when she announced the date change for the Miss Junior Licking contest. You can hardly blame her."

Tucker walked over to the fridge and helped himself to Mama's extra-large bottle of Yellow Tail chardonnay and a giant coffee mug from the cabinet.

"Leon dated Hiram Fuller!" I cried. "The professional whatsit!"

Brooks took the mug out of Tucker's hand and replaced it with a glass pitcher. "This'll fit more," he murmured.

Tucker eyed me. "The basketball player?"

"Yes!" I cried, pointing at him with one hand and my nose with the other. "Got it in one." That man always did know how to read my mind.

"Why'd they break up?" Ava asked. "Probably couldn't handle balls as well off the court as on."

"Ava Marie Siegel," Mama chided.

Ava batted her eyes innocently at Mama. "I meant on the golf course. You know how much Leon loves to hit eighteen."

"There!" I shouted again. "Something else you have in common with him. I forgot. Leon loves golf. Tuck, you do too. You're great at golf. You're a golfing… stud."

The room suddenly felt a little awkward, but I thought maybe it was the amount of wine Tucker was still pouring into the pitcher.

"Anyway," I went on. "Even if things don't work out with you and Leon, you have to admit it'd be nice to have someone to meet up with on the course since you won't play golf with me anymore." I tried not to sound pathetic and hurt about it, but it still stung.

Tucker's jaw dropped. "You peed on the green. In front of the Licking Thicket High golf team."

I tried to remain calm. "I told you it was an emergency. And I hid behind a bush. It wasn't like anyone saw me."

"*I* saw you!" he said, slapping a hand on his chest. He had a nice chest. "And I'm pretty sure everyone out there heard you moaning in relief."

I searched my memory for the truth of the matter. "It was a really good pee," I admitted. "You know the kind."

Mama sighed. "On that note, let's eat."

When we moved to the dining room, Mama and Ava jostled me until I was practically falling into Tucker's lap. "What the hell?" I asked, moving to the chair next to his. I couldn't help but notice he smelled funny. "I normally sit over th—"

"That's Ava's seat, dear," Mama said before moving to the end of the table. "She's gotta sit next to the high chair."

I leaned over and sniffed my best friend. Like you do.

"What the hell?" he asked, jerking away.

"Why you smell like fried onions and spicy sausage?" I glared at him. "And do not lie to me, Tucker Wilber Wright, because I know you and I will know if you're lying."

"My middle name isn't—"

"If you went to CarrieBell's brunch buffet out on Highway 50 without me, we're going to have fucking words."

Mama's sharp inhale caught my attention, and I glanced up at her with an apologetic expression. "Sorry."

"Dunn Johnson. Watch your mouth in this house and anywhere else the Lord has eyeballs and earlobes," she hissed.

I wasn't sure the Lord had either of those things anymore, but I wasn't about to argue with my mother about Jesus semantics on a Sunday. Brooks shoved a casserole dish in my face. "Humble pie?"

I dished out some potato salad before handing the dish back to Brooks.

"Aren't you going to pass it to Tucker?" Brooks asked with a knowing grin.

"No need. Tuck's probably still full from CarrieBell's brunch buffet. Aren't you?" Besides which, he hated potato salad and almost any other salad made with mayo, with the exception of cheesy broccoli salad, deviled eggs, and the lemon chicken salad out at Thelma's Sandwich Shack.

Tucker didn't answer, and that was fine by me. How dare he go to CarrieBell's without me? How. Dare. He.

"Hey, Tucker?" My mom's voice sounded weird, like the

time she subtly took charge of a town meeting and wound up somehow convincing sixty people into volunteering to have their hair dyed pink for the breast cancer fundraiser walk. It was like... one minute there was a roomful of normal people, and the next it was a cotton-candy-colored free-for-all.

Something was up.

"Yes, ma'am?"

Poor little innocent Tucker. He had no idea. This was how she lured people into her trap.

"Your receptionist's still out on maternity leave, isn't she?"

"Yep," Tucker agreed. Brooks, the giant traitor, passed the broccoli salad in his direction, and Tucker took a big helping. "Annie won't be back until May."

Considering my mom and half the Corps had been at Annie's shower—and heck, even *I* knew she'd only had her baby a week ago—this question was further proof my mother was machinating.

Machinat-inating?

Machininating?

Plotting.

"You haven't filled her spot yet, have you?" she asked, all casual. Too casual.

Like a gazelle sensing he was about to become prey, Tucker blinked a little. "Uh. No, ma'am. Remember I mentioned that Vienna and I thought we could probably just muddle through without a receptionist, since it'd only—"

"I ask," Mama interrupted with a beaming smile, "because Jenn Shipley's between jobs again—"

Silence reigned around the table. Even baby Beau stopped his happy babbling.

"Oh, yeah? Thought she worked at the wrap place?"

Tucker speared some broccoli with his fork and shot me a look.

I shrugged. Jenn hadn't mentioned a new job to me. At least, I was pretty sure.

"Mmm. Well, as it happens, she feels like making sandwiches isn't the best use of her talents. And also, she has a sincerely held belief about eating meat and cheese."

"She's vegan?" Tucker looked from my mom to me, like somehow *I* was supposed to know what the heck Jenn Shipley ate. Who paid attention to that stuff?

"Oh, no," Mama said. "No, she doesn't believe it's right to eat a sandwich *without* meat or cheese, and she doesn't think anyone else should either. So she quit." She shrugged. "I think she's still not over losing her job at Summer Honey. Selling highfalutin bath and body products was her dream career. She thinks Abilene had it out for her personally, rather than being justifiably upset when Jenn handed out free products to several ladies on the Beautification Corps."

"As if we can be bought," Ava scoffed.

"She's hoping Dunn'll get her job back for her," Mama continued.

"And a spot on the Beautification Corps," Gracie added behind a fake cough. I ignored her.

I looked up from my plate in surprise. "Me?" I said around a mouthful of potato salad. I swallowed. "What'm I s'posed to do?"

"Talk to Abilene, I guess, since you supply all the milk for their products?" Mama shrugged. "I don't know, honey. That's your business."

I was glad something was.

"But in the meantime, Jenn's out of a job and low on marketable skills. She's real good at talking on the phone, though, Tucker, and I'm guessing she could write things down and whatnot real well."

Tucker blinked. "Well, that's… ah…" He stuffed some broccoli in his mouth instead of replying.

"Besides, how cute would it be if Dunn could see his special girl every time he came by to see you?" she continued.

I narrowed my eyes at her as I felt Tucker's gaze on my face. "No need, Mama," I said through a lump in my throat.

For some reason the idea of Jenn around Tucker that much made my potato salad go down the wrong way.

"I think she's a shoo-in at the Dollar Barn. They need an overnight stocker."

Everyone gaped at me. "What?" I asked. "It's good pay, and she can handle it."

Mama shook her head. "No. I think if you're still serious about Jenn, you should give her a chance to get to know Tucker better, don't you?"

No. No, I did not. Not only no, but hellfire and damnation, no.

"Who said I was serious—"

"That's fine," Tucker interrupted in his polite *I'm lying through my teeth* voice. He did not like Jenn Shipley. "It's just for another six weeks while Annie's on maternity leave anyway."

Mama nodded firmly and dusted her hands. Mission accomplished. Although I wasn't quite sure what the mission was exactly.

Mama made it sound like she was Jenn's biggest fan, but for some reason, every time her name came up, Mama asked me about Tucker instead.

I called her on it one time, and she'd told me she thought Tucker would make a better "helpmate" for me than Jenn. Ha. As if. I told her she was seeing gay where gay didn't exist. Which, okay, maybe made sense after everything that had happened with my brother.

"Fool me once," Mama had said. "Shame on me. But you aren't fooling me, Dunn. I see the way you look at Tucker. He's your person. It's only a matter of time till you get your head out of your derriere and do something about it."

That's when I'd replaced her frozen vodka bottle with the Yellow Tail Chardonnay.

And maybe now that she was trying to help Jenn get a job, that meant it was working.

Paul sat forward and reached for a hamburger bun from the basket in the center of the table. "So fill me in on this twine festival I keep hearing about in town," he said. "I missed it last year, since little Beau, here, was a newborn and our idea of romance was letting each other sleep for an hour."

"Still is," Ava sighed. "But the Entwinin' is where we pull down the old, dried-out wisteria vines and twist them into little mementos for loved ones. I've told you about it a million times."

My parents shared a secret gaze across the length of the table.

I cleared my throat. "It's, ah, it's kinda special. Like, um…" For some reason this festival, out of all the others, got me right in the feels. Tucker shifted next to me until our thighs pressed together. I swallowed. "My dad always makes his in the shape of a daisy for my mom."

Dad nodded and glanced at my mom with a look of utter adoration on his face. "The day we met, we took a walk in a meadow outside of town and I told Cindy Ann her dress reminded me of the pretty daisies growing there. Ever since then, whenever I want her to know how I feel about her, I give her something in the shape of a daisy. Each year for the Entwinin' I get to remind myself how impossible it is to make old wisteria vines into a circle," he finished with a chuckle.

Ava let out a happy sigh. "My dad makes different ones each year to commemorate his favorite memory of my mom from that year. The year of the Centennial Lickin', he made his in the shape of a tree house because he still thinks it's hilarious Mom put Mal out in the tree house when he first came to visit."

Mal rolled his eyes but then gave my brother gooey love-stupid eyes. "Brooks made me one in the shape of a bucket of milk that first year."

I glanced at Tucker out of the corner of my eye. Every year I twisted a vine into a different kind of fish and left it for him in his tackle box. We never spoke of it. Ever. Because it wasn't something you did for your best friend. I just… I knew how much he wanted that. How much he wanted someone to care about him like that, and I never ever wanted him to spend a single day not knowing that someone did.

I cared about him like that, even if I couldn't be the boyfriend he needed.

It was why I was so desperate to find someone to fill his other needs so we could get back to our old way of being. Him and me, together forever, as best friends.

"The thing to remember, Paul, is that handmade is always best," my dad instructed, "even if the best you can do is a rough circle. Last few years, the florists in town have tried to get in on the act. For a hundred dollars or more, they'll make you a big ol' wreath in any shape you like and deliver it to your sweetheart for you. *Pah*." The disgust in his tone made it clear how he felt about that. "The whole point of the Entwinin' is to tell your person that you want your lives to be wound together. And I'm sure you know, being committed to someone for the long haul has more to do with stepping up and trying your best than with achieving perfection."

My mother's eagle eyes bore down on me. "Tucker," she said lightly, even though her gaze on me was heavy as a Loony Tune anvil. "I've heard Leon Morton is good with his hands."

I damned near choked on my burger.

"I'll bet he weaves a delightful vine," she said, still pinning me with those laser beams. Why was she staring at me instead of him?

I swallowed thickly. I didn't want anyone weaving a fancy vine for Tucker Wright but me. Clearly, I was having issues, but that was fine. I simply needed to take myself out back behind the proverbial woodshed and remind myself I was not, in fact, Tucker's person.

I mean… I *was*. Just not… like *that*. There was going to come a day when someone else twined his vine, and I was going to have to come to terms with it.

"You know," Tucker replied thoughtfully, "you might be right. I'll ask him about it at dinner next week."

I closed my eyes and took a deep breath. At least he'd finally agreed to keep the date.

3

TUCKER

11-ACROSS: Annoyed; provoked (5 letters)

"STILL WORKIN' on that seltzer water, Doc?" Alana Jackson cracked her gum and hugged her empty drinks tray to her ample chest.

"Yep." I gave her the weakest smile in existence and chopped the ice in my glass with my straw. "Strong stuff. Gotta take it slow."

"Right." She smiled a smile that held more pity than humor. "You want any food, or..." She looked half-expectantly at the door.

I looked at my phone, which said it had been five minutes since the last time she'd asked me that. "I'm gonna look at the menu for five more minutes, but thanks, Alana."

"M'kay. But, like, if it helps?" She leaned forward and put a hand on my shoulder. "Skeeter's got more of that Triple Chocolate Heartbreak Cake from Annie's out back. Same kind you ordered after your date last week. And the week before."

I nodded. "Thanks. That's... fortuitous."

She twisted her mouth up to one side. "Not really. He's started ordering it special on Fridays, just 'cause..." She glanced at the door again. "You know."

I grimaced and nodded again as Alana patted me on the shoulder and left.

I did, indeed, know why Skeeter had started ordering that cake on Fridays. And the Thicket being what it was—heck, my *luck* being what it was—there'd soon be a freakin' holiday where everyone ate chocolate cake for ten successive Fridays in the spring to commemorate Ol' Doc Wright's Terrible String o' Dates. The Datin', they'd call it.

Or the Sighin'.

Or the Shamin'.

All would be accurate.

And, given the way this particular Friday was going, the Shamin' might last an unprecedented *eleven* Fridays. At least the kids in town would remember me fondly, even if the dentists burned me in effigy.

Ethan Howe, another server, came over and set a glass of white wine down in front of me.

I shook my head. "Sorry, Eth, but I didn't order this."

"Compliments of the gentleman in the back," Ethan said, wiggling his eyebrows significantly toward the back of the restaurant. He ruined the effect by snorting and adding, "Saw that on TV once. Always wanted to say it."

"Well done, you," I approved.

I didn't have to turn around to know who "the gentleman" was, but I did anyway, just so I could glare at him. Dunn Johnson sat alone at a booth, eating a giant cheeseburger with one hand and drinking a chocolate milk with the other. When he saw me looking, he smiled around his mouthful and raised half his burger in salute.

No one should look sexy drinking chocolate milk. Ever. It defied reason. It had to be against the law. And yet there was that big man, taking up half the booth, smiling at me like I was the sun after a long, long rainstorm, and he wanted nothing more on earth than for me to smile back.

I was going to kill him.

Literally kill him.

Possibly using the straw from my eleventh weekly tonic water.

"Thanks, Ethan," I said, summoning half a smile.

I grabbed my phone off the table and fired off a text to Dunn.

Tucker: Leave. Now.

Dunn's reply came more slowly, probably because he was typing with only his burger-free hand.

Dunn: Who, me? I'm just enjoying a meal. Best burgers in the Thicket.

I ignored this, as well as his next messages.

Dunn: What time's your date coming?

Dunn: You look real nice in that shirt.

Dunn: Bernadette's been asking for you.

Dunn: How's your water?

Seriously, the only thing worse than enduring this farce was having Dunn watch me endure it.

"Hey, Ethan?" I asked, as he strode past my table. "See that potted fern over there?" I gestured to a plant about ten feet away, directly between me and Dunn. "Could you do me a huge favor and move it, like… six inches to the left? I'm having an allergic reaction."

Ethan looked at the fern and blinked. "To the… to the fern?"

"Something like that." I smiled widely. "I'd so appreciate it."

He smiled readily. "You got it, Doc!"

My phone vibrated a second later.

Dunn: Rude and uncool.

I shut my phone off before I could type out something blistering and friendship-severing like, *"No, what's uncool is the whole freakin' situation you engineered"*… but then, that wouldn't be true, would it?

It was Dunn's fault, sure, in the sense that he'd set me up on all these fucking apocalyptic dates, but whose fault was it for allowing it? It was like people who claimed they cared about the environment but still littered. Or people who claimed they hated graphic violence on television but still let their friends con them into watching *Game of Thrones*…which was another thing I'd done because Dunn had flashed me those big green eyes and had lived to regret.

All in all, Operation Healthy Boundaries was going swimmingly, thanks for asking.

I tapped my finger on the table and glanced around the restaurant. It was packed with the usual crowd of Thicketeers as well as a few of my Shamin' Greatest Hits.

Leon the Lecher, date number nine, sat at the bar. He'd greeted me on our date with an "I'd like to see you wearing nothing but a smile and my cum," which I'd thought was a bit of a forward response to "Leon! Nice to meet you! I've heard you play golf," but apparently he'd gotten the wrong impression of me after Dunn had spent forty minutes bragging about my honest, direct nature while the two of them were waiting in line at Levon's Lucky Lube for an oil change.

Kevin, sitting with his back to me by the window, had looked sweet enough, but he'd opened my sixth date with, "I like to get creative with my nuts," which had killed the conversation quickly. It recovered for half a second when I realized he'd literally meant *nuts*, since his family owned a peanut farm just south of town that used the same alfalfa distributor that Dunn used, and that Dunn had gone on and on to him about how open-minded I was. But the conversation had withered and died for good after he'd spent two and a half hours extolling the virtue of the humble legume, which could be used in place of all kinds of things, including conditioner, shaving cream… and lube.

And there in the booth by the door was Devraj, date ten. He'd returned my "Hello" with a breathless ramble of "I'm sorry, I shouldn't even be here, I'm still in love with my boyfriend—*ex*-boyfriend, *oh my God*, Jeremy's really actually my *ex*-boyfriend for *good* this time— and I wasn't gonna come, but Dunn said you were a really good listener, so I figured what the hey and I'm *sorryyyy*." That date hadn't actually been too awful. We'd spent a long time commiserating about men we couldn't have, and after I'd counseled him a little, he'd said he was going to try to work things out with Jeremy. Considering he was sucking the face off his booth-mate, I was pretty sure it had worked.

But I had to hand it to those guys. At least they'd been up-front about who they were and what they wanted. Meanwhile, here *I* was, waiting for date eleven, because I was unable to tell my best friend *no*.

It was one word.

One syllable.

Two tiny letters.

I mean, I could *say* it. I had said it. Ten times and counting. But I hadn't stuck to it, and that was the problem. I kept caving, partly because I knew Dunn loved me and he wanted what was best for me—though frankly, my mom had used that rationale for years to try to make me eat collard greens and it hadn't worked. The other part of the equation was something more complicated, and I couldn't puzzle it out no matter how much cake I consumed or how many nights I lay awake in my bed, pounding my pillow and thinking about it.

The door opened and a guy with thinning, sandy hair and a phone pressed to his ear walked in.

I sat up straighter, trying and failing to find something handsome about him, but in the end, he seemed to spot someone in the corner of the bar behind me, because he hurried off in that direction.

I sagged back down in my seat.

I couldn't keep doing this to myself week after week, not only because I'd soon weigh more than Bernadette — who rang in at a cool 450, but don't tell the other girls — but because it was taking a toll on the most precious thing in my life: my friendship with Dunn.

For those unaware, Dunn Johnson was pure goodness. Yes, even when I wanted to impale him with a plastic straw.

Oh, he could crack wise, and he could play pranks, but there wasn't a mean bone in his body. He worked hard and he loved harder, and he was loyal as the day was long. He got my sense of humor. He made me feel safe and strong. And he was never competitive or jealous, which was more than I could say for other folks, including my little brother. I'd even heard Dunn tell Thom off once, when he'd complained that everything came easily to me.

Ha. Little did Thom know.

Trouble was, it was hard to be around Dunn and all his goodness without... well, loving him. And it was impossible to love him and not love him *too* much.

In ways he couldn't return.

So I'd been trying to stay out of his path... at least as much as I could, considering he was a Doberman who could scent me out and happened to know all my hiding places.

I never went by to see Bernadette anymore, and even though Dunn had been begging for help remodeling his house, I hadn't bitten. I hadn't gone fishing but once the whole winter, and that was when Mal and Brooks and a whole bunch of other folks had been along. I only went to the Johnsons' house when I knew he wouldn't be there. And it turned out having Jenn as my temporary receptionist had actually been a stroke of genius, because Dunn hadn't come by the office since the day I hired her.

I figured he didn't wanna fuel any jealousy leftover from the Pickin', but honestly, I wasn't sure, since Jenn was a subject I'd flat out refused to discuss since that night at the Steak 'n Bait.

I looked at my phone again, ready to call time of death on Date 11, when the front door opened once more and a really adorable guy walked in. He ran a nervous hand over golden-brown hair and straightened his sweater. He smiled at the host and nodded at the bar, and I was almost positive he was looking for someone.

Okay, wow. Maybe Dunn hadn't done too badly this time.

I surreptitiously ran a hand through my own hair and fixed my posture.

He approached the table, and I summoned a tremulous smile. Oh, he *was* cute, with little gold freckles and a Cupid's bow mouth. *Be cool, Tucker.*

He smiled and extended a hand—Cool! Dry! And merciful heavens, the man had all his own teeth!—then said, "Hey! I'm Aiden. You must be Kevin?"

For half a second—okay, three-quarters of a second—I debated saying *yes*, but…

"Uh. No. Kevin's the dark-haired guy by the window." I held his hand a fraction of a second longer. "You don't have a nut allergy, do you?"

"Pardon?"

I let go of his hand and smiled. "Nothing. Not a thing. You have a lovely evening."

He lifted his chin and hurried off, and I closed my eyes and sighed.

When I opened them, it was to find Sandy-Haired-Phone-Man standing by my table.

"I think I found him," he barked. "*Finally.* You Tucker Wright?"

"I... yes?"

The guy pursed his lips and looked me up and down, from my head to the fifth button of my shirt, just visible over the table. "Mm. She said you'd be taller."

I looked down at myself. He... he did realize I was seated, right?

"S-she, who?" I demanded, as Sandy-Hair threw himself into the opposite side of the booth.

"My mother." He set his phone on speaker in the center of the table. "She negotiated the terms of this meeting with a... what was his name again, Mother?"

"Dunn Johnson," said a tinny voice from the phone. "We met at the feed store. Good Lord, that man is a tall drink of water on a hot day."

I blinked at the phone, then at the man. I clenched my fingers around my straw. "You must be Gordon."

He snorted. "Obviously." He gave me a look like he doubted my intelligence. "Thought they said you were a doctor."

I inhaled sharply. "Could you just... excuse me one quick li'l second?"

I grabbed my phone off the table, turned it on, and

began texting rapidly while Gordon snapped his fingers —*snapped his fingers!*—to get Alana's attention so he could order two orders of jalapeño poppers with a side of mayonnaise for "his side of the table" and made sure to ask for separate checks.

Mayonnaise? Ew.

Tucker: The. Flippity. Flipping. Feed. Store?

Tucker: You set me up on a DATE…

Tucker: Through his MOTHER…

Tucker: At the SEED AND FEED?

Tucker: I cannot describe on how many levels this is WRONG. And he ordered MAYO, Dunn!

Dunn: Ingrid and I had a lovely discussion about the merits of alfalfa versus corn for young pigs.

Dunn: You know, she breeds potbellies?

Dunn: Not that I'd ever personally have a pet pig, but she showed me pics of her baby Moxie and they're adorbs.

Tucker: THEN YOU DATE HER.

I clicked my screen off and set the phone on the table so hard I nearly cracked the screen.

"Pardon me, Gordon. I think there's been a misunderstand—"

"Gordon? Gordon, what's happening?" came a fractious voice from the phone. "I can't see what's happening!"

"The man was playing on his phone, Mother. And now he's looking at me… peevishly. Sort of like Moxie when she's constipated."

I sucked in a breath. In a lifetime of insults, comparison to a constipated potbellied pig was a new low.

"Now he's trying to ignore me," Gordon narrated. "And he's looking… irked. Decidedly irked. He's chugging his wine. He's… what's a stronger word than irked?"

"Ahh, angry?" Ingrid suggested. "Enraged. Murderous?"

"Testy," Gordon said as Alana delivered his poppers. "Very definitely— Wait, hang on, Mother. Excuse me, miss. *Miss*?" He snapped his fingers again until Alana turned around. "Did I or did I not ask for mayonnaise?"

Alana looked at Gordon, then at his two plates, each of which had a fair-sized ramekin of mayonnaise. "Yes, sir. But it's right there on the side of your plate."

"This?" he scoffed, tapping a mayonnaise container with his fork. "No. Oh, no no no. When I ask for mayonnaise, I mean I need an *appropriate quantity* of mayonnaise. You cannot eat poppers with... with... this. It's a slap in the face."

"Ah, Gordon," his mother said happily. "You do love your condiments."

Alana looked to me like I might know what the hell was happening, but all I could do was shrug helplessly. I had been unaware that poppers required *any* quantity of mayonnaise.

Medical school had not prepared me for this.

Life had not prepared me for this.

Alana hurried away, and I wet my suddenly dry lips. "As I was saying, Gordon, I think there's been a misunderstanding. My friend Dunn—"

"Your *best* best friend," Ingrid said warmly from the speaker.

I barked a little laugh. Was he, though? Was he *really*? As I watched Gordon cramming three mayonnaise-coated poppers in his mouth at once, I had to wonder.

Last fall at the Pickin', I'd have told you there wasn't a soul on this earth who knew me better than Dunn did, but with each successive loser he set me up with, I began to doubt whether he knew what I wanted—what I *deserved* —at all.

I grabbed my phone to text him that he needed to get

me out of here immediately, but before I'd begun typing, the man himself pulled up a chair and flipped it around backward so he could face the table.

"Howdy, gents. Tucker, looking magnificent as *always*. And you must be Gordon. You're… you… have a little, ah… popper juice on your chin there."

Gordon grunted and ran the back of his hand over his mouth.

"Hey, Dunn," Ingrid drawled from the speaker flirtatiously.

"Uh." Dunn looked at my incredulous face and shrugged helplessly. "Hey, Ms. Cooper. How's Moxie?"

She giggled. *Giggled*. "Oh, she's just great. How's Bernadette?"

"She's alright, thanks for asking. Old Spots are a hardy breed, for all that they're rare." Dunn darted another glance at my face and bit his lip nervously, like he'd finally clued in to the fact that I was displeased — possibly thanks to my laser eyes, or maybe my expression of absolute rage.

Alana plunked a soup bowl of mayonnaise down on the table, then flounced away.

"This, *this*, is an appropriate amount of mayo!" Gordon groaned with satisfaction.

Dunn pressed his leg against mine in a silent gesture he'd done a hundred times — a gesture that was familiar and soothing, or would've been at any other day and time, but in this moment just pissed me off because it was a reminder that Dunn Johnson didn't just know the hiding places in my house, he knew the hiding places in my heart too, and I was fucking helpless against it.

"So, Gordon, you and Tuck have a lot in common! You both like science fiction."

Gordon slurped his jalapeño popper. "You ever seen

Game of Thrones? I freakin' loved it. Red Wedding was a cinematic *classic*."

I shuddered.

"Pity your sow's past breeding age, Dunn. We could've had some beautiful babies," Gordon's mom tittered.

Aaaaand that's when I was officially done.

More than done.

Overdone.

"This has been great, but I'm leaving. Thanks so much for—" I shrugged, unable to think of a way to end that sentence "—you know." I dropped some cash on the table to cover Alana's service, since I was pretty sure Gordon wouldn't. "Y'all have a great night." I pushed out of the booth.

"Packed this up for you to go, Doc," Alana whispered, pushing a small container of what I fervently hoped was chocolate cake into my hand. "On the house."

"Wait. Wait, what's happening?" Ingrid demanded. "Gordon? Gordon! Who's leaving?"

Gordon licked popper juice off his finger. "Tyler."

"*Tucker*," Dunn corrected hotly.

"Yeah, Tucker," Gordon repeated. He looked up at me. "Oh, hey, if you see the waitress again on your way out, can you ask her to keep the poppers coming?"

Not if you were starving in the desert and that popper stood between you and certain death, Hippocratic oath or nah. "Sure."

"Tuck." Dunn's oh-so-reasonable tone that suggested *I* was the one acting like a toddler here. He made a grab for my wrist, and I dodged it.

"I'm going home."

"You can't!" he insisted, hurrying after me. "Not yet! With me sitting down to be an interpreter for you, you and Gordon could…"

"Could what? Eat our way through the restaurant's

entire popper supply? Slather ourselves with mayo and *wrassle*? No, thank you."

"'Course not," Dunn said, following me out to the sidewalk. "You hate mayo, and you're a terrible wrestler."

With the sun down, there was a distinct wintery chill in the air, like spring would never come.

I felt this on a deep, cellular level.

Without sparing my "*best* best friend" a look, I turned left and marched down the street toward home with my cake.

Dunn sighed loud enough for me to hear from two doors down. "Don't forget too many cookies before bed give you a sugar hangover, babe," he called. "Drink water! Make good choices! I promise I'll do better with the next guy!"

The next guy?

I stopped dead in the middle of the sidewalk and whirled to face him. Panicked, horrified laughter shook my chest.

"No. *Nope.* Nooo. Nuh uh. EN-to-the-OH. Nein. Nyet. I am being very, absolutely serious, right now, so please, *please* hear me when I tell you, Dunn: you have set me up on *eleven* terrible dates, and that is plenty. You will *never* set me up on another date as long as I live. Do you understand that? Please tell me that you understand. You and me, no more dates."

Dunn rocked back on his heels. He rubbed his jaw, which had looked smooth in the Tavern, but was usually covered with fine blond bristles this late in the day and —*shit*, I did not need to remind myself that I knew things like that. He licked his lips and nodded thoughtfully.

"You're angry."

Give the man a prize. "Yes, I am. You wasted everyone's time. Gordon and I had nothing in common."

He winced. "I get it. But in my defense, his mom made him sound like a total catch, and she never mentioned the mayonnaise thing, because I promise I knew better— sorry, sorry!" He held up his hands like he wondered if I might attack him. "I can see that I shouldn't have taken her word for it," he insisted. "My bad."

I nodded once, firmly. "So that's the end of that."

"It is." Dunn nodded again and drew an X over his heart. "I promise."

I took a deep, calming breath and nodded again. "Thank—"

"I'll vet every dude myself from now on. Extensively. And I'll ask about mayonnaise *and* ex-boyfriends."

I clenched my free hand into a fist and clutched my cake with the other. "Sweet baby Jesus, your continued existence on this planet is the greatest proof of a merciful God I have ever encountered, Dunn Johnson."

"Aw." His mouth quirked up, and he wrapped an arm around my shoulders, pulling me against him. "Thanks, boo. Back atcha."

I sighed. Even now, *even now* when I most desperately wanted and needed to, it was impossible for me to stay mad at the man. I shook my head—at him, at myself, at the whole impossible situation.

"How is it, Dunn Johnson, that you know me so well in some ways and so little in others? You know I don't eat spicy food. You know I'm going home to eat a truly worrisome amount of sweets from the freezer—"

"The one in the garage labeled 'Bacteria Samples' that's actually full of baked goods. Genius."

I pressed my lips together. Vienna had never cottoned on to my stash, but naturally Dunn knew. Dunn knew everything... except the most important things.

"—but you don't know the first thing about what I want

in a man? If you tried on purpose to find me terrible candidates, you couldn't have done worse. Why the heck are you so obsessed with this?"

"I just..." He looked guilty, then embarrassed. "I told you back in November. I said, 'I can't be happy when Tucker's not happy.'" He shrugged. "That's the long and short of it. I want you and me to have what Mal and Brooks have... with Ava and Paul."

I nearly whimpered. So close to what I wanted him to say and yet so far.

"You want me a-and *Gordon*... to be besties with you... and Jenn."

He frowned. "Well, no. I mean, Jesus, not Gordon. Unless you wanted to give it a second chance?"

I sighed, suddenly overwhelmingly tired. "I need a break, Dunn. This isn't working."

"Yeah?" He nodded. "Okay, no, I can respect that. Even NFL players get a bye week. So we'll take next week off, we'll come back the following week, and we'll hit it hard. I have, like... a dozen more candidates, and I find new ones all the ti—"

"No, Dunn. Not a break from dating, a break from *this*. From you." I shook my head up at the cloud-covered moon. "God, maybe a break from the Thicket entirely, I don't know."

Maybe I'd go and visit my parents for the weekend. Or head someplace where the breeze was a little less chilly. Something.

"But, Tuck—"

His pleading voice almost killed me, but it occurred to me right then and there what the missing piece was, the thing that kept me hanging on Friday after horrible Friday: these setups were a connection between me and Dunn. A way of knowing I was always at the forefront of his brain, even when he was at the mechanic or the feed store. A way of knowing I had his attention and focus, since that was the most of him I could have.

"But nothing," I said softly. "If you care about me, Dunn Johnson, leave me be."

4

DUNN

17-Across: Not aware of or not concerned about what is happening around one (9 letters)

"Next time I won't be so quick to trust a woman," I promised her, raking out the mucky straw that had accumulated near the open barn door. "Which, honestly, is a life lesson someone ought to put on a cross-stitch sampler and hang somewhere."

Bernadette regarded me with interest. She was always such a good listener.

"And, alright, maybe Brooks had a point about digging a little deeper into what makes a good match. I can do that. There's a ton of stuff about Tucker Wright I can use to narrow it down to the absolute perfect pick. And since he's going to fight me tooth and nail on this, I need to make sure the next guy is the one, you know? I don't mind telling you, he scared the bejeebers out of me the other day, talking about taking a break from the Thicket. Wouldn't be home without Tucker here."

Bernadette made a snuffling noise of agreement and wandered over to nose the pile of debris I'd collected. I hadn't checked it for anything dangerous, so I didn't want her picking through it.

"Get out of there," I snapped. "Nothing good for you in there."

She turned to me with hurt-filled eyes, and I cursed as my phone began to ring. "Damn it, Bernie. I didn't mean to lose my temper. C'mere." I squatted down and waited for her to lumber over before scratching her jaw and scritching her ears. "Good girl. Daddy loves you. Who's the best girl?"

I held the phone up to my face in time to hear my mother's voice. "You'd better not be talking to that pig."

I shot Bernie a look of apology and mouthed, "Sorry," before turning and walking away so she couldn't hear my mother's hateful words.

"Hey, Mama."

"I need your help with something. Can you come over?"

"Yeah, sure. What's going on?"

"After Tucker fixed the shutter for us, I realized I wanted to put some on the shed out back to be all matchy. Tucker can't do it this weekend because of his date, so I thought I'd see if you could come by and hang them for me. You know I don't like to ask your dad to do anything strenuous on account of making his stents pop out."

No matter how many times we'd all tried to explain to her that arterial stents didn't work that way, she still didn't buy it. But that wasn't the part that bothered me. "Wait. What date? I didn't set Tucker up with a date this weekend. He told me not to."

Mom sounded awfully nonchalant about it. "Oh, you didn't? Hm. Guess it's with someone else, then."

"Who? Who would it be with?" I scrambled my brain up and down the list of single guys in the Thicket. It had better not be Kort Blanchard or I was going to have to intervene. That guy was shifty as hell, what with all his... classic cars and stuff. Who needed that many cars? No one, that's who.

Mom's voice sounded distracted. "Honey, there's someone at the door. See you when you get here. And thanks a bunch."

I growled as I pulled the phone down to text Tucker.

Me: Who you going out with this weekend?

There was no response, so I tried again.

Me: I just want to cross them off the list so I don't double-book you. That's all.

Still nothing. I tried calling him. No answer.

"Fuck," I muttered, trying the office line.

"Thicket Med, how may I help you?" As soon as I heard Jenn's familiar voice, I both ducked and threw the phone away from me at the same time.

As if she was here on the farm, watching me.

"Shit," I hissed. "Stupid, stupid."

I duckwalked over to the debris pile and began to pick through it in search of my phone. I tried not to notice Bernadette's judgmental stare. Or the one from my young farmhand, Luisa, who always seemed to be lurking around judging me even more than the pig.

"Mind your business," I muttered. I picked up the dirty phone, grateful for the military-grade case I had on it. Ever since I'd run over my phone with a tractor a couple of years ago, Tucker had made sure the case I had was inde-structible.

"Dunn, is that you?" Jenn's voice sounded tinny and far away. I hit the speakerphone button so I didn't have to put the dirty phone to my ear.

"Oh. Yeah, uh. Hey. Sorry. Dropped the phone."

Her voice went weird. "Heeey."

Hadn't we already covered that part? "Hey. Yeah, uh… Tuck there?"

There was silence for a few beats which was a little weird since Jenn had never met a silence she couldn't fill. "We going out Saturday night?" she asked.

Hellfire and hay bales. "Uh, sure? Yeah." I thought of Tucker's date. "Yeah. That's a good idea actually. I'll pick the place." I just needed to find out where he was going and it'd be all set. And this time I wouldn't let him see me. I'd just be there in case of emergencies.

"Oh good. Hang on for Doc Wright. Bye, cutie."

It seemed to take forever before Tucker came on the line. "Dr. Wright speaking."

"Hey, it's me. Listen, Mom said—"

"Dunn? Jesus. I'm working here."

Bernadette rolled her eyes, and I nodded in agreement. "You can't take a break to answer one text?"

"It was two texts and a phone call—now two phone calls—and I already told you. No more dates."

"Okay, but—"

"Dunn, I mean it. Stop this." He sounded harried, but I figured he was probably just having a busy day. It happened to the best of us. Hell, I'd already been up since before dawn dealing with two heifers who were in a mood.

"Okay, but—"

He cut me off again. "No. No okay buts. I'm done with the dates. Done. Besides, this weekend's thing isn't even a *date*-date. I'm going out with Carter Rogers, your dad's temporary cardiologist. He called me the other night 'cause I guess your mom gave him my number, and we're going out to have a meal and, ah…" He took a breath. "Catch up. As former… you know… colleagues. Not a date. Got it?"

I let out a breath and let my shoulders drop. "Okay.

Phew. That's… good. That's good." I wasn't sure why it was good, but the words just came out anyway.

Bernadette made a snorting noise of relief too.

"That Bernie?" Tuck's voice sounded softer. "Give her scritches for me."

I reached out and ran my fingers behind Bernadette's ear. She closed her eyes and leaned into my touch. "Nah. She's in the pen with the rest of the hogs," I said, clearing my throat.

"Mm-hm. Sure. Hey. Maybe drop by your mom and dad's place. She said she had some work that needed doing, and I can't help her this weekend."

I sighed and stood back up, kicking some mud off my boots and heading for the house. I ignored the dirty look Luisa shot me. Teenagers were pains in the butt. If she wasn't so darned good at farm work, I'd have tossed her out on her ass by now.

Well, not really. But I would have given her a stern look or two.

"Heading over now," I told him. "I'll let you go."

There was an awkward beat of silence which made my stomach hurt. Tucker and I never had awkward silences. Ever.

"Dunn, you need to give me some space. Stop calling and texting me. Just… just stop for a little while. Alright?"

"Mpfh."

"That's not an agreement, D."

"Gotta go."

I hung up the phone and hopped in the truck. It was a good thing Mama needed help because I was in the mood to bang something.

Hard.

AFTER HANGING THE SHUTTERS, I joined Mama on the back porch for some cold lemonade. She was sitting on a blanket stacking old wooden blocks with Ava's little boy when I threw myself down on one of the chairs. Ava lifted an eyebrow at me.

"Gordon Cooper. Really?"

I groaned and leaned my head back on the flowery cushion. "I know already. I don't need to hear about it from you too."

Mama lifted her head up as little Beau swatted at one of the blocks with a plastic hammer. "Oh, that reminds me, Ingrid is spearheading the cookbook project for the Beautification Corps next year. I told her you might be willing to tell her your bacon cornbread recipe if she asked real nice." She stopped and frowned, which hopefully meant she'd realized how ridiculous and assumptive that had been. "Wait. Gordon Cooper? And *Tucker*?"

"Exactly," Ava muttered. "I can't think of two people less suited for each other. First Frank Derring and now Gordon Cooper."

I opened my mouth to argue, but Mama beat me to it. "But Tucker was raised Episcopalian, and Frank comes from a long line of Southern Baptists. That doesn't even make any sense."

Before I could cut in, she added, "And Gordon... don't even get me started on a man who couldn't even move out of his mama's house to go to college. The poor man got one of those internet degrees because he was too afraid to leave the county. Meanwhile, Tucker spent his junior year in Italy. Italy! I can't think of a worse match."

I threw up my hands. "It's slim pickings for gay guys in the Thicket! I'm doing the best I can."

Mama frowned at me. "Honey, there are eighty-two members in the Thicket-Lurch chapter PFLAG alone.

Have you tried anyone from Pecker Lurch or Great Nuthatch? What about Rafe Whitney? He loves crosswords and Christmas trees, just like Tucker."

Ava clapped her hands. "Heck yes. Perfect pick! Plus, he's hot as hades."

I shook my head emphatically, picturing the firefighter from the town to the east of us. Rafe with all the height and all the thick dark hair. The man looked like some kind of… superhero on his day off. And he was a firefighter, in case I forgot to mention that part. So… kind of an actual hero. Which Tucker needed no part of. None. "They're too similar, Mama."

Ava got a look on her face, a look I remembered from her scheming high school days.

Mama handed a block back to little Beau before zapping her eyes on me. "Dunn, why is this even a situation? How come you and Tucker can't see —"

Ava choked on her lemonade and began to sputter. I reached over and whacked her on the back, while I could have sworn she shot my mama a look.

When she finally got herself under control, she shook me off. "Dunn, why don't you let your mama and I handle this?"

My skin felt prickly all of a sudden. "Handle what?"

"Good idea," Mama said. Now she was looking schemey too. Didn't these people know scheming was wrong? I never did like people butting into other people's business.

"No," I clarified. "Not good. Not good at all. Tucker doesn't need other people setting him up. In fact… in fact, he's asked that we stop. He doesn't want to be set up anymore."

Ava took another sip of her lemonade and looked thoughtful. "I have some great ideas. What if we…"

Mom made a happy sound. "Ooh! We'll get the Beautification Corps involved. They love a good charity project."

"Now see here!" I cried, standing up to emphasize my point. "Tucker Wright is not a damned charity project. I can't believe you just said that."

Both women blinked at me, and Beau giggled.

Mama clutched the neckline of her blouse. "Dunn Johnson."

"Sorry for cursing, Mama. I just… I don't want him to be unhappy."

Mama's face softened. "Of course you don't, sweetie."

"I want him to find the perfect man for him."

Ava patted my knee after I sat back down. "Of course you do."

I sighed. "I don't want him to ever feel unloved or… or lonely, you know?"

Mama's eyes looked extra sparkly in the afternoon sunshine as she exchanged a look with Ava. "Yes, baby. We do know. Don't you worry. We know just the right man for him."

I tried to tell myself this was a good thing. Mama and Ava did have a good track record of matching people up when it came right down to it. But… I still had my reservations.

"Just not Rafe," I said, standing back up to leave. The day was getting away from me, and I still had more work to do on the farm.

Ava tilted her head at me and smirked. "Why not?"

"He's too slick," I muttered. "Always doing good deeds for people and stuff. I don't buy it."

The women exchanged another knowing look before shooting me innocent faces with little spinny halos above their heads. "If you say so," Mama said.

I studied them for a minute before nodding. "Good."

The sound of their laughter as I made my way out of the back gate followed me all the way to my truck. Lord only knew what was going to happen, but at least I could keep my promise to Tucker.

I wasn't going to set him up on any more dates.

My mama was.

5

TUCKER

4-ACROSS: Useful for screwing or nailing (4 letters)

I TURNED down the gravel lane to Dunn's farm like I'd done a billion times over the years, and I swore to myself that this time — *this time* — when I talked to him, it was going to be different.

I wasn't gonna let him do that thing he did with the charm and… and… and the wounded doe eyes, and the disarming smile that said, "I know you from the inside out, Tucker Wright, and I like you lots." This time, I wasn't going to let him talk his way out of accepting total responsibility for his actions.

This time I was going to be immune to his wiles.

And this time, for maybe the first time, I was going to *make* him listen to me… because this time he'd gone too far, and I was one hundred percent pissed off.

I hadn't seen Dunn in the six and a half days (not that I was counting) since I'd laid down the law outside the

Tavern and told him I needed a break. He hadn't even texted in the two days since I'd *re*-laid down the law and told him to leave me be.

But, Dunn being Dunn, that hadn't stopped him from finding a way to be *allll* the way up in my business. Oh, no. Instead, the man had infected half the town with Find Tucker A Date disease—a plague twice as contagious as chicken pox and three times as annoying—and suddenly gay men were popping up all over the place like a bad rash.

First there'd been Carole Phipps, who'd ended up in my office yesterday with her five-year-old, Little Timmy—not to be confused with his daddy, Big Timmy, our town plumber—because Little Timmy had somehow managed to bruise his, er... *littler* Timmy while climbing a tree. As if that weren't traumatizing enough, at least for Timmy and me, as soon as I'd given him some ice and pain relievers and Mrs. Phipps had distracted him with her phone, she'd turned to me with a gleam in her eye.

"Doc Wright, while I'm here... What would you say you look for in a partner?"

Naively enough, I'd thought this was some kind of cry for help. "Well, I'd want him to be patient and kind. Never rough or abusive. You know, if you ever feel—"

"Right, sure. But what about, like, eye color?" She'd gotten her phone out like she was making a note and looked at me expectantly. "And would you say you're more of a lake man or a mountain man?"

"What? Uh... lake," I'd replied absently, thinking of Dunn's cabin on Bull Lake. "Carole—"

"And for eye color, I'll just say lake green?"

I thought of Dunn's eyes and nodded. Then I shook my head. "Wait, what's going on here?"

"Not a thing, Doc! I'll just ask Jenn to book us a

follow-up for next week." She'd winked, stood, and carried poor Timmy—and his ice pack—to the car.

Then this morning, after listening to Vienna complain for a literal hour about how Jenn had de-alphabetized my patient files and instead put them in order of who drove the best cars in the Thicket because "That's just how they organize themselves in my brain, Vienna! *God*, open your mind," I'd walked down the street for a coffee, only to be *accosted* by Amos Nutter on the sidewalk.

If you've never been accosted by an octogenarian, you cannot understand how horrifying this was.

He'd seen me coming and raised his cane in salute, and I guess I must've telegraphed my intent to avoid a conversation, because he'd immediately clutched his side and cried, "Oh, no! Catch me, Emmaline! There goes ma' hip!" I'd detoured back to offer assistance, of course, and that's when the man had slow-motion bodychecked me, right up against the Wisteria Cafe's window.

"Doc Wright," he'd yelled in my ear. "Fancy meeting you here."

"Are you okay?"

"Who, me? Just fine. Fit as a fiddle." He'd leaned his body weight more heavily against me and spoken even louder. "But while I have you, have I ever mentioned my nephew Elmer? He's a mechanic over in Dooberville. From what I heard, the boy knows his way around some hot fluids, and he'll take real good care of your crank shaft."

"What? But… but I don't need a mechanic?" Did I? Was this some kind of mechanic shakedown? Was Amos Nutter the mafia?

"You need *this* mechanic. He's got fuel injectors for days, if ya know what I mean." He'd wiggled his eyebrows and popped his tongue meaningfully.

Even *I* couldn't pop my tongue.

"Wait… you mean…Is he…? Are you trying to…?"

"Elmer's a young, gay Adonis," Amos had assured me. "In fact, lotsa folks say he's the spittin' image a'me when I was that age, sooo." He'd smoothed back his thinning hair and grinned so widely his teeth nearly fell out. "Whaddya say? You wanna take him for a test drive?"

"I say… um… no, thank you? Sir, are you on any medications, or…?"

He'd sighed. "Ah, well. Cain't say I didn't try."

But he didn't move. And he was breathing really, really close to my face.

"Mr. Nutter…"

"I might could use an assist, as it happens, Doc," he admitted finally. "Hip's locked up for real this time. Could you maybe…?"

When I'd finally gotten him settled on a bench to wait for his son to come fetch him and gotten him an appointment with the chiropractor in Pecker Lurch for his trick hip, I'd needed coffee more desperately than ever before.

"Iced coffee, please, Fee?" I'd begged. "The biggest one you've got."

After paying, I'd gone to take my place in the line to get my drink.

"Well, hey, there, Doc Wright." Lurlene Jackson's use of blue eyeliner had been as on point as ever. "Don't you look a mite frazzled?"

"Just a bit," I agreed. "Thoughtful of you to point it out."

"Poor thing. You need a man to look after you," she'd said sympathetically. "Someone who'll make you coffee at home."

I'd given her a half-smile because heck yeah, that was exactly what I needed.

She'd taken a step closer, until she was invading the

personal space Amos Nutter had so recently vacated, then glanced left and right before whispering, "So, do you like it... vanilla?"

"Oh." I'd frowned. "Uh. No. More of a hazelnut guy, I guess? Though some days, like today, I just want it straight. And the bigger the better, you know?"

Her eyes went wide. "*Really?*" she'd tittered, clutching her imaginary pearls. "Why, Doc Wright, you sly dog!"

"Huh?"

But Lurleen had already collected her coffee and left with a little curled-finger wave.

"Fee," I'd demanded, after she handed me my coffee and I'd taken my first grateful sips. "Do you have any clue what's gotten into people the last couple days? Everyone's acting *weird.*" Which was saying something, considering what the baseline was around here.

"Not really." She'd shrugged. "Just trying to win the prize, I guess."

"Prize."

She'd nodded. "You know, the prize folks are offering for finding you your perfect match?" She counted off on her fingers. "Free soft drinks for a month at the Tavern. Free Doc Wright Triple Chocolate Heartbreak Cake at Annie's. Free lube job over at Levon's—but frankly I think Levon just threw that in there to drum up business... Uh... let's see..."

I held up a hand. "Got it. Thanks. That's... real helpful. I understand now."

I understood that I'd inadvertently, *unwillingly* become a contestant in a dating show, where my friends and neighbors were competing to find me a boyfriend, and now instead of trying to convince one well-meaning doofus to back off, I now had to convince four dozen. Or more.

And what's more, Annie's Bakery had named their heartbreak cake after me.

I'd stalked out of the cafe and down the street to my house before the penny had dropped.

Vanilla, not as in coffee but as in…

Oh, fuck. And I'd told her I was a *hazelnut*? What the hell had I just confessed to?

More to the point, what the hell had my *former* best, best friend gotten me involved in?

I'd called Vienna and told her to have Jenn cancel my afternoon appointments, then I'd immediately gotten in my car.

Suddenly nowhere was safe. I couldn't be in town. I went stir-crazy staying up in my living area all by myself when I could practically see the ghost of Dunn sprawled on my sofa. And Lord knew I couldn't be in my office because literally every time I walked past Jenn, she narrowed her eyes, snapped her gum, and started talking about how she and Dunn had a date on Saturday.

She reminded me of the singing fish plaque Dunn had inherited from his great-uncle Waylon along with his fishing cabin. Billy the Bass would erupt into song and start flapping its tail anytime it sensed motion… and it only knew one song too.

I sighed. And now I was being mean to Jenn when her only real crimes were having all the equipment Dunn liked best — which I could hardly blame her for — and being jealous of Dunn — which I couldn't blame her for either.

She was also possibly the worst receptionist anyone had ever had — how many times did a person have to be told that recommending Botox to patients was unacceptable? — and I *did* blame her for that, but that wasn't why I was salty.

This situation was utterly, epically, incontrovertibly, and

in all other ways unacceptable. And I was almost positive it was all Dunn's fault, so I was going to freaking tell him so.

I pulled in to my usual spot on the driveway just under the big oak tree in front of the farmhouse, slammed the door, and took a deep breath to center myself.

True story, I'd always loved Dunn's place. The little white house was tiny—one open living space and a half bath downstairs, two cozy bedrooms and a bathroom tucked under the sharply slanted metal roof upstairs—but it was so comfortable that just looking at it gave me the same feeling I got after taking off my shoes and stretching my toes at the end of a long day.

Dunn had redone the outside with white board-and-batten, which set off the original multicolored stone foundation from back in the early 1900s. The wraparound porch had two comfortable rocking chairs near the front door, where Dunn and I had spent many an evening watching the sun set over the trees while the fireflies gave us our own personal fireworks show on the lawn.

Now that Dunn was renovating the inside, he'd gone full-on Chip and Joanna with shiplap and slate and...

And holy crap, that was not remotely what I was here for.

Good Lord, Tucker Wright, can't you stay mad at that man for more than thirty seconds? He had a heartbreak cake named for you, for crying out loud.

But it appeared I couldn't, which did not bode well for me.

My phone jangled in my pocket, and I almost hoped it was Dunn texting, just so I could get properly worked up again, but it wasn't Dunn. It was Carter Rogers.

Carter: *Hey, handsome. We're still on for tomorrow night, right? You, me, dinner... dessert?*

Uh, so. Semi-important information about Carter. He wasn't just a former colleague; he was actually a former boyfriend. As in, the guy I'd once imagined would be my Once Upon a Time and Happily Ever After, until I'd realized my dream future involved putting down roots someplace close to home, and Carter had realized he wasn't ready to put down roots anywhere just yet.

We'd parted amicably—meaning we'd fucked around for maybe a month or so after the breakup, even after I'd moved to the Thicket—but then things had shifted, and we'd grown apart for some reason.

The whine of a saw cut through the air from the general direction of Dunn's workshop just off the pig barn, followed by a very enthusiastic, *very* off-key rendition of his mom's favorite country song "Maria," including all the falsetto bits.

I sighed.

Okay, maybe I knew *exactly* why Carter and I had stopped fucking around after I'd moved to the Thicket, and why I'd quickly rewritten my Happily Ever Afters with another Prince Charming in mind.

And maybe that meant it was a good thing Carter had picked right now to get back in touch. It might be nice to have dinner with a man who might actually want to kiss me at the end of the night, even if I didn't plan on letting him.

Tucker: Yep. Looking forward to it. Where should we meet?

Carter: I'll pick you up at 7. I remember your house. I made us a reservation at someplace called Steak 'n Bait.

The Steak 'n Bait? With Carter? My stomach fluttered at the idea—and not in a good way—but I pushed past it.

Tucker: Sounds great!

It wasn't a date, I told myself. It was still just old colleagues reconnecting. Those colleagues just happened to have seen each other naked. Regularly. For a couple of years.

And the strange, guilty, gnawing feeling in my gut was a perfect example of the feelings I needed to *stop* feeling. Which would be a heck of a lot easier if Dunn Johnson kept his giant nose out of my business.

I nodded once, pleased that I'd managed to work myself up enough to stalk my way to the barn. I took a breath to yell his name, but when I stepped inside and got a good look at the man, I found myself choking on my tongue instead.

Dunn Johnson stood half-naked in a shaft of sunlight that fell through the open double doors at the front of the barn. God's most perfect blue jeans cupped his ass and his thick, thick thighs, which were braced wide apart, but from his glorious shoulders down his thick chest and over his rippling—*yes, rippling*—abs, his golden skin glistened with sweat and flecks of pine sawdust.

He held a heavy table leg in one hand and drilled it into place with the other, as though it were the simplest thing in the world... which for him, it maybe was, though I could see the effort it required in the bunch and flex of his biceps and the sweat that dripped down his neck despite the cool March temperatures. He moved around the table with an odd grace, belting out a song—he'd moved on to some old-school Zac Brown—and only stopped every once in a while to smile at his audience.

All four hundred fifty pounds of her.

"I don't want you, but I need you... Sing it, Bernadette!" he yelled, and I swear to God that sow let out the world's most musical piggy grunt. Her pitch was certainly better than Dunn's. "That's it! You got it, baby!"

I couldn't honestly tell you which made my stomach flip harder, those shiny abs or the wide grin he bestowed on his pig—total lie, it was the abs—but like always with Dunn Johnson, I found myself grinning like a fool in return…

Which was exactly what I was doing when his eyes found mine.

"Holy shit! Tucker!" he cried, tossing down his probably-very-expensive drill and running at me like I'd been away fighting a foreign war, not across town avoiding him. He caught me up in those big, strong, sweaty arms, pulled me against that dirty, sweaty chest, and spun me around in a circle, so my head was filled with the mingled scents of pine and Dunn.

Holy shit.

"Thank goodness you're back! Come see Bernie!" He half carried me to Bernadette's pen. "Or did you wanna go up to the cabin and catch some big bass? Oh, speaking of! Lemme show you the new swimbait I got. It's in the garage." He started heading in that direction but stopped himself. "But the rod I ordered's not here yet. Oh, wait, are you hungry? Did you want some pizza? Or to watch a movie?" He headed toward the side door and the house but stopped again, like he wanted to do all the things and couldn't figure out which one to do first.

He was like a puppy. A really skilled, talented, loving, excitable, hot-as-hades puppy.

"Dunn, I'm not here for any of those things. I came here to… to… tell you again that you need to back off." I reached over the pen gate and scritched Bernadette's head, just behind her ears. Her bristles tickled. "Didn't I, sweet girl? 'Cause your Daddy needs to slow his roll and listen to me when I talk, yes he does."

Bernie grunted her agreement.

"Wait, what? You came all the way out here to see me, to tell me you can't see me?"

"I asked you to leave me be, didn't I?"

"You did," he agreed. "And *I* did, even though it's been nearly two weeks!"

"It's been less than one," I corrected. I glared at him over my shoulder, which was a mistake because he was standing in the sunlight again looking like some kind of glowy, woodchip porn star, and I had to swallow hard and try to remember why I was there. "And it's not leaving me be when you get Carole Phipps or Amos Nutter or *Lurleen* to do your dirty work for you. When I said no more dates, I didn't mean I wanted you to delegate, for heaven's sake, let alone set up a contest with prizes. I came to tell you that you need to call off your dogs."

"I have no idea what you're talking about." Dunn sounded genuinely bewildered. "Amos Nutter? And Lurleen? You mean Lurleen Jackson, my mama's...? Oh. *Oh.*"

"Oh?"

"Well." Dunn frowned and rubbed his chest, like it was painful being that sexy. "I maybe mentioned to my mom that I hadn't had any luck setting you up, and she told me it was because my choices of men were... not... you know..."

"Good?" I supplied.

"I was gonna say *ideal.* Anyway. She said to leave it to her." He shrugged. "So I did."

I blinked. "What do you mean 'so I did'? She said she wanted to set me up and you said, 'Sure, Mama, sounds great! Find Tuck a man'? Without asking any questions about how she was going to do it?"

His guilty face suggested this was *exactly* what had happened.

"How could you, Dunn Johnson? It was bad enough when *you* were the only one setting me up. I do *not* need Lurleen Jackson asking about my kinks in the coffee line so she can win free sandwich wraps for a year!"

Luisa's voice rang out from somewhere behind me. "I'm waiting for Thicket Piercing and Ink to throw in a discount before I hook you up with my uncle Pete, Tuck. I promise you he's worth the wait. I once saw the guy swallow a banana whole by accident."

I turned and gaped at her. "Inappropriate! Also, you're overdue for your tetanus booster, so I'd better see you in my office before your next shift. You promised me. Also, Dunn could get in trouble if you get hurt on the farm."

She rolled her eyes at me but reluctantly agreed. "Yes, Dad," she grumbled before driving off in the utility vehicle.

Dunn snorted.

"Don't encourage her," I snapped.

"Be kinda funny if you were really her dad."

"Be kinda scary, you mean," I muttered. "I'm fine just being her group leader at Rainbow, and don't change the subject. The setups. The whole town's in on it now."

"I bet it all spun way outta hand," he soothed. "You know how my mama gets excited and… Wait." His green eyes got impossibly wider. "You said kinks. *Do* you have kinks?"

"What? I… no. Not… exactly. Irrelevant." I felt my face flame. "Stick to the topic."

But Dunn stared at me with a new sort of interest, like I'd just declared that I had gills or a magic wand.

"But I'm your *best* best friend." His voice was a deep rumble in the quiet afternoon, and his gaze was weirdly intent, watchful. Totally unlike Dunn. For the first time ever in our friendship, it felt almost, sort of like… flirtation. "If anyone's gonna know that kind of thing about you, shouldn't it be me?"

I swallowed hard, my mouth suddenly dry as a bone, and holding his gaze was a challenge. There was a kind of awareness ping-ponging back and forth between us—his

newfound awareness of me, and my awareness of his awareness, and his awareness of my awareness of his awareness,
which was honestly the point when I thought he'd look
away... but he didn't. Instead, he doubled down.

"I missed you this week, Tucker Wright," he said softly.
"And I get you were mad at me, and I get you needed space,
but... I missed you. You're like the other part of me. Being
without you's like walking around with only half of my
body."

I fought hard against the pull of that gaze and forced
myself to roll my eyes. "You *couldn't* walk around with only
half your body."

"*Exactly.*" Dunn's cheeks twitched, more like a flinch
than a smile. "It's been a real shit week."

I sighed, and Bernadette squealed in sympathy.

It really *had* been a shit week.

"And I learned my lesson," Dunn swore, all innocence.
"If you don't want another date, then *no* more dates. Pinky
promise, super swear. I'll let you find your own dudes. A-
and I'll have a word with my mama too and tell her to
cancel everything, effective immediately. Just say we can be
friends again, Tuck. I've got whole seasons of that baking
show I haven't watched 'cause you haven't been here, and
Bernadette's grown so much you probably don't recognize
her"—he thrust a hand out toward the pig, who looked
exactly as rotund as the last time I saw her, but who never-
theless gave the pitiful whine of an abandoned orphan
—"and last night I ordered a large pepper and onion with
half black olives."

My stomach clenched. "You hate black olives."

"But I never order pizza for just me, do I?" He heaved a
frustrated sigh. "I just don't *work* without you. And I don't
want to."

Ugh. It was a good thing Dunn had never turned his talents toward, say, a life of crime. He'd have made entire countries throw open their borders and lay down their weapons with the power of those big, green eyes. Bank managers would open their vaults and wave him out with a smile. Spies would type up all their secrets, with footnotes, and just fork them over.

So how the heck was *I* supposed to resist him?

"You're impossible," I groaned, rolling my eyes to the rafters.

He grinned like he was suddenly sure it was all going to be okay. "The kind of impossible you want to pick you up at six tomorrow morning for fishing and tie your clinch knots for ya?"

"Fine." I sighed, which sounded a whole lot like letting out a breath I'd been holding for six and a half days. "Fine."

Dunn whooped and wrapped those big arms around me again, pulling me into the overwhelming heat and scent of him so I could rest my cheek against his naked, sweaty pec. Exactly where I most wanted to be.

I pushed myself away. "I have to be back early tomorrow, though. I have a… a dinner tomorrow night."

"Oh, right," he agreed. "Your old colleague?"

I nodded slowly. "Carter. He made us a reservation at the Steak 'n Bait. He, ah… he's new in the area."

"So, you wanna stick around tonight? I can order some burgers and show you my swimbait and —?"

"No! I… I can't. I have paperwork to catch up on, since I stormed over here today." Not to mention the fact that I was more than a little hard, and I'd be damned if I'd let him see it.

Boundaries. Healthy, healthy boundaries.

"Ah, okay. Sucks, but you made the right choice, 'cause

I was *dyin'* over here." He grinned broadly, and I had to laugh out loud. "So... tomorrow, then?"

"Tomorrow," I agreed.

And I prayed that by then I'd figure out how to be just friends with Dunn Johnson, because not having him in my life wasn't an option.

6

DUNN

12-Down: A person who says one thing and does another (9 letters)

IT WAS a gorgeous morning on the lake. The kind of morning that reminded me of how Tucker and I had originally struck up our unlikely friendship.

"Stop tapping your foot," Tuck mumbled, nudging my arm with his elbow.

I finished tying his lure with a clinch knot and handed it to him. "Stop nagging me," I muttered back. My foot obeyed Tucker without asking me permission, as if my body lived to serve the fussy physician sitting next to me.

"How're those heifers you were having trouble with?" he asked after casting his line and sitting back in his folding chair.

"Fine. You were right. I think one of them is pregnant. Not sure about the other." I cast my own line. "Hey, you remember the day we met?"

I felt his eyes on me even though I kept my own on the water. I wasn't quite sure why I was feeling strangely sentimental this morning, but there it was.

"I believe you were like eight years old and I was asked to watch you while your parents took Brooks and Gracie into a haunted house at Halloween."

I turned and gaped at him. "Say, what? I was talking about the time we found the same fishing hole out by Fossie Creek."

Tuck let out a warm chuckle. "Wasn't the first time, D. And you know it."

"I do *not* know it. What the hell are you talking about?"

"You were mad as a hornet they wouldn't take you into the haunted house. When they saw me taking care of my brother and the two of you recognized each other from school, they ditched you with us so they could go in. As soon as they'd disappeared into the entrance, you turned around and kicked me in the shin. Hurt like a sonuvabitch."

His words brought back the memory, but I was surprised we'd never discussed it before now. "I coulda handled it," I muttered.

Tuck's barked-out laughter probably scared all the fish out of the damned lake. "Dunn Johnson, you're so easily scared, you pissed yourself last year watching *Aquaman*. *Aquaman*."

I shot him a look. "You promised on your granny's grave never to mention that again," I hissed.

My anger didn't make him drop his smarmy smile. "Granny hates when I do that. Also, she sent some peanut brittle for you in my St. Patrick's Day care package. Forgot to tell you."

"You forgot to tell me because you ate it."

He laughed again. "Perhaps."

We sat in silence together for a while to let the fish return. I finally couldn't stand it anymore. "I meant Fossie Creek," I said in a low voice.

"I know you did, Dunn."

"It's just… why there? You're afraid of heights, and the bridge over Fossie is super high. I never did ask you that."

Tucker stayed quiet so long, I wondered if he was going to simply refuse to answer. I should have known better.

"I thought I'd had my heart broken, and I was feeling dramatic."

I turned to stare at him and mighta accidentally screeched a little. "*What?*"

The birds shot from the trees, and Tucker winced as the fish most likely tore off toward Kentucky and away from our lures at my raised voice. "Sorry," I mouthed.

Tucker shrugged and reeled in his line before setting his rod on the dock next to his chair. "It's not like I was going to jump or anything. But I kind of wanted something to scare me out of my routine, you know? Like face a fear and conquer it."

"Didn't work," I muttered with a smile. "At least according to the crescent-shaped scars on my arm from where you gripped it on the Ferris wheel last year."

"No, it didn't. But it was nice getting away regardless. I was exhausted from years of nothing but studying, working, and living under fluorescent lights. I wanted some time outside, *alone*, and I wanted time to calm down and be still. But then, of course, I met you instead."

I smacked his chest with the back of my hand. "Asshole."

He caught my hand and held it there, close to his heart for a split second. "Best damned thing I ever caught while fishing."

Tucker let my hand go and gave me a cheeky grin to take some of the whipped topping off the lovey-dovey sundae, but I still allowed myself to take a giant bite of the sweetness.

"I'm sure grateful," I said, clearing my throat. And then I added a bit so as not to seem too mushy. "Mostly because I need some help with picking out paint colors for the renovation."

What I'd really wanted to ask him about was the heart-break before Fossie Creek, but I didn't feel like it was my place. We'd already made up from our fight the day before, and I was afraid talking about his love life was a one-way ticket toward Angry Tuckerville.

Tucker closed his eyes and let out a frustrated growl. "I told you, jackass, just because I'm gay doesn't mean I know shit about paint colors."

"You have to know more than I do. It's like... virtually impossible to be worse at that stuff than I am."

"Can't you ask Brooks? Or Mal? He's an artist. What about Ava? Or your mom?"

I started reeling in the big fat nothing on my line. "My mama would paint giant bovines all over my house and well you know it. As for Mal, if the baby-puke green he suggested for Ava's nursery was any indicator, he's color challenged. And don't even get me started on my brother."

He stood and began packing. If we'd scared away the fish, there was no point in sticking around anyway.

"I would, D. But I volunteered for a shift at the hospital. Maybe ask the folks at the hardware store? If Sully's working today, they'll fix you up." He hesitated and then spoke with some kind of fake casual. "Or Jenn. She's off today. You could ask her to help."

I stood up and stretched. "Nah, it'll be fine. Maybe

you're right about Sully. They helped Diesel with his chicken chateau thing, and it turned out real nice."

But when I dropped Tucker off at his house, I almost forgot all about the paint. As he leaned out of my truck, his shirt rode up, exposing a strip of bare skin and the tiniest sliver of his underwear waistband.

It was dark pink.

I'd never seen dark pink underwear on a guy before, which was probably why my eyes glued onto it, and I couldn't seem to unstick them for anything. What did those undies look like? Were they his usual boxer briefs or something else? Did he wear little briefs sometimes? And why the hell did I care?

I cared because it was something about him I didn't know, and I liked knowing everything about him. Lately it seemed like new Tucker details were popping up all over. First it was the way his mouth tasted when I kissed him at the Pickin'. Then he revealed the whole ex-boyfriend thing. After that it was the revelation he was at Fossie Creek in the first place because of heartbreak.

It was like I didn't even know my best friend anymore. And now the freaking underwear thing.

My eyes wandered all over his body, looking for other clues. As I drank in the familiar sight of him, my skin got all hot and weird. He was… really nice to look at. Like, *really* nice. The man was fit and healthy. Tight muscles under smooth skin. His hair was dark brown, and he had the kind of face that could look serious and professional one minute and mischievous and boyish the next.

I adored that face, but now… now I was starting to think about other parts of him. And that was weird.

I forced myself to focus on the things I needed to do today. I swung by the paint store, but Sully wasn't there. Mayleen sold me a ten-dollar pack of stapled-together colored paper pieces called a "fan deck" and told me to take it home and think on it. When I pulled up to my house, I thought maybe I'd leave the thinking to someone else like Tucker had recommended.

Before I had a chance to open the front door, I heard tires crunching on gravel.

"Hey, Dunn!" Jenn waved excitedly from the open window of her car. "I brought you some wisteria vines my daddy pulled down this morning." She got out and waved the scraggly brown vines around like cheerleader pom-poms.

Oh Lord on a Lilliputian. The Entwinin'.

"I'm not... I mean. I'm not all that great with..." She didn't let me finish. She shoved the vines in my chest and yanked the fan deck out of my hand so I could cradle the unruly vines to my chest. "It's just that me and vines don't really—"

"Whatcha painting?" She fanned the colored pages open with excitement.

I threw out my hand to encompass the house and the barn. "All of it. Tucker said I should consider something besides a white farmhouse and red barn."

"Oooh! I love picking out colors. You want my help?"

I tossed the vines down in a heap on the front porch and plucked the fan deck back from her. "I don't need help," I said, tossing the fan deck on a table on the porch before turning and hopping back down the porch steps to the yard. "I've gotta check on one of the heifers. You're more than welcome to come with."

Jenn jumped back and almost slid into the mud left over from last night's rainstorm. She picked her way delicately through the puddles spotted here and there between the house and the main barn. I noticed she wore light pink canvas shoes that weren't going to bear up well on the farm.

"You want some boots?" I asked. "Tucker keeps a pair here, and his feet are smaller than mine. They're around back. I'd say you could wear Luisa's extra pair, but she'd probably shank you if she saw you in them."

"Who's Luisa?" she asked in a not-very-happy voice.

I frowned at her. "Luisa, as in Lu. My right-hand... cowhand. Or whatever. 'Bout five feet nothin' and full of snark?"

I knew for a fact that Jenn had met Luisa on any number of occasions. It always ruffled my feathers that Jenn could remember the names and details of every piece of gossip in the Thicket but couldn't seem to recall the conversations we had. Sometimes she could be really sweet and attentive, but other times it felt like she only heard what she wanted to hear.

"Anyway, Lu's pretty possessive about her stuff, so you're better off with Tuck's boots. He'd never shank you. I think it's against his doctor code."

I led her around the side of the house to the mudroom door. As soon as I opened it, Bernadette pushed her way out and came trotting over to sniff Jenn's legs.

"I don't need someone else's nasty boots," she said, dancing around to evade the pig snout.

"Suit yourself." I took off my running shoes and slipped my feet into my boots. Bernadette trotted ahead of us toward the barn, sniffing happily at all of the puddles on the way.

"I was going to bring lunch," she offered. "Pick up your favorite sandwich at Thelma's, but they weren't open yet. I thought maybe you and I could—"

"Aw, man, I love that place. I usually pick up..." I let the sentence drift off as my brain caught up with what I was getting ready to say.

"You usually pick up sandwiches from Thelma's for you

and Tucker on Wednesdays. I know. He sneaks out the back door and meets you in the park." She rolled her eyes and sighed. "It's like some kind of illicit affair with you two."

I blinked at her in surprise. "Jenn, don't be ridiculous. It's not like that."

"Might as well be," she said.

"Except for the fact I'm not having sex with the man." Even though I knew firsthand how sweet Tucker's mouth tasted, since I'd kissed him last fall. For some reason I felt peevish now. And my heifers hadn't been seen to.

She threw up her hands. "Well, you're not having it with me either!"

I winced. How could I tell her that I was withholding the goods in an effort not to lead her on? "I've told you I'm not ready for a relationship."

"When will you be ready?" Her hands fisted on her hips, spooking Bernadette into stepping sideways right into a nearby mud puddle. The muck splashed onto Jenn's pristine shoes, causing her to squeal which caused Bernadette to squeal louder and look at me with brokenhearted eyes.

"Jenn, you know she doesn't like sudden movements," I chastised as gently as I could. "On account of the time she—"

"I don't care about your pig, Dunn. I care about you!"

Luisa's voice came from deep in the barn, and it was low enough not to draw Jenn's attention. "Can't have one without the other. They're like PB&J."

I coughed to cover Lu's muttering. She wasn't Jenn's biggest fan even though she thought Jenn—and I quote— had a killer set of breasts. "Well... thank you. I guess?"

"I need this relationship to move forward, Dunn. For both our sakes." Jenn looked upset, and I could hardly blame her, really. I'd kind of been stringing her along for a while now because I was a chickenshit. Relationships scared me. They were a lot of work, and there were too many chances to get things wrong.

"I don't make rash decisions," I said, moving over to reach for a bale of straw so I could toss some handfuls in the nearest mud puddles.

Jenn made a point of staring at the two rare-breed alpacas watching us curiously from over a nearby fence.

"Those don't count," I muttered, waving my hand dismissively like Johnny and June weren't important. I'd apologize to them later. "Tucker said he'd read an article on the sustainability of alpac… you know what? Never mind. They're very sweet, and they don't take up much of my time."

Jenn squinted at me. The calculating look in her eyes made my stomach sour. "I have a proposition for you."

"Uh…"

"No strings, no commitments. I want a ninety-day trial."

I didn't like the sound of this. "Trial of what?"

"Us. This. A relationship."

Now my stomach was pressing up under my ribs. "I don't think…"

"It's time for you to take a break from thinking. I've given you long enough, now it's time to fish or cut bait, Dunn Johnson."

I never did like that expression. "I don't rightly understand exactly what we're saying here," I admitted.

She stepped closer to me and softened her face into a smile. She really was a pretty woman when she smiled like that. Her brown hair caught the sun and her eyes sparkled, reminding me of why she'd gotten my attention in the first place. "We're going to date full-on for ninety days. At the end of the ninety days, we're going to make some decisions. *Lifelong* decisions, you hear me? Decisions about me moving in here with you, and helping you run your business, and taking a post on the Beautification Corps with your mama, just like all Johnson women have done."

Good Lord, the very idea of her moving into my space was enough to make me feel like I was roasting alive, let alone the thought of her becoming a Johnson. Then again, maybe everyone felt this way before they got serious about someone. Maybe I'd feel different in time.

"I'm not ready for sex," I blurted, unsure why exactly that was.

She glared at me. "Fine. No sex until you're ready."

"I'm not ready for monogamy either. That's... that's part of my hesitation," I clarified.

"Damn it, Dunn. I just want to start being able to rely on you for a Friday night date. Can we at least get to know each other on a more regular basis? I already said no strings for ninety days, jeez."

I swallowed. Maybe she was right. Maybe it was time for me to get serious. How could I expect Tucker to find his special someone if I wasn't willing to put in the time doing it for myself too? "Yeah. Yeah, okay."

She leaned in and kissed me full on the lips. She tasted like cherry lip balm and Diet Coke. I noticed a piece of hay had floated into her hair, so I plucked it out.

"You told me when you called the office the other day that you'd take me out tonight," she said coyly.

"Oh, right. I mean, obviously. I didn't forget." I'd totally forgotten.

"Good. Pick me up at seven," she said, stepping backward. "We're going to the Steak 'n Bait."

Steak 'n Bait. Where Tuck was meeting his old friend? This could work out. I could meet someone from Tucker's old life, maybe ask him questions about what Tucker was like in med school. Maybe see for myself why my dad said his new cardiologist looked like a fashion model.

"Okay," I said. "It's a date."

Luisa laughed at me long after Jenn's car had crunched its way back down the drive.

7

TUCKER

15-ACROSS: An enlightening experience... or a biblical apocalypse (10 letters)

"OKAY, I've got another one. You remember Char Beck?" Carter Rogers's familiar blue eyes danced at me over the Steak 'n Bait's snowy-white tablecloth. "Pretty girl with the dark hair?"

"Of course I remember." I sipped my sangria—the *one* alcoholic beverage I was allowing myself on this date-that-wasn't-a-date—and leaned forward in my seat to catch more hot gossip about people I used to know in another lifetime. "Your neighbor who used to bring you those boozy chocolates at Christmas. My friend Dunn loves those." I shuddered a little. I hated anything that tasted too much like alcohol.

"That's the one. She's about to become country music royalty. She just got engaged to Jack Gray from August Sanctuary, and they're building a 17,000-square-foot house shaped like a castle complete with pointy turrets and one of those metal thingies over the door." He mimed a gate going up and down.

"The word you're looking for is *portcullis*," I informed him.

"Of course it is." He grinned a devastating grin, complete with a pair of dimples guaranteed to make almost any human under the age of ninety-two stammer and blush, and clasped a hand over his heart. "My vocabulary has shrunk exponentially since my crossword-loving boyfriend left me a few years ago. Soon I'll be reduced to communicating through a series of grunts and rude gestures. Remind me again why we broke up, Tucker Wright?"

"Because I wanted to stay home and do crosswords, and you wanted to go out and save the world," I said, returning his smile. I sucked down a bit more of my drink and relaxed back into my seat, totally unfazed by the dimples. "Stop trying to distract me. I have questions—"

Kelsey, our server, placed a basket of warm bread in the center of the table and eyed the two empty chairs at our table. "Evening, Doc Wright. Dunn on his way, then?"

"Ah. No." I frowned. "Friends do go out without each other sometimes, you know, Kels."

"Oh." Kelsey looked as confused as if I'd offered her salt without pepper. "Okay, then. So, you gents know what you want?"

"I'm afraid I need to beg you for just a few more minutes." Carter brushed back his artfully shaggy hair with one long-fingered hand and turned the full force of his smile and his soulful eyes on her. "If it wouldn't be too much trouble."

Kelsey nearly tripped over her own feet standing stock-still. "S-sure," she breathed. "You can take all the time you need."

As she walked away, Carter sighed contentedly. "Thank God. I worried I was broken for a second there."

I rolled my eyes. "Nope. It's just that time and distance have made me immune to your charms."

"Hmm." He narrowed his gaze. "Is it time and distance, I wonder? Or is it something else?"

"I must be thinking of the wrong Char," I continued hurriedly. "Because the Char I knew was with dude bro Josh for *years*. Remember, the guy who used to chant, 'Keg stand!' every time anyone asked if he wanted a beer?" I snickered, inviting him to laugh along.

He didn't.

"Sometimes I forget how long you've been gone, Tuck. Char and Josh haven't been a thing since... uh." He cleared his throat and swished the wine in his glass. "Well. One night after you and I stopped talking, Josh and Char had a huge fight and broke up—for the twelfth time—so Josh brought over a bottle of Southern Comfort, and... you might say we attempted to give each other a little Southern Comfort." He wiggled his eyebrows. "Char came looking for him the next morning and found more than she bargained for."

I choked on my drink and ended up coughing into my napkin as Carter grinned. "Wait, what? You? And Josh? Josh who wore those Sigma Nu windbreakers like he was still back in college Josh? Josh with the boat shoes Josh?"

"I prefer to think of him as 'Josh who's packing *heat* under those khakis Josh.'" Carter sighed, eyes to the ceiling and a fond look on his face. "And let's just say, keg stands took on a whole new meaning with him."

I laughed out loud. "Oh my *God*. I cannot believe... you and... just... wow. And how do the Rogers of Belle Meade feel about Josh?"

"Like I'd inflict my family on the poor man," Carter

scoffed. "Besides, it wasn't like that. You know I refuse to settle down until I'm forty-five."

"Used to be forty," I noted.

"Until I turned thirty-five and suddenly forty was in spitting distance." He chuckled at himself. "Anyway, Josh was just having fun. Curious, I guess. Probably also looking for a good reason not to marry his on-again-off-again girl-friend." He shrugged. "It was very temporary, and we moved on. No harm, no foul, and we stayed friends. Last we spoke, he was dating a woman who looked remarkably like Char and his itch had been scratched."

"Oh, wow." I laid a comforting hand over his on the tabletop. "I'm so sorry."

"Don't be," Carter said. Before I knew what was happening, he turned his hand over so our fingers were clasped. "It wasn't serious at all. Not like we were. So tell me for real, Tuck, why'd you stop calling? And more impor-tantly—" He dropped his voice an octave to a low purr. "What would it take to get you to *start* calling again, espe-cially now that I agreed to spend the next six months covering for Dr. Symmons in Great Nuthatch—which, I swear to God, is the worst name anyone ever gave a town."

"Ah…" I laughed nervously. "Spoken like a man who doesn't know there's a town called Pecker Lurch just on the other side of the Thicket." I tried to withdraw my hand, but Carter held it fast and lifted one eyebrow.

"Spoken like a man who's dodging my question."

"What? Dodging? No. I…" I took another healthy swig and licked my lips. "See, the thing is…"

The thing was, Carter Rogers was handsome and charming and funny and smart and Lord a'mercy, he was sexy, with his windblown hair and broad shoulders. Plus, he made me laugh… *a lot*. There were entire minute-long stretches of time tonight where I'd purely enjoyed myself and not felt like

I'd left the house and forgotten to do something vitally important—like shut off the stove, or unplug the iron, or tell Dunn I loved him—which was how I'd felt every single day since I'd realized I'd fallen head over heels for my best friend.

But I swear, the moment I let myself enjoy Carter's conversation or the way his button-down bunched over his big biceps, the ghost of Dunn Johnson would appear right on the table between us, smack on top of the bread basket, waving his spirit fingers and kicking his heels in the air, forcing me to remember that Carter Rogers was not the man I wanted.

He should have been. Oh, he should have been. Carter was gay, for one thing, and attracted to me, for another. One quick *yes* and he'd have me home and naked in no time flat, and I could potentially go to sleep on a Saturday night feeling satisfied instead of pounding my pillow in frustration until I dropped off.

Except... I couldn't.

Because it was not Carter's arms I wanted wrapped around me. It was not Carter's chest I wanted to lean my head on when I'd had a hard day. It wasn't Carter I wanted to call when I heard a stupid joke, or an interesting story on the news, or when I wanted to get outdoors and go fishing.

"Are you seeing someone, Tuck?" Carter prompted, his head tilted to the side like he already knew the answer. "I probably should have asked before I invited you out tonight, but I figured, worst-case scenario you'd just tell me you were engaged or married or something." He grinned again, totally unrepentant. "And at least then I'd have gotten to see that handsome face again, right?"

I smiled back a little wanly. "I'm not seeing anyone... exactly. It's complicated," I admitted. "And a little hopeless."

"Ah. Then tell Dr. Rogers all about it. I'm here to solve your problems."

I blinked at him. "You are? *You*? The man who just reiterated his desire to not have a committed relationship for at least ten more years?"

"I am *literally* a heart doctor, Tucker. I have the fancy diplomas to prove it." He winked. "And I have an opening for precisely one new patient."

I snorted.

"Besides, I know it's been a long time, but I care about you. I always have."

"Aw." I gave him a sappy grin, and after a second's hesitation, I leaned forward and took a deep breath. "Fine. Okay, so I have this friend, Dunn. Actually, he's my best friend. And he—"

A commotion near the front of the restaurant caught my attention, and I looked up... right into Dunn Johnson's scowling face.

For a split second, I thought it was ghost-Dunn again, tired of hovering over the bread basket, so he'd decided to put on the heathered green cashmere pullover I'd gotten him for Christmas—the one that exactly matched his eyes— and hang out by the door.

But then I saw Jenn Shipley, wearing a pink wrap dress designed to make even a man like *me* notice her boobs, with her two arms wrapped around his bicep, trying to pull him along so the host could show them to one of the nicer tables near the fireplace at the back of the restaurant... and that was when I knew this was no ghost.

There was no realm in which I'd *ever* conjure Jenn with him.

To be fair, there was also no realm in which I could have imagined Dunn rooted to one spot and staring at Carter's hand clasped around mine like he was trying to incinerate it with superhero laser eyes.

Shit.

I felt weirdly guilty, which was silly. I mean, sure, I'd said Carter and I were old colleagues, but that wasn't a lie. Exactly. Besides, Dunn *clearly* didn't tell me every time he went on a date with Jenn.

Dunn called the host back and murmured something that made Jenn's nostrils flare like flames might shoot out of her head at any moment, but the host shrugged and nodded. She led Dunn and Jenn back toward the front, then took a right and headed...

Oh, holy mother of noes.

"Well, *hey,*" Dunn said from mere inches away as the host placed a pair of menus on the table directly next to mine and Carter's. "Tucker Wright, as I live and breathe! What a coinky-dink!"

I swallowed hard and once again tried to move my hand back, but Carter held it tighter and even smoothed his thumb over my knuckles.

"Friend of yours, babe?" Carter asked lightly.

Babe? Had I somehow miscommunicated something? But no, Carter's eyes were dancing again, full of unholy amounts of mischief. My heart thumped double time, and I made a strangled noise. I really might need a cardiologist by the end of the night.

"Dunn," Jenn whispered, yanking on his arm in a way that was sure to dislocate something. "Sit *down.* People are looking at us."

"Just being polite first," Dunn told her without lowering his voice one decibel. "Hey, Tucker, you know, Jenn, right?"

The woman who'd tried to send one of my elderly

patients to wait on the porch because his hair disturbed the "whole vibe" of the waiting room? Oh, I knew her.

I nodded. "Evening, Jenn."

Jenn sighed a sigh so deep it came from the center of the earth and rolled her eyes heavenward. "Yep, hey."

Dunn rocked on the balls of his feet, waiting for me to reciprocate the introduction, but I didn't know where to begin.

Carter kicked me lightly under the table. "I'd take this one, but I can't introduce myself as your heart doctor, Tuck. HIPAA regulations and all," he murmured.

I was so glad he was enjoying himself. "If you do, a HIPAA violation will be the least of your troubles," I muttered back.

Meanwhile, I could sense Dunn's anger, pulsing like a telltale heart. "Excuse me? Aren't you gonna introduce me to your old colleague?"

I sighed. "Yeah. Uh. Dunn, this is Carter Rogers. He's the cardiologist covering for Dr. Symmons. Carter, this is—"

"Dunn Johnson," Dunn said, sticking out his right hand, while his left came to rest on my shoulder. "Tucker's *best* best friend."

Good Lord. The man was all but pissing around me in a circle. Who the heck got that territorial over a friend?

And mother*fucker*, why did I find it so hot?

I needed an intervention, I really did. Or maybe meditation. Or maybe...

"Uh, hey, Kelsey?" I flagged our server as she passed. "Another sangria, please?" I tossed back the dregs of my first one.

"Nice to meet you," Carter said after a beat, shaking Dunn's hand. "I think Tucker might have mentioned you earlier."

I shot him a warning glare.

"Of course he did," Dunn scoffed. "We do everything together."

"Not *everything*," Carter said lightly.

Dunn scowled, but before he could reply, Carter turned his smile up from *stun* to *kill* and shot it directly at the fourth member of our group. "You must be Jenn. A beautiful name for a beautiful woman."

"Oh, I..." Jenn fluttered her eyelashes and blushed. "Oh."

Dunn's scowl, which was already blacker than the night outside, deepened. "So, Tucker said y'all were colleagues." He glanced pointedly at our joined hands.

"Oh, we were," Carter agreed. His smile dimmed not at all. "Roommates too. During all those long, *hard* nights of residency." He winked at me. "I'm sure this wild man's told you all the stories."

Wild man? I narrowed my eyes at him. All the stories? There were no stories except the ones that involved me working eighty or more hours a week and falling exhausted into bed, and Carter knew it.

Was he trying to make Dunn jealous? What for?

"Dunn," Jenn demanded. "Would you sit the heck down?"

Dunn shot me a look like I'd betrayed him somehow and turned his back on me. He smiled at Jenn. "Sorry about that."

"I can't believe you made us switch tables." She pouted.

"It was the smoke." Dunn smacked his chest a couple of times and cleared his throat. "My lungs get weird sometimes, you know?"

I couldn't help overhearing. "Is your asthma acting up again? You're carrying your inhaler, right?" I asked a trifle worriedly. "You know you're always more sensitive at the change of seasons, and it's been—"

Dunn set his elbow on the table and blocked the side of his face, pointedly ignoring me. "What were you saying, *Jenn*?"

"Hey, I know it's cumbersome," I insisted. "But Dunn, you can't take chances when—"

"I was *saying*, I had to call a week in advance to get a spot near the fireplace." Jenn ignored me also and proved that she could give Dunn's little niece Myleigh lessons in sulking. "And now I don't even get to enjoy it."

"I'm sorry, Jenn," Dunn said, all patient and calm like he was talking to one of his animals, not acknowledging my presence at all. "But… we only talked about coming here this afternoon, remember?"

I set my teeth. In all the years of our friendship, I couldn't remember a time when Dunn had ever tried to ignore me before. I'd tried to ignore *him* plenty—see also: the last few weeks of our lives—but whenever I cast a glance in his direction, he'd always been right there, ready to literally and figuratively embrace me.

Safe to say, I was not a fan of this ignoring business. At all.

Carter tapped the back of my hand with two fingers. "You're staring," he mouthed.

Pfft. Of course I was staring. Dunn Johnson was ignoring me. I turned my attention back to his table.

"I planned it as a surprise for you," Jenn was saying. "To celebrate us officially *dating*, honey bunch. I just knew you'd want to fight for us!" She beamed.

Dunn's back stiffened. "Uh. That's not… You remember what we talked about, right?"

"Of course I do," she assured him, round-eyed. "Every word. It was the most meaningful discussion of our entire relationship." She gave him a dreamy smile. "So far, I mean. So, when do you want to tell your mom?"

My jaw dropped. Dunn and Jenn? Officially dating? Telling Cindy Ann?

Since when? Since *how*?

Hurt and fury churned in my gut. Dunn didn't even *like* Jenn, not really. He might like the way she filled out that dress, but he went out of his way to avoid her. Heck, he'd made *me* sneak out of my own office to avoid her. And now… and now…

"Here you go!" Kelsey arrived with my sangria.

I snatched it out of her hand before she could set it down and sucked back half of it. "Thanks a billion, Kels."

"Sure. Y'all need a few more minutes?" She smiled between Carter and me.

"Hey, chill out over there, Dr. Wright," Dunn said grudgingly. He stared at his menu and didn't turn his head in my direction. "You know red wine takes a minute to hit you, but if you have more than two, you'll be singing Gloria Gaynor before bed and making love to the porcelain goddess by morning."

How fucking *dare* that man know me so well and also be officially dating Jenn Shipley, who was right that minute shooting a satisfied little smile in my direction?

"I'd love another sangria, please, Kelsey," I sang, showing that my ignoring powers were by far superior. "Make it extra large."

Carter ran his tongue over the front of his teeth. "*Oookay*, then. And I think we're ready to order, since it'll probably be good to get some food in that stomach. I'll have the filet, medium, with the baked potato. Tuck?"

"Salmon gremolata, please."

"And to start, we'll split the Cobb salad," Carter decided, handing her our menus. "Thank you."

"Tucker doesn't eat Cobb salad." Once again, Dunn addressed this comment to his menu, but Kelsey hesitated.

"Sure he does," Carter said. "We've split one a million times. He loves it. Don't you?"

"Well, I... that is... I..."

"Doc Wright?" Kelsey said.

"Tucker no longer consumes pork products for moral reasons, and he hates blue cheese," Dunn gritted out through clenched teeth.

"No, he *doesn't*." Carter gave me a mystified look. "Do you, Tuck?"

"Dunn, honey, I'm thinking I want steak and tater tots," Jenn said with a desperate sort of brightness. "What do you think? Steak and tots? You and me could split an order and..."

I inhaled sharply. Buying your date tater tots was a well-known Lickin' Thicket code for being in a serious relationship. There was no way on God's blue earth I could sit here and watch them eat shredded potatoes together. Death would be preferable.

"Dunn doesn't eat processed potato pieces," I lied. "Tater tots go against his life philosophy."

Jenn pursed her lips. "Doc Wright, I think you might be deluding yourself about Dunn's potato preferences."

"Uh, no. I am Dunn's *best* best friend. I know every spud-based desire of his heart. If anyone at this table is deluded—"

"Erm, so it's looking like maybe no bacon," Carter cut in. He smiled at Kelsey, who was still waiting with her pen poised above her notepad. "Tucker, blue cheese, yes or no?"

"What? Yeah, fine." I was too engaged in my tater tot stare-down with Jenn to pay him much mind.

Dunn gasped and pushed his chair back with a squeal. "I can't sit here anymore. I need air."

"But, Dunn, we haven't ordered!" Jenn made a grab for his arm. "Dunn?"

"It might be his asthma," I lied. I pushed my chair back too. "I'll go."

"Nonsense. He and I are dating. *I'll*—" Jenn began.

"Nah, Tuck's a medical professional," Carter reminded her, dimples winking. "Let him do his thing, Jenn. Meanwhile, you can tell me more about yourself."

I was pretty sure I was going to owe Carter my first-born child by the end of this date-that-wasn't-a-date, but I didn't care. As I pushed out the main door into the cool night air of the parking lot, all I could think about was Dunn Johnson.

I spotted him off to one side of the parking lot, pacing under the brightly lit Steak 'n Bait sign that proudly declared, "2,542 YESSES AND COUNTING." He looked supremely pissed off, clomping around in circles and muttering under his breath, which was great because I was too.

He also looked tall and broad and gorgeous, wearing his one pair of "good" jeans and that sweater I'd searched high and low for last year, and that made me even *more* pissed off.

"Take off that sweater," I demanded, stalking toward him.

"What?" Dunn stopped his pacing and whirled to face me.

"I said, you take off that sweater I bought you." I poked him, right in the center of his big, broad, cashmere-covered chest. "You know how hard I looked for a sweater that was the same green as your eyes? *Hours*, Dunn Johnson. You don't get to date Jenn Shipley while you're wearing *my* sweater."

"You're bein' ridiculous," Dunn scoffed.

"No, you are!" I set my hands on my hips. "You don't even *like* her. Name one thing you have in common."

Dunn's already scowly face scowled harder. "We…" He opened and closed his mouth like a fish for a second.

"Yeah?" I made a gimme motion with my hand. "You what?"

"…are…"

"Uh-huh. Good start. Keep going. Lay it on me. I'm ready for it," I taunted.

He swallowed hard. "…both appalled that you didn't tell me the truth about your date tonight being a *date*. After all I've done for you, Tuck!"

"Done for me? For *me*? You haven't done anything for me! You only tried to match me up so you could feel free to date Jenn!" Oh. Wow. Those were a lot of words I was saying, huh? I wasn't even sure where they came from — Dunn may have had a small point about the sangria — but they felt true, so I kept going. "And Jenn is *not* appalled. She's in there trying to climb Carter like a tree." I hooked a thumb over my shoulder.

"Ew. She is *not*." Dunn wrinkled his nose. "Not much of him to climb, anyway. He's all white teeth and soft fingers." He made jazz hands in the glow of the sign. "I hope you know, those fingers couldn't tie a clinch knot on a sunny day with no breeze."

"I know I'm about to shock you right now, Dunn? But fishing's not everything! Carter has other qualities."

"Like what? That man touches people's hearts." He paused. "And not like a Hallmark card."

"He doesn't *touch hearts*. He's not a surgeon. And besides, you rectally probe your heifers to see if they're knocked up." I smoothed a hand up my arm from my wrist to my elbow. "Let's not play that game."

"Not playing any games." Dunn crossed his arms over his chest. "You *said* he was a colleague."

"Yeah? Well, you never said you and Jenn were officially dating, so we're even." I folded my arms over my chest too. "You're leading her on."

His jaw dropped. "Nuh-uh! She and I talked about it. We're doing a free trial!"

"A what?"

"Her and me. Ninety days. Risk-free. No commitment. Cancel at any time. To see if we're suited."

He said this *proudly*. Like the concept should be obvious. Like it was a real thing that people did with their relationships all the time.

Meanwhile, I stared at him like he was spouting gibberish because he fucking was.

"Money-back guarantee if you're not totally satisfied?" I demanded. "Is she some Chuck Norris gym equipment? Or a human being with feelings? You two have been dating off and on for *years*. You need to fish or cut bait."

"You know I hate that expression," he said mulishly.

"Yes, because you don't like having to narrow your options, and you don't like having to hurt anyone's feelings. But too bad, so sad, Dunn Johnson. Sometimes you *have* to, because hurting someone now is better than leading them on and hurting them later." And I really wasn't sure whether I was talking about myself or Jenn anymore. "There is no such thing as a risk-free trial for a relationship. She's gonna fall for you, Dunn, if she hasn't already. And *shit*. Why am *I* out here worried about Jenn's feelings when she's not remotely worried about mine?" I poked his chest again. "*This* is how messed up you make me."

Dunn grabbed my wrist when I went to move my hand back and held it in both of his. He stared down at it angrily. "You let him hold your hand."

"Who? Carter? He's done a lot more than that. We were friends and roommates and… and we dated, okay? But I haven't seen him in years before tonight, because he lives in Nashville and travels around a lot, and I… live here." And why was I explaining all this to him, anyway? "Besides, why do you care who holds my hand? What did you think I was gonna do with any of those guys you set me up with, huh? What are *you* gonna do on your ninety-day trial? Why don't I get to do what I want?"

With my free hand, I poked him again… though this poke was maybe more like a shove.

It didn't move Dunn an inch, the stubborn asshole, and in fact, he grabbed that hand too.

"Because you're *Tucker*, that's why. You're the good person of the two of us. The one who always knows how to protect someone's feelings. You're the one with the million-dollar words. And the one who doesn't half-ass things, ever. You're the person I know best in the whole world, and that's not allowed to change. And you *don't* like blue cheese. And you don't get to like anyone better than me, for God's sake."

I blinked at him. Then I blinked some more. "What?"

"What, what?" Dunn repeated impatiently. "I *said*, you don't fucking like blue cheese. The first time we ordered hot wings and I asked if we could get ranch 'cause I hate blue cheese, you said…"

"I said I hated blue cheese too." I shrugged. "Because I wanted you to get the sauce you wanted. But forget that bit. I meant—"

"Forget that bit? Forget that our whole relationship was based on a *lie*, Tucker Wright?" His green eyes were stormy. "How can I ever—?"

I grabbed one of my hands back so I could capture his chin in my fingers and force him to look at me. "Shush.

What do you mean I don't get to like anyone better than you?"

"I mean... you don't. *Duh*. Just like I don't." He shrugged. "That's what being best friends is about. Isn't it? I never had a best friend before. Not like you and me. Someone who just... gets me like you do. But... but when you have that, you don't let anyone interfere, right? So, who cares if Jenn and I date? Who cares if we get married? She's nice enough. But I don't need anything in common with her, because... I have you."

Oh my God. This man's brain was a fucking labyrinth.

How could a functioning human be so foolish?

How could he be so impossibly sweet?

I stared at him mutely for a second, just processing it.

Dunn misunderstood my silence. "I *do* have you, don't I, Tuck?" he whispered.

His fingers slid against mine as he pulled our joined hands to his chest, and the kaleidoscope of butterflies that had hibernated through my entire interaction with Carter jumped to life in my stomach and started beating their wings in time to my pounding heart.

I licked my lips. "Most people want their boyfriend or girlfriend to be their best friend also," I said, just as softly. "Like Mal and Brooks. Like Ava and Paul. Heck, like Cindy Ann and Big Red. Best friends and lovers at the same time."

He swallowed. "Is that what *you* want?"

I nodded vehemently. That was exactly what I wanted. It was what I'd wanted for *years*, even though I knew it was impossible.

Dunn moved half a step closer, so the toes of his boots touched the toes of my shoes, and angled himself so his body acted as a windbreak to protect me from the chilly breeze. "And you think this... this Carter person is the answer to that? He seems boring as fuck."

I snorted out loud and clapped a hand over my mouth to stifle the sound. "You've met him for ten minutes and heard him order a salad. You don't know what his life's like. And besides, I hate to break it to you, but *I* am boring as fuck. I do crossword puzzles to relax. I go fishing, an activity that requires me to sit without moving or speaking for long stretches of time. Your *best* best friend just might be the least lively human on the face of the planet."

"You're not."

I grinned up at him. "Super am."

"Not," he insisted in that same soft voice. It felt like we were in a cocoon, right there in the parking lot, just him and me. Dunn and Tucker. In our own little world. "Know how I know?

I shook my head. "How?"

"Because every fucking second I'm with you, Tucker Wright, you make me feel... alive." Dunn lifted his free hand to my cheek. His nostrils flared. He swallowed hard.

And then before I could ask him if he was okay, he bent his head and laid his soft lips on mine.

Holy... holy... just *holy*.

It was not the first time Dunn Johnson had kissed me, but it was the first time he'd kissed me like this, in the dark and quiet with just the two of us and the stars and the sign of twenty-five hundred *yesses* bearing witness. It was the first time his arm came around me to pull me against him, flattening our clasped hands between us, and it was sure as all fuck the first time his *tongue* ever licked at my lips, demanding entrance.

I gasped, just a little, because I couldn't believe this was actually happening. My free hand fluttered in the air over his bicep, and I was weirdly afraid to touch him, afraid it would make him stop.

But then Dunn's tongue slid against mine, and he groaned like he was really into it and... yeah, no lie, that was the last conscious thought I had in a while. After that, it was all just flashes of his cinnamon toothpaste taste and the way his fingers dented the skin of my lower back, the softness of cashmere over the flex of his muscles and the way he stroked into my mouth with the same confidence that he walked into my office, like he knew he was welcome.

Like he knew he belonged there.

8

DUNN

7-Across: Confused, perplexed or flustered (9 letters)

It wasn't the first time I'd kissed Tucker, but it was hands down the hottest time.

I was brainless and stunned, like a newborn calf who'd just been spit out of his mom into a strange and dazzling new world. Tucker's lips were like sweet candy, and the very air around us was permeated with his familiar scent.

I couldn't get enough of him. Before I knew it, the kiss had turned from some kind of meek, experimental thing to something entirely out of my control. It was like heat and anger and begging and rejoicing all mixed up in the tangle of two tongues. No other kiss I'd ever had in my life had come anywhere close to this one. My brain filled with bright sparks and a jumble of mismatched thoughts.

Why did I hate sangria but love the taste of it on his tongue? Was my late-day scruff hurting his clean-shaven cheek? And why had he shaved for this Carter guy if it wasn't a date? Also… no wonder my brother was gay. Men just plain kissed better.

What the fuck was I doing? My best friend had finally, finally gone out with an actual viable prospect, and I'd stormed in there like a terrier in a pissing contest.

"Gah!" I yanked myself off him and shoved him away. "Go back to your date. I should have never —"

"Don't you dare say it!" Tucker's voice was sharp with anger despite the rapid panting of his breaths. His fingers came up to touch his mouth, but I wasn't sure if he was holding on to the kiss or wiping it away. I wished I could have said I didn't care which it was, but that would have been a damned lie.

"Fine. I won't. But I…" I wanted to say I never should have interrupted his date. I never should have screwed things up between the two of us. I never should have opened a Pandora's box worth of shit I wasn't going to be able to stuff back inside. "I need to get back to Jenn, and you need to get back to… Carter."

"This isn't over," Tucker warned. He stuck a hard pointer finger in my chest. "Don't go getting any stupid ideas about acting like this didn't happen, Dunn Johnson. I know you and —"

He was right. I wanted to rewind time to before it had happened. If left to my own devices, I would have smiled and nodded and gone back to my same old ways as if I'd never felt the life-changing effects of Tucker Wright's kiss on my lips.

I held up my hands in surrender. "Okay. Okay, I won't."

His eyes steadied on mine. They were lit with anger and resignation. I hated to see him upset, especially knowing I'd been the cause of all of it. "Don't freak out either," he added.

"Fat fucking chance. I'm already freaking out."

Tucker grabbed the front of my sweater and yanked me close until we were nose to nose. I couldn't help but suck in another comforting whiff of him, only this time it was more than just comfort I felt. My head spun with a million thoughts, and my dick did a little jig in my pants. Maybe I had a secret desire to be manhandled. This wasn't the best time to learn about it, though, so I did my best to ignore it.

"Dunn," he said in a crazy-soft voice. The kind of voice that made it extra hard to ignore my dick. "Do not freak out. It was just a kiss. Do you understand?"

"Yep. Sure." Part of me wondered if I could ask for another kiss as a kind of… "sealing the deal" type thing.

His eyes bounced between mine assessing the truth of my words. Both of us knew I was lying. I didn't understand jack shit.

"Go," he said in the same low voice. "Go home with Jenn." He shoved me gently away from him, and I turned to jog back into the restaurant like hellfire flames were licking at my heels.

It was going to be fine. I would go back inside, enjoy the steak and baked potato dinner, and enjoy a healthy make-out session with Jenn before the night was over. I'd just let friendship jealousy go a smidge too far, but I could rein in this baby and get back on the horse. No problem.

Jenn's mouth widened into a relieved smile when I sat back down at the table. "Everything alright?" she asked.

"'Course it is."

Jenn's brows furrowed. "I didn't know you have asthma. It's not in your medical chart. Don't you think that's something your *girlfriend* ought to know?"

The word hit me like a fork on metal siding. I didn't want a girlfriend. If I had a girlfriend, I couldn't do things like kiss other people out in the parking lot of the Steak 'n Bait. Could I?

"Why are you looking in my medical chart?" I asked instead, trying not to notice Tucker returning to his table flush-faced and beautiful like a damned shining star. "You know what? Never mind. We should order."

Carter stood up and helped Tucker into his chair like he was some kind of Disney princess. I bit my tongue to keep from telling the guy Tucker had been helping himself into chairs for decades now.

"So... tots okay?" Jenn asked.

I side-eyed her. I knew what tots represented around here. I wasn't stupid. "I thought you said no strings, no commitments," I began. "Are we... we're not exclusive, are we?"

She rolled her eyes and huffed. "Fine. No tots. I get it, jeesh."

I leaned forward and tried to meet her eyes. I didn't want to feel guilty for the kiss since I couldn't exactly take it back.

"No, but for real," I tried. "We talked about this before, remember?"

Her face broke into a sheepish grin. "But I really like tater tots."

"Fine. Get the tots." I sensed Tucker stiffen somewhere behind me, so I made sure I said the next part just as loud. "But we're not sharing them."

I spent the next several minutes trying desperately not to listen to every smarmy, conniving, charming word out of Carter *Snake-In-The-Grass* Rogers's mouth. He talked about things I didn't understand like cardiac electrophysiology fellowships and antithrombotic therapy studies. It was a stark reminder of the kind of people Tucker hung out with at work. Smart people. Well-educated people.

Not dairy farmer people who barely scraped together

enough brain cells for a high school diploma and some after-hours business courses at the community college.

Jenn told me about a few job leads she had for when Tuck's receptionist returned from maternity leave, and I tried my best to give her my full attention and contribute.

"I heard Alva Nichols might be looking for help at the veterinary clinic," I suggested. "She might even be willing to help you get classes to become a vet tech if you want. She did it for Petey Winchell, remember?"

Jenn sighed. "Everyone there has to wear those white smocks. Ew. I was thinking about trying for the cosmetics counter in Jester's."

"You'd be on your feet all day, and the pay is probably awful."

"Yeah, but think of the discount on makeup. Besides, I need to have a flexible schedule in case I get nominated for a spot on the Beautification Corps." She shot me a beseeching look I wasn't quite able to translate.

"Okay?"

The sound of Tucker's laugh broke the soft background noise around us, making me both happy and so very annoyed. Where the hell was Kelsey to take our order?

"It's just that I was wondering..." Jenn batted her thick eyelashes at me, and I realized maybe she'd be a shoo-in for the job at Jester's since I swore her eyelashes looked a thousand times longer and thicker tonight than they had even a few hours earlier.

"Yeah?"

The low rumble of Carter's voice was interspersed with Tucker's laughter now like the man was doing his own damned comedy special. None of my business. Jenn was my business. "You were saying about the Beautification Corps?" I prompted.

"Maybe Cindy Ann could nominate me."

I blinked at her in confusion.

"For the Beautification Corps opening," she clarified nervously.

Well, hell. Maybe my sister had been right.

The Licking Thicket Beautification Corps was harder to get a seat on than Jesus's own last supper table. You didn't "get picked" for the Beautification Corps. You were either born into it or had it bestowed upon you by heavenly angels of deceased Beautification Corps corpses. Or so it seemed.

One didn't simply "nominate" someone without a lengthy and confoundingly elaborate sponsorship ritual.

As I stared at her, wondering how to inform her that I could no more suggest that to my mother than declare my candidacy for president of the United States, I heard Tucker bold-face lie to Carter Rogers.

"I could take you to the Gatlinburg Sky Bridge if you want. It's beautiful there."

That was it. I was officially done with this bullshit. Tucker Wright was terrified of heights. I slammed my hand down on the table. "Let's go. We'll get better service at the Sip and Save for God's sake."

I reached for Jenn's hand and yanked her up, waiting only long enough to drop a twenty on the table before marching us out of the restaurant.

"What in the world?" Jenn asked breathlessly as I hauled her up into the passenger seat of the truck. "I was hungry."

"Yeah, well apparently Steak 'n Bait no longer sells actual food," I said, moving around to the driver's side. "We'll pick up a pineapple pizza from Stan's."

Her lips curved up a little. "You hate pineapple pizza."

I looked over at her and noticed her hair had blown partway out of a little clip it had been in. I reached over to tuck the loose strands behind her ear. "I do. But it's your favorite," I said, taking a breath to calm down. "And you deserve to have something you like tonight."

Her smile widened. "Can we take it back to your place and watch a movie?"

I nodded and leaned over to press a kiss to her cheek. "Sorry about tonight."

She shrugged. "That's okay. I didn't really want to stick around listening to all of Doc Wright's bragging anyway, no offense."

Her words took me aback. "Bragging? What do you mean?"

She flapped a hand in the air. "You know. He uses all these big words like he's always trying to remind people how much smarter he is. Then he talks about medicine stuff the same way. Highbrow, my mom calls it."

"He uses big words because he spends hours working on crossword puzzles," I said. "It's a habit he started when he used to take his aunt to her doctor's appointments when he was in high school. He'd wait hours in waiting rooms with nothing to do but crosswords."

"Well, whatever. It makes me feel stupid."

"You remember Nina Wright? She used to teach math at the high school."

"The one who died?"

I remembered the crowds at her funeral, the families from three counties all coming together to honor her memory as one of the community's most beloved teachers. Most of all, I remembered noticing my friend Thom start to cry right there in front of everyone before his older brother Tucker pulled him into the tightest hug imaginable.

I cleared my throat. "Nina was Tucker's aunt. His mom's twin sister. They were really close. She died of lymphoma when Tuck was in college. She's the reason he wanted to become a doctor."

Jenn's hand landed on my leg and squeezed. "I'm sorry, Dunn. That must have been hard for Tucker. I didn't realize they were related. I should have."

I let out a breath. "Yeah. Anyway, that's why he uses big words. He has an enormous vocabulary. Don't ever get into a game of Words with Friends with him or you'll live to regret it."

We pulled out of the lot and drove into the middle of town to pick up the pizza before heading to the farm. When we got inside, I shooed Bernie outside and into her holding pen.

The pizza hit the spot, but the movie definitely did not.

"*Mama Mia*? No." It was one of Tucker's guilty pleasures, and I'd seen it enough times to have the damned thing memorized.

Jenn shot me a look from her spot on my sofa. "You owe me."

So that's how I ended up with "SOS" playing on repeat in my head. After enjoying one of the only scenes I actually liked, I'd finally reached my limit and decided I'd rather distract Jenn with a make-out session than watch the part with all the "Slipping Through My Fingers" sentimentality bullshit—i.e., the part that made Tucker ugly cry and me feel itchy.

I cupped her cheek and leaned in to drop a soft kiss on the side of her mouth.

"Mm," she said, turning to face me so I had better access. I kissed her full on the lips and felt...

Absolutely nothing. Nothing at all. *Worse* than nothing.

I felt confused, surprised, disappointed, and terrified. My heart hammered against my ribs in a rhythm that might as well have said *Tuck-er, Tuck-er, Tuck-er*. My mind's eye flashed with scenes from the Steak 'n Bait parking lot when Tucker's mouth molded against mine like it had been created as part of a matched set. I remembered his hand in mine and the sweet fucking promise of things I never knew were possible.

Why hadn't I ever let myself go there before?

I eased back from Jenn and gave her an apologetic look. "Can I run you home?"

She nodded and sighed before grinning at me. "You're the champion of playing hard to get, Dunn Johnson."

"I don't mean to," I said, standing up and realizing my dick had gotten hard after all.

You were thinking about Tuck.

I squeezed my eyes closed and shook my head. This was crazy. It wasn't like I'd never imagined it, Tucker and I being together.

Why can't you?

My face ignited with heat at the thought. Naked Tuck underneath me, Tuck's hot mouth on my dick. I groaned, and Jenn shot me a teasing look. "You know… I could help you with that," she said, glancing down at my crotch.

"Naw, I'm good. Thanks, though." I wiggled my hips a little as I grabbed the keys to the truck.

After giving Jenn another quick peck in the driveway of her place, I promised I'd give her a call tomorrow. Then I headed home.

Except, of course, I didn't head to *my* home.

He didn't even look surprised to find me there, but I was.

"Carter not here with you?" I asked gruffly before moving past him into the mudroom. I kicked off my shoes and tossed my jacket on a hook by the door before following Tucker upstairs to his living area.

"No. I told you, it's not like that."

When I got to the small room he used as a den, I noticed a wood fire crackling in the brick fireplace. A glass of wine sat on a side table next to the sofa, and two lamps cast enough warm light for the book he'd been reading. Those adorable black-framed glasses of his were perched on the side table like he'd just taken them off.

I turned around and threw out my hands. "I'm dealing with some unexpected shit here, okay? I wasn't expecting this. My head's all turned-around right now and I don't know what to think." The panic crawled at me from the inside, because the last thing I wanted to do was hurt him. "Why did I feel more while kissing you—a *man*—than I did kissing a beautiful girl who'd do anything for me? Huh? Tell me that." My voice broke on the last word, but his clear brown eyes remained steady and warm, the same way he'd always been as long as I'd known him.

He held out his arms.

And I walked right into them.

9

TUCKER

14-ACROSS: Hashtag carpe diem, baby (4 letters)

IT'S A STRANGE THING, getting exactly what you thought you wanted.

For years, I'd fantasized that one day Dunn Johnson would turn around and see me—*really* see me—and realize how perfect we could be together. I'd daydreamed about him saying that kissing me was better than kissing a woman. I'd imagined him showing up at my house late at night and taking me in his arms.

The reality of it was both better… and worse.

I'd never pictured Dunn's voice catching as he told me he was "all turned around," or those green eyes I loved hazed with panic. And in my wildest imaginings, I'd never thought his big body would tremble in my arms as I comforted him… all because he'd kissed me.

I never, ever wanted Dunn to feel scared or unhappy. Not for a single minute. So it was hard not to feel… guilty. Like I'd made this happen somehow. That I'd wanted it so much, I'd willed it into being. That aiming all my unrequited love in his direction all these years had caused some kind of alchemical reaction, transforming his friendshippy feelings into more.

Which was ridiculous, obviously...

And here I was, making this about *me* and *my* feelings, when it should have been about Dunn. About giving him the unconditional love and support he deserved.

"Hush now." I led him to the sofa and rubbed my hand up and down his warm back as he dragged in big, calming lungfuls of air. "I've got you, D. I've got you, baby. Hush now." As we sat, he laid his head on my chest and grasped the waist of my shirt in two tight fists, like he thought I might try to escape. As if I wasn't exactly where I'd always wanted to be.

"I don't think you realize how important you are to me, Tuck," Dunn whispered into my sweater. "Like, if I didn't have you... I don't know what I'd do. You make everything about me make sense. You make me feel strong." He slid his cheek against my chest, and I clasped him tighter. "The idea of not having you in my life scares me to death."

Good Lord, the man was sweetness personified.

I ran a hand over his silky hair. "That won't happen," I whispered into his ear. My breath raised gooseflesh on the sensitive skin of his neck, and his grip on me tightened. "You know I love you, Dunn. You're my *best* best friend. You'll always have me, no matter what. Talk to me. What's going on in that head?"

I was close enough to count the freckles on his jawline —precisely *four*—and see the little flecks of golden stubble glint in the firelight. Close enough to smell his cologne and the faint tang of woodsmoke that clung to him. Close enough to feel the soft nap of his sweater beneath my fingertips and the play of his muscles under that. It was painfully thrilling being this close, and my heart was so full of tenderness for him, it was liable to beat out of my chest.

There was nothing I wouldn't do for this man.

"I'm so messed up right now," he whispered. "Am I gay? Or bi? That seems to be a thing a guy should know before he gets to be twenty-eight, you know? A-and why is it that I can look at a guy like Carter and think he's attractive, but not wanna get with him at *all*, but then want to drag you out of your chair and kiss the shit out of you right in the middle of the damn Steak 'n Bait?"

My breathing hitched.

Seriously, this jealousy thing should *not* be hot.

Dunn shook his head against me. "And then… shit. What if… what if I'm not good at it?"

I blinked, wondering if I'd missed something. "At what?"

"Bein', you know, gay." He swallowed hard. "You know how you can't tie your own clinch knot on your fishing line to save your soul, no matter how hard you try? What if… what if *I'm* like that, but with gay sex? What if I told you all the stuff that's going through my brain and you were freaked-out? Or, God, what if I told you something and it hurt your feelings?" He lifted his head so he could look at me, and his eyes were troubled. "Seriously, Tuck, what then? Because if I ever fucked this up with you…"

I cradled his jaw in both hands. "Dunn, you can't. You and me… we're un-fuckup-able."

"You promise?" He quirked one eyebrow.

"I swear." I marked a cross over my heart with my fingertip. "You can tell me anything. All your fears and doubts and… anything. Really."

And I would not judge, I vowed to myself. I would not make this about me. Even if he wanted to talk about women. Even if he wanted to talk about—*gah*—Jenn.

My job was to be his best friend. To be reassuring and accepting.

"Okay, well." Dunn scrubbed his hands through his hair. "The thing that's been on my mind the most…" He bit his lip.

"Go on." I tried to project safety and calm.

"…is that I got hard earlier tonight, thinking about that mouth of yours," he confessed in a whispered rush.

My jaw dropped and wheezed out a cough. That… was not where I'd seen this going.

Okay, rewind. Just because he was thinking of these things didn't mean he actually wanted to do them. It could be like that time he'd been *thinking* of free-climbing the giant water tower on the Lurch side of town, but we'd gone fishing and the urge had passed.

A supportive friend would not make assumptions.

"M-my mouth," I stammered, trying and abjectly failing to sound casual. "M'kay. Like, um… thinking about us kissing, you mean?" I stopped just short of asking, "And how did that make you *feel?*" like I was his therapist or something.

"Not exactly that. Kissing too, though, because that kiss was the most intense sexual thing I've ever experienced. But, um, I was thinking more like…" He paused to wet his lips. "Your mouth on my dick."

"My… oh." I nodded encouragingly. "Uh-huh. Yes. That's… very…"

Jesus on a jackhammer, what was I babbling about? In my defense, my entire brain had liquified when he started talking about my mouth and started spilling out my ear when he mentioned my dick.

Supportive friend.

Supportive. Friend.

"Very… what?" Dunn bit his bottom lip again and

stared at my mouth like he was imagining things right then and there.

My whole body flashed hot and then cold, which was totally a hypothalamus thing caused by a surge of adrenaline.

In other medical news, I was very concerned that my cock might actually harm itself in its desire to break free of my pants.

"Very *good*," I wheezed. "All very normal. I'm not freaking out, see? Keep going."

"Yeah? Okay, well… you were naked underneath me in these thoughts."

I pushed my lips together so hard it was painful. "Mmm. Mmhmm" was about the best I could manage. My cock throbbed in my pants—literally throbbed. I'd always thought that was hyperbole when I read it in books, but as it turned out, *it was not.*

At all.

This was a day of revelations.

"And you did this thing where you kind of… I'm not sure of the vocab. It was kind of a shimmy?" He moved his shoulders a bit. "But lying down?"

"Lying down?" I croaked. "Maybe we should…"

"Did you feel it too?" Dunn blurted out. "I mean, before. When we kissed. Is it always that overwhelming with a guy? Or was that… us?" His green eyes were earnest and molten hot, and I could no more have stopped myself from kissing him than I could have stopped myself from breathing, it was that reflexive. That necessary.

My liquified brain could not process all the ways this could go spectacularly wrong, so I simply didn't think about them. I just tunneled my fingers into his hair, pushed him back against the arm of the sofa, laid myself out on top of him, and kissed the stuffing out of him.

You only live once, right?

Dunn moaned a little, and one of his big hands came up to hold my head in place while the other crept up under my sweater.

Holy shit. I was almost positive I was on fire, boiling from the inside out. The heat and taste of him on my tongue, the feeling of his calloused fingers against my back... I couldn't help writhing against him a little, desperate for relief.

Dunn broke away and gasped for air, his green eyes fully dilated despite the dim light. He looked down at our fully aligned bodies, then back at me. "Shit, Tuck," he breathed. "You're hard. I *felt* it."

"Oh, uh..." I looked down at the two of us too, but my reaction was less shock and more like overwhelming desire. "Yeah, I am. And so are you." I watched his face carefully. "Does that bother you?"

He shook his head wordlessly, but his eyes were wide as saucers. "It's *hot*, but... I have no idea what to do now." He spread his hands out helplessly. "I want to touch you, but I don't... know how."

"You can touch me anywhere, Dunn. Do... anything. Okay?" I reached behind me and yanked my sweater over my head before I became the first person in the Thicket to die of heat stroke in March. "I'll show you. You tell me if there's anything you don't like."

Dunn's big palms coasted up my naked back, and his nostrils flared, like he couldn't believe this was happening any more than I could. He looked almost drunk, with his kiss-swollen lips and fever-bright eyes. "I trust you, Tuck," he whispered. "Show me."

I sat back on his thighs just long enough to shimmy his sweater up and off him, taking care not to stretch out the neck. Dunn watched in amusement as I folded it before tossing it gently onto the side table.

"Something funny?" I demanded.

"Just remembering you stomping out of the Steak 'n Bait, ready to rip off that sweater 'cause I'd dared to wear it out with Jenn." His lips quirked. "What would you have done with me, half-naked in the parking lot?"

"I'm sure I would have thought of something." I leaned forward and laid my palms flat on his chest, which brought our jean-covered cocks into alignment. Dunn's eyes went unfocused, and I moaned.

Shit. I tried to remind myself that I'd seen his naked chest a thousand times—heck, I'd rubbed sunscreen all over him *ten* thousand times, 'cause he was so fair I made him reapply religiously—but suddenly everything was different. I could run my eyes over his flat, pink nipples and not have to hide my arousal, because I *wanted* him to see how much I wanted him. Heck, for this one night, I could put my *mouth* on him if I wanted to.

And I really, really wanted to.

Breathing suddenly became tricky.

"Is this staring and hyperventilating thing what you were gonna show me?" Dunn whispered in the same warm, teasing tone he used when we were fishing and it was my turn to go inside and get us fresh beers... and that was when it clicked—*really* clicked—that this was *Dunn* underneath me.

And tomorrow... well, tomorrow Dunn was one hundred percent gonna realize all the reasons why he needed to stick with someone like Jenn, or hopefully someone better for him than Jenn, but still someone who wasn't *me*, and my poor heart was gonna shrivel up and crack into dust and blow away. *Goodbye, Tucker Wright.*

But this moment, right now? This was the shot I'd never thought I'd get. This was the undying dream of my foolish, foolish heart. I had never wanted anyone or anything the way I wanted Dunn Johnson under my hands, to have the opportunity to show him how incredible he was. And now I could.

And I was going to savor it.

I hooked a finger in his waistband and raised an eyebrow. "These look uncomfortable."

"Do they?" His voice was rough. Needy. And it made an answering need fizz through my blood.

"I mean, I know mine are." I stood up without waiting for him to say anything else and shucked my pants entirely, kicking them under the sofa.

My erection bobbed against my stomach, sticky with fluid and really, unmistakably *there*. Dunn's gaze locked on it... and his breathing ramped up.

I toyed with the button on his jeans, and his eyes met mine, a little wary and a whole lot excited. "Yes?"

"Yeah." He nodded. "Definitely yes."

I unbuttoned and unzipped him, and then Dunn took over, wiggling out of his jeans and briefs and kicking them off so hard they sailed over the back of the couch.

I snickered... and then laughed out loud. "Excited?"

"Maybe."

I looked down at him splayed out on my couch and... fuck. He was long, and cut, and mouthwateringly perfect— everything I *never* needed to see if I ever wanted any hope of being content just being friends, but that was tomorrow-Tucker's problem. Today-Tucker was living in the moment, so I reached out a hand to stroke him.

Dunn's entire back bowed up off the sofa like he'd been electrocuted. "Oh my flippin Lord."

"Dunn? Y'okay?" I asked softly. I wondered if this would be the part where it all got a little too real for him, and if it was, I was going to be a supportive friend. I *was*. And I'd maybe only cry a *little*.

"Tucker?" Dunn's green eyes lifted to mine, confused and aroused. "God, you're gorgeous."

He sounded nearly as shocked to say it as I was to hear it, and I hadn't known just how badly I needed to hear that from him until the words were out.

"Yeah?" I huffed out a little laugh. This… this was not real life. I had no idea what kind of alternate reality, parallel universe, dream world I'd stumbled into, but I didn't wanna go home.

"Come here," he whispered. "Come back here and hold me down and kiss me again. Everything makes sense when you do."

I felt kinda the same, so that's exactly what I did. I climbed on top of my *best* best friend and let him wrap his arms around me. I took my time exploring his mouth, then yanked his head to the side so I could lick each of his four freckles as I made my way down his jaw to his neck.

Dunn's breath shuddered out of him, and his hands tightened on me as I ran my teeth over each of his nipples in turn. His body writhed under mine, needing friction, so I straddled his leg and rubbed against him while I took my time worshipping every inch of his gorgeous chest and his smooth, defined abs.

And then I moved lower, pushing his knee off the couch to give myself room.

"Tuck?" Dunn asked softly.

"Shh. Let me. Just like you were thinking earlier," I told him. I wrapped a hand around the base of his shaft and licked a stripe up the side of his cock.

"Shit, Tuck!" Dunn shouted. He grabbed the back of the sofa like we were on a boat in choppy water, and I chuckled darkly... then I braced a hand on the cushion beside his hip and sucked him into my mouth.

It had been years since I'd done this, and I was pretty sure anyone else would've found my technique a little sloppy, but Dunn didn't seem to care, maybe because I made up for it with some serious enthusiasm, jacking him in time to the pulls of my mouth until his breath came in little moaning pants.

Dunn's hand—the one that wasn't anchored to the couch—came to rest on my hair, but it seemed like he wasn't sure what to do with it besides pat it gently, when gentle was the last thing I wanted.

I stared up at him, over the gorgeous expanse of his chest, until our eyes met, then grabbed his hand in mine and pushed down firmly. I wanted him to do whatever he wanted with me. I wanted him rough and earthy and impolite and *Dunn*.

His eyes widened in understanding, and I swear his cock jerked in my mouth.

"Holy fuck," he breathed. He held my head in place and thrust into my mouth once, twice... then he cried out my name and came down my throat.

A second later, I was on my knees between his legs, jerking myself off to the sight of Dunn Johnson—*Dunn Johnson!*—splayed out naked in my den in the firelight, and with his lust-glazed eyes watching my every move, I came all over his chest.

"Oh my God." I braced a hand on his shoulder to catch myself, squeezed my eyes shut, and panted like I'd just run six miles. "I have... no feeling... whatsoever... from my thighs down. I might... be dead."

Dunn's shuddering breath fanned my face, and I blinked my eyes open. "Dunn? That was a joke."

But Dunn had lifted a hand to trail his fingers through

the spattered cum on his chest—*my* cum—and some emotion I couldn't recognize was working behind his eyes. "Well, okay, then," he said softly.

For maybe the first time ever, I couldn't read him *at all*. I couldn't tell if what he was feeling was disgust or satisfaction or something in between. I couldn't tell if he was happy or sad or freaking out or just really tired.

"What's that mean?" I demanded.

"It means… Thank you, Tuck. This helped. A lot." He smiled.

I blinked. Like, helped how? Helped him decide he was bi? Helped him decide he never wanted to do this again?

Before I could ask him, he stretched out his arms and legs with a groan and yawned hugely. "I am so sleeping over tonight."

"You are?" I shifted backward, then scrambled off the sofa. Where were my damn jeans?

"Totally. I feel more drunk than you were on sangria. Like, I've never felt this loose in my life." He stretched his arms to the ceiling and grinned at me, totally unconcerned by his nakedness. "Mind if I use your shower? Hey, you still use that herbal shampoo I like?"

He walked off down the hall, not waiting for my answer, which was fine, since I didn't know what to say.

I'd been trying to comfort him, pretty sure, like a sensitive friend… and he seemed pretty comfortable.

So, mission accomplished?

I followed him down the hall after a quick stop in the hallway half bath to clean up, and I'd just pulled on a pair of flannel pants when the shower turned off in the attached bath and Dunn emerged in a cloud of herbal-scented steam, wearing his boxer briefs and rubbing his head with a towel.

And what was the first, most essential thing I said at this juncture?

"I was not drunk on sangria."

"No?" Dunn snorted and lay down on my bed like this was a thing we did all the time, then curled himself around my pillow. "Sure seemed like it. You were cute. I mean, when you weren't pissing me off."

I understood the feeling.

Acutely.

"Dunn, what are you doing?" I folded my arms over my chest. "There's a guest room down the hall with your pajamas in the drawer."

"Mmm. But I'm here now. And it's not like we've never shared a bed." He yawned so hard his jaw cracked. "We do it all the time out at the cabin."

All the time was a serious exaggeration, and the amount of sleep I'd gotten on those nights could be counted in minutes. I'd been too afraid I'd wind up wrapped around him or start muttering, "Fuck me, Dunn Johnson!" in my sleep or something.

"Come to bed, Tucker. I can feel you thinking from all the way over there."

I sighed, still nonspecifically annoyed. "I usually sit up and do crosswords until I feel sleepy," I complained.

"That's okay. You won't bother me."

"How magnanimous of you," I grumbled. But after rolling my eyes *hard*, I went out to the den and made sure the fire was out, shut out the lights, brushed my teeth, grabbed my crossword puzzles and glasses, and got into my side of the bed—by which I meant the 25 percent of the bed Dunn didn't occupy.

Dunn's breathing was deep and even, and his damp hair was tousled around his head, begging for my fingers to comb through it. I bit my lip and decided that this was still *tonight*, right? So I let myself do what I wanted. I stroked my fingers through those soft golden-brown locks.

Dunn sighed contentedly, and I snatched my hand away.

"Today y'almost fought Jenn over tater tots," he chuckled sleepily.

Yes, that was indeed the most important takeaway of this day.

"Y'all ordered them anyway," I grumbled.

"But she din' *eat* 'em," he mumbled. "So it does'n coun'." He rolled even closer, stretched out a hand and banged it around the mattress until he found mine, then set it back on his head. "Mmm. G'night, Tuck."

Maybe for him it would be, but there was absolutely *no* way I'd ever be able to sleep like this, when I didn't know what Dunn was thinking or what would happen the next morning.

The next thing I knew, Dunn was standing beside the bed fully dressed and staring down at me. Thin, gray light seeped through the shutters on the window.

I quickly shut my eyes and kept my breathing even, hoping he couldn't tell I was awake.

"Tuck?" His voice was sleepy-gruff, and it was sexy as all hell. I did *not* need to know that. "Gotta go milk the cows."

Did he want me to go with him? I sometimes did, when we had to head home from the cabin or whatever, and I even enjoyed it, but today? When it was time for the reckoning, where I'd learn the cost of last night? "Mph. Sleeping."

I could *feel* him hesitate. "You and me... we'll talk later, okay?"

Oh, sure. We'd talk. Yeah. That totally didn't strike fear into my heart. "Mmmmph," I muttered noncommittally.

He hesitated again, then leaned down and brushed a

kiss over my forehead. "My best, best friend," he said affectionately.

The second he left, my eyes popped open.

His best, best friend? That... did not sound promising for continuing shenanigans. Which was *fine*.

I was pretty sure.

But then, the kiss... that was very, very new.

Was it a romantic thing? Or an "I'm so comfortable with my heterosexuality after a night of unsuccessful experimentation that I can now kiss all my friends" kind of thing?

Jesus Christ, I had no idea. I was more mixed up than a milkshake, as my Nana Aarons used to say.

I jumped out of bed and was in the shower with a head full of herbal suds—which now reminded me of Dunn, even though it was my shampoo, which was *unfair*—when I heard Carter's voice in my head from last night.

"Josh was just having fun... Curious, I guess... looking for a reason not to marry his on-again-off-again girlfriend... his itch had been scratched."

I blinked the shampoo out of my eyes.

That was really the most likely thing, wasn't it? So... I was going to do what I'd promised I'd do last night. Be a supportive friend. If being with me this way wasn't his thing... well, then... okay.

I puttered around the house for a couple of hours, rinsing out my wineglass from last night, taking stock of my secret stash of cookies, tidying my office, and even doing a crossword, but I couldn't settle to anything. Sundays were usually my free days, the days I spent with Dunn or with the Johnsons or *both*, but I felt weirdly out of sorts. I took off my glasses, grabbed a jacket, and headed down to the coffee shop for a muffin.

Just the walk helped get me out of my head, and so did the ten or so people who stopped me to say hello and have a quick chat. There *was* more to my life than Dunn Johnson, and I needed to remember that.

I pulled open the door to the shop, and Ava Siegel tackle-hugged me. "Oh my God, if you didn't show up I was gonna fake appendicitis so I could come talk to you! What happened at the Steak 'n Bait last night?"

"What? Nothing!" Oh, motherfucking duckbills. Had someone seen me and Dunn in the parking lot? I could barely swallow. "We are *friends*."

"Not what Jenn said," Ava singsonged.

Wait, *Jenn* knew?

"She said y'all were holding hands. And *he* said he's known you for years." She grinned broadly. "And he made it sound like it was in a biblical sense."

"Huh?"

Ava nudged her head toward the back corner of the shop, where Carter sat chatting with Jenn Shipley and Cindy Ann Johnson.

Three of the four people I least wanted to talk to just then, all together. Yay.

But it was too late to turn around, especially with Ava dragging me over to the table by my elbow. And when we got close, Carter looked up and flashed me a "Save me!" look.

"Uh. Hey. Morning, all." I lifted a hand in greeting.

Jenn gave me a surprisingly friendly smile, all things considered, but Cindy Ann looked a little concerned.

"Honey bear!" Carter said, pulling out the chair beside him. "Come sit by me. Mrs. Johnson—"

"Cindy Ann," she corrected, wagging a finger.

"Cindy Ann," Carter agreed. "She's just been telling me *how many* gay men there are in Licking Thicket and the surrounding towns." He gave me a desperate look. "Who knew?"

"Tucker did," Cindy Ann said proudly. "He runs a charity to raise money for LGBT youth programs."

I smiled wanly.

"She's offered to introduce me to them," Carter said, a little edge of panic in his voice. "*All* of them."

"Oh, that's so sweet."

"But unnecessary," Carter said. "Since I have Tucker here." He threw an arm around my shoulder, pulled me against his side, and pressed a kiss to the top of my head. "Right, Tuck?"

"Well, now," a gravelly voice behind me said. "Seems like you maybe forgot to tell me something, Doc Wright."

Shit.

The fourth person I least wanted to speak to had just arrived.

10

DUNN

1-Across: Causing or feeling embarrassment or inconvenience (7 letters)

WAS THERE anything better than waking up wrapped around your favorite person on earth? No. No there was not.

I walked out of Tucker's house like a brand-new man. I wanted to shout my relief and happiness from the rooftops. Bernadette and the cows heard more about Tucker Wright's body than was decent, but I needed to get some things off my chest.

By the time I met my brother outside the coffee shop, I felt like the man at the front of a parade—the one with the giant stick he got to lift up and down and the cheesy grin on his face for everyone around him. I was just so damned... joyful.

"Christ on a cracker, are you high?" Brooks asked when I approached him and Mal on the sidewalk. "You look like you just swallowed a handful of Doc Wright's special pills."

I puffed out my chest. "I swallowed his *somethin'*."

Brooks blinked. Mal tilted his head. "What?" they asked at the same time.

I deflated. "Well, not literally. But, you know. I'm sure it won't be long before we do that too."

Mal didn't take his eyes off me but leaned over to whisper at Brooks. "Is he really on special pills?"

Brooks ignored him. "What are you talking about?"

"Me and Tuck. We did it. *Finally.* And I'm just so... relieved. But I wanted to ask you guys. Where do I get my flag? Does Mama keep a stash? Isn't that what PFLAG means?"

Brooks blinked. "You're not telling Mom!"

Mal grinned. "No, because he's going to let me do it."

Brooks elbowed his boyfriend in the gut. Not nice. "Dunn. What are you saying? You and Tucker finally..."

"Did the nasty?" Mal suggested eagerly. "Knocked boots? Went cave diving? Buried the weasel?"

Brooks turned to him and lurched forward until their noses were touching. "Enough, you. This is serious." He turned back to me. "What exactly happened? I thought he had a date last night and so did you."

"Carter Rogers." I lost a little bit of my joy at the reminder. "That guy was too good-looking for his own good."

"No such thing," Mal muttered.

"Tuck deserves better," I added.

"And you're better?" Brooks asked.

Mal nodded his head energetically.

I appreciated the support.

"No one cares more about Tucker Wright in this entire world, and yes, I'm including his mama in that statement." I felt my face heat at the strong assertion, but I stood by it.

Brooks looked confused. "So you just ran in there like a bucking bronc and took charge of him like some kind of—"

Mal flapped his hands in the air. "Oooh! I love it when you get Southern. Keep going!"

Brooks sighed. "How far did you two go? And what about Jenn?"

"Jenn and I aren't exclusive. I made sure of that before I agreed to her free trial."

Mal opened his mouth, but Brooks slapped a hand over it. "And Tuck?"

I sighed. Were little hearts and stars floating out of my eyes? I felt like maybe they were. "He's everything. *Everything*."

The two of them stared at me again. It was getting a little weird. I held up a hand. "But don't worry. We're not going to rush anything. I don't want to scare him off, and I know I can be somewhat… overwhelming."

Mal shook his head. "No. You're the right kind of whelming. I love your whelming."

Brooks frowned. "Slow is good. Slow is really good."

I nodded. "Except I have to tell Mama. It's going to break her heart, but I don't want her hearing it from anyone else. It's going to come as a huge scandal to the town, and Licking Thicket is going to get nuts for a while with the shock."

Mal clapped a hand in front of his mouth and tried to hold in his emotions. I understood his distress. It probably brought up bad memories from when he and Brooks got together.

"The… shock," Brooks said carefully. "Of you and Tucker being a thing."

"Exactly," I said. "No one would expect this. Ever. And I don't want to upset anyone, especially Mama."

Mal bounced on his feet. "Please, please let me come with you to tell Cindy Ann and Big Red."

Brooks sighed. "And there's no way I can dissuade you from doing this?"

I shook my head. "No, sir. I owe it to Tuck to be all in. I don't want him to think I'm ashamed of him or anything."

"You're going to need to pick up a cake," Brooks said. Mal nodded his agreement. "And not just any cake. Maggie's apple crumble cake."

"Ooh. Good call. Let's get coffee and the cake before we head on over."

I opened the door, all bright-eyed and bushy-tailed, feeling a bit like I'd been dressed by twittering animals and danced my way through my chores this morning. So when I stepped inside and saw my Tucker being manhandled by that smarmy big-city doctor... well, it wasn't pretty.

"The fuck," I said under my breath.

Mal made a little sound of excitement in the back of his throat, and Brooks immediately tried to shush him.

"*Hey*," I said abnormally loudly. "*It is us. Me, I mean. Us. The three of us. Here in this house of coffee.*" I gestured in a generalized circle with a stiff arm.

Everyone in the shop seemed to stare. "Well, hey, Dunn, buddy," Cornell Higgins called from behind his giant latte. "You having a hearing problem?"

"*No.*"

Brooks stepped out from behind me. "Oh look," he said dryly. "It's Mom." He swallowed. "And Tucker. And some super-handsome rich-looking dude."

Mal shoved me out of the way. Tuck hadn't even looked over yet. Obviously whatever Dr. Jerkus was saying was way too interesting for him to spare a glance at little ole me. I moved closer.

"Well, now." I spoke as calmly as I could. I'd seen

scenes like this in movies, and I didn't want to alarm anyone or start something melodramatic. "Seems like you maybe forgot to tell me something, Doc Wright."

Tuck squeezed his eyes closed. Probably the wince of guilt. "Dunn?" he asked, as if confirming it was, in fact, the person who'd been in his bed this morning.

Naked.

"That's my name. Don't wear it…" I stopped and sighed. That was stupid. "Yeah, it's me. Didn't know you wanted coffee. I could have made you coffee. You certainly didn't need *other* people to get coffee for you. I was gone for an hour. Jesus."

"Dunn Johnson," Mama snapped. "Taking the Lord's name in vain and on a Sunday, no less."

"Sorry, Mama." I leaned over and pecked her on the cheek before grabbing a chair from a nearby table. "I was gonna come see you, but I guess now there's no reason to."

I gave Tucker significant eye contact, but he just squinted at me in return. "Your eyes hurting, D?"

"Mr. Rogers," I said with a nod in the man's direction. I shoved the chair between him and Tuck and sat down.

"It's Doctor," he said, lifting an eyebrow. "Good to see you again, Dunk."

I lurched forward, but Tuck grabbed me smoothly by the back of the collar and sat my ass back down in the chair. "It's Mr. Johnson to you," I snapped.

Mal sat down in a chair on the other side of the guy and placed his hand on Carter's arm. "Actually, his daddy is Big Johnson, so you can call him Little Johnson." Then Mal turned to me with flippy eyelashes. "Isn't that right, Little Johnson?"

Brooks snickered, and I shot him a look that promised retribution on his man. Then I turned to Tuck. "Hey."

He blushed and looked down at his lap. "Hey."

Carter laughed. "So, Tucker. You were saying you were going to show me around this charming little burg of yours."

"Is that what you want to do?" Tucker asked, as if actually considering it. The loud clattering and chatting noises in the crowded cafe were getting on my last nerve. "I do have the day off."

Carter leaned back and crossed his outstretched legs under the table. "Either that or you can take me fishing to all those pretty little spots you used to tell me about. Wasn't there one on a bridge you liked?"

That was *enough*. I couldn't sit here and listen to any more of this nonsense. If Tucker wasn't going to put him in his place, I would. "He can't," I said. "I'm coming over to snake his drain."

The entire coffeehouse went dead silent like someone had turned a giant off switch on the back of the building.

"Finally," Mama muttered.

"Is that right?" Mal asked innocently.

Tucker's face bloomed deep red in slow motion as his face turned from slightly, awkwardly uncomfortable into mottled fury.

Shit.

"You *what*?" he asked between tight teeth.

I stood up and put my hands up so everyone would hear me. "It wasn't a euphemism," I said to the room. "I swear. It's just that when I was in his shower last night, well, closer to this morning I guess, it was draining really slow."

Mama put her face in her hands and began to shake. And that's when I realized she wasn't going to take the news of the two of us as well as I'd hoped.

I shot a frantic look at Tucker. He always knew how to help me get my mouth out of trouble. "Tucker, do something. You know what I mean."

But Tucker just stood up and turned to Carter. "Come on. We'll go fishing."

Just then a booming crack of thunder shook the café, and God's own drain didn't need snaking. Rain came down in a torrent and lashed against the windows of the cafe.

Tucker sighed and his shoulders drooped. Brooks stood and clapped him on the shoulder. "Bring Carter fishing tomorrow. We'll all go together."

I let out a breath of relief and tried to meet my brother's eyes to thank him, but he grabbed Mal's hand and bolted for the end of the coffee line.

I turned to Tucker. "I'm… sorry?" I whispered, unsure of how everything had gone to shit so fast. I had to figure out how to fix it before things went from bad to worse. "Can I talk to you? Please?"

He shook his head and looked… *squirrelly*. Not at all like a man who'd had his future decided and his love life locked down tight the night before. "Not right now, D. I gotta think about some things, alright?"

I glanced between him and Carter. I did not like the sound of that one bit. "Naked thinking, or…?"

Tucker's eyes narrowed to angry slits, and his lips pursed the way they did when I accidentally on purpose shoved him in swimming pools whenever he got too close to them.

"Okay, okay. So… I'll see you tomorrow? At the lake?" I tried not to sound too needy, but it was a close thing.

"Fine," he muttered. "Bring your Damiki Armor Shad lure."

He grabbed Carter's arm and yanked him toward the door. Before they got to the exit, Carter turned back and winked at me. Cocky fucker.

I turned back to my mama, who seemed to have gotten

herself under control a little. "Um... I was gonna stop by and pick up a crumble cake at Annie's..."

That perked her right up. "Well, at least something good might come out of this morning," she said, standing and brushing off her clothes as if she'd been in a dust storm or something. "Let's go. And then you can tell me all about what happened between you and Tucker."

I dragged my heels as I realized my celebration cake had turned into what Mama and Gracie had always called a "boy problems" cake.

Yet another thing about being bisexual I was going to have to get used to.

11

TUCKER

10-ACROSS: Baffled, confused, screwed (10 letters)

"IF ONLY DUNN JOHNSON could *want* me," I singsonged under my breath as I stared up at a faint crack in the plaster ceiling over the exam table in my office. "Then I'd be the *happiest* man in the *universe*. We'd live happily ever after!"

I snorted and shoved another dark chocolate Milano in my mouth.

What a fool I'd been.

Dunn and I had just barely gotten back on track after an awful week apart, and what had I done? Comforted him with an orgasm—you know, as all platonic buds do—when the poor guy had just *barely* started questioning his sexuality, and ensured that things went right back to weird between us. Now I couldn't look at my *best* best friend without thinking about the precise taste and texture of his dick in my mouth—a singularly interesting experience while sitting with his mama at the coffee shop, let me just tell you—and when the man had shown up with his tool bucket to snake the drain in the master bathroom, all I'd been able to think about was him *snaking my drain* in the master bathroom... which was why I'd squeaked out something about an "emergency situation!" and fled downstairs to the exam room, leaving Carter in the living room with my crossword puzzle books unsupervised, damn it.

Dunn and I needed to talk and clear the air about last night, *obviously*. But I felt like the apology I owed him for jumping him while he was vulnerable would be more sincere and effective if I weren't springing wood all over the damn place while I made it. This meant that no talky-talky would be happening today.

I reached down to adjust my jeans, making the vinyl-covered exam table squeak.

Someone knocked at the door, and I froze.

"I'm... I'm *bivvy wite* now!" I hastily swallowed my cookie and brushed the crumbs from my sweater. "Doctor things. Medical emergencies."

The doorknob rattled, and a second later, the door swung open to reveal Carter Rogers leaning against the jamb, looking way too put together in his khakis and pastel sweater. How the hell had he known to come look for me?

"Key was above the doorframe." He glanced up, and his lips twisted into an unimpressed face. "You'd make a terrible spy."

I scowled. "Then it's just as well I'm a *doctor*. And as I mentioned, I'm busy."

"Yes, I see. Is a Milano deficiency a medical emergency now?" He glanced at the package of cookies still in my hand.

I scrambled off the table and peered around him into the hall. "Don't be ridiculous, Carter!" I said over-loudly. "I'm simply eating a cookie while I ponder this complex, confidential... situation. Involving medicine."

"Ahhh, that must be how real doctors do it. I saw that on an episode of *House* once." Carter brushed past me and hopped up onto the end of the exam table, stealing my spot. "Your boyfriend's gone, by the by. It's just you and me —"

I whirled to face him. "Dunn's *not* my boyfriend."

"— aaaand I got tired of drawing anthropomorphic penises on your crossword puzzles —"

"Damn it, Carter!" I shook the cookie bag at him. "I knew it!"

"— so I figured I'd come down here and consult with you on your emergency. Little did I know just how badly you'd need your personal heart doctor." He lay back and stacked his hands behind his head. "Lay it on me, Doc. What's happening between you and the handsome and oh-so-jealous Farmer Johnson?" He swung his feet back and forth like he hadn't a care in the world... but he watched me closely.

I closed my eyes and sighed. "Dunn's gone? You sure?"

"Yep. And he looked none too pleased when I lied and told him I might just stay the night, since we'd need to get an early start for fishing tomorrow. He said, 'I think it's only fair to warn you, Rogers, that I'm bringing out my Armor Shad and my *Magnum* Squarebill tomorrow.' I'm ninety-nine percent sure that was fisherman-speak for challenging me to a duel." Carter wiggled his eyebrows.

I groaned. God, I was a sucker for Dunn Johnson and his proprietary friendship.

"Do I even want to know what you said after that?" I demanded.

"Oh, I just reminded him it's not about how big your Squarebill is, it's about knowing how to use it." Carter studied his nails innocently. "Wasn't that right? I'm not up on all the fishing lingo."

"Oh, God, you didn't." I thought of Dunn last night, all

bewildered, saying he wanted to touch me but didn't know how. I smacked my forehead with the hand that wasn't still clinging to the cookie bag. "*Carter*!"

"What?" He sat up, his blue eyes sparkling and unrepentant. "I have to say, I only agreed to cover Dr. Symmons's practice 'cause my old man asked me to, and I'd kinda dreaded it. Who knew small towns could be so fun?"

"Hush! You've just taken a bad situation and made it even worse. *And I didn't think that was possible.*" I stormed out of the room and up the main stairs to my kitchen. This situation required something stronger than Milanos.

"What did I do?" Carter demanded, following along behind me, his long legs matching my shorter ones stride for stride. "Dunn's jealous of me, I know he is. Which, a) is hilarious, since I'm almost positive he was the reason you dropped me like a hot and sexy potato three years ago, and b) indicates that the 'hopeless' situation you mentioned last night isn't actually so hopeless. What's so bad about me poking him along a little?"

I pawed through the freezer, chucking packets of frozen vegetables to the side, until I found the holy grail—one extra-large slice of Annie's Triple Chocolate Heartbreak Cake. I stuck it in the microwave.

"What's wrong is... is..." I hesitated. I didn't want to tell anyone Dunn's business, but Jesus, I needed to talk to someone. "Okay, I need to know that if I tell you something, it'll stay in total confidence."

"Doctor-patient confidentiality," Carter agreed solemnly. He boosted himself up onto my soapstone counter. "Spill."

"Well." I blew out a breath. "Last night after that debacle at the Steak 'n Bait, Dunn came over."

"Came over? So?" Carter's eyes widened. "Oh! *Ohhhhh*! You mean he *came over* came over! You two did the deed?"

"We did *a* deed," I allowed. "*Some* deeds. Not *all* deeds. But he'd never done *any* deeds before. Not with a man."

"Ah, shit." Carter sounded momentarily contrite. "And I inadvertently suggested he didn't know what he was doing, did I?"

I nodded once. Then I retrieved my cake, grabbed a fork, hunched over the island, and dug in without offering Carter *any*. Meddlesome fucker could get his own.

"Holy hot damn! Guess Farmer Johnson was further down the path to self-awareness than I figured, huh?" Carter sounded impressed. Then he frowned. "Wait, if Dunn *came over*… why the hell are you self-medicating with cake instead of sucking his face off?"

"Beckuv," I said around a mouthful of chocolate.

Carter lifted one eyebrow.

I swallowed. "*Because*," I repeated. "It was like we opened Pandora's box last night, only worse. *Tucker's* box. The box of unrequited feelings. And I can't seem to close it again." I stabbed my cake viciously. "It's going to destroy us."

Carter pushed his lips together like he was trying not to laugh. "Honey, I'm not gonna accuse you of being a drama queen, but you might wanna lay off the cake. Opening the feelings box is a good thing."

"You don't understand." I licked my fork. "See, Dunn was confused. He kissed me in the parking lot last night during dinner—"

"Oh *ho*." Carter's eyes lit up. "That's a weird way to treat his asthma, Dr. Wright. Guess they do things more hands-on in the Thicket, hmm?"

"Hush," I told him again. "The point is, after the kiss, Dunn got all kinds of freaked-out about his sexuality. I wanted to talk then, but he wouldn't. Instead, he went back inside to finish his date with Jenn." And I hadn't realized how much that hurt until I said it aloud. I chopped the cake into crumbs. "They ordered tater tots, Carter. *Deliberately.*"

"Mmm." He stroked his chin. "Yeah, Jenn explained the tater tot thing last night while you were giving Dunn a tonsillectomy with your tongue. I think she thinks we're best friends, since *my* date was besties with *her* date, which was convenient since she was very forthcoming on a whole bunch of subjects—and once again, let me just say, this town is a fucking *hoot.*"

"Delightful." I shoveled in another mouthful of cake. "Congwats on yow new fwienship."

Carter chuckled lightly. "Tuck, tater tots or not, every time you fake-laughed at one of my incredibly witty rejoinders, Dunn's shoulders crawled up closer to his ears, and I've never seen someone look so mortally offended by my discussion of antithrombotic therapies. Pretty sure you're Dunn Johnson's true-tot-love."

God, I wanted to believe that, but for the sake of my sanity, I couldn't let myself. "Nope. No."

"Oh, but *yes.*" Carter grinned. He waved a hand magnanimously. "Anyway, go on with your tale. Dunn swung around for a booty call, and?"

"No, see, it wasn't like that at *all*! He came over here looking for comfort. From his friend. And instead we ended up frotting and, ah, other stuff." I winced guiltily. "And then we slept in my bed, and this morning he said he wanted to *talk* in this super-serious voice. And no wonder, right? Who does that, Carter? Who gives a friend a com-frot?"

"A really, *really* good friend." Carter snorted. "A *com-frot.* What the hell is in that cake?"

"Sugar, and stop being judgy." I pushed the rest of the cake away and pressed a hand to my stomach, suddenly nauseous. Every single time I thought about this, the situation seemed worse and worse, and I was more and more clearly at fault. "In my greedy lust, I may have ruined the most important friendship I'll ever have. Pardon me if I'm slightly panicked over it."

"You're slightly something alright." Carter hopped down, grabbed a jelly jar from the glass-front cabinet, filled it with water from the fridge door, and handed it to me. "Drink this and listen up. Tucker, Dunn Johnson is an adult. An adult with a gay best friend, a gay brother, and at least eighty other gay male neighbors in the greater Thicket environs according to Cindy Ann, all of whom he probably knows and likes. Right? He's hardly awash in homophobia."

"Right," I agreed cautiously.

"And he also looks at you the way you look at chocolate —like he will cut anyone foolish enough to stand between you. He knows you, Tuck. He *loves* you."

"He does." I guzzled some water. "But as a friend."

"Maybe friendship is how he's let himself define his feelings for you in the past." Carter opened my fridge and pulled out something wrapped in paper. He set it on a plate. "Maybe he's defining it differently now. Maybe he's genuinely attracted to you."

I thought of Dunn's face staring down at me as I worked him, and I swallowed hard.

"It doesn't work like that. Not really." I reminded myself of this fact daily. Sometimes hourly. Sometimes more. Especially since last fall, when I'd stupidly let myself hope after he kissed me at the Pickin'.

Carter led me away from the cake, over to the little table in the breakfast nook. He pushed me onto one chair, then took the seat opposite, and set the plate on the table between us.

"Except sometimes it *does* work like that. I'm sure I

don't need to remind you that bisexuality is real, do I?" He narrowed his eyes. "That sexuality exists on a continuum? That many, *many* people identify as straight until they find themselves attracted to someone of their own gender, which sometimes doesn't happen until they're in their twenties, or thirties, or *later*?"

"I know." I did. Theoretically. And the very idea of Dunn being one of those people, and that *I* might be the someone he was attracted to, made my chest hurt, because I wanted it so much. "But then there are people like what's his name that you slept with there..." I waved a hand. "Who are just experimenting and decide it's not for them."

"You mean Josh?" Carter's jaw dropped. "Oh, come *on*, Tuck. I know for a fact you've got brains in that skull, so use 'em. Josh and I fucked around 'cause it was fun. We were never close friends, let alone *best* friends, let alone... whatever you and Dunn are, which is something past that. You really think Dunn would risk your relationship on a whim?"

"No," I admitted. "He wouldn't."

"No," Carter agreed. "He definitely wouldn't. Even *I* know that."

"But that doesn't mean he wants it to keep happening. Or that, deep down, he's not upset that I took advantage of him and it made things weird between us. Or that things would be all sunshine and rainbows if he *did* come out as bisexual. You know it's no picnic, Carter. Being queer might be easier in an accepting town like Licking Thicket than in most places around, but that doesn't mean it's *easy*. I've volunteered with enough kids to know that. Heck, my own parents were enough to teach me that." They hadn't disowned me or anything dramatic, but they hadn't exactly joined Cindy Ann's PFLAG chapter either. In an attempt to change the subject, I pointed at the plate. "What's that?"

"Oh, *this*?" Carter nudged the plate. "This here is a chicken salad sandwich. After you disappeared, Dunn told me, and I quote, 'Tucker's down there eating cookies, and he'll make himself sick and shaky. He needs protein and water. Give him this sandwich. And if he won't open the door, use the key above the jamb once I'm gone.' And FYI, that was before he threatened me with his Magnum-sized Squarebill."

"Oh." I stared at the sandwich, and tears filled my eyes. It was from Thelma's Sandwich Shack, the only place in town that made their chicken salad without covering it in mayo, just the way I liked it.

"To state the obvious," Carter continued, "snaking your drain and buying you a sandwich to save you from imminent hypoglycemia are not the actions of a man who's pissed off because your unbridled lust ruined your friendship... nor, indeed, the actions of a man who feels like your friendship's been ruined at all."

"I guess not," I whispered.

"So what exactly did he *say* about your com-frot, then, that got you so doom and gloom?"

"He didn't," I admitted. "He, um... fell asleep. Smiling. And then this morning he said the thing about talking."

"Ah. Truly, he sounds enraged." Carter nodded sagely. "I can see how you came to this logical conclusion about Little Johnson."

I unwrapped the sandwich and picked up half. "Don't call him that. It's unkind and very, *very* untrue." I licked some chicken off my thumb and pushed half the sandwich and the plate back toward Carter. "Look, I have to talk to him. Clearly. I already knew that. But..."

"But?"

I chewed a bite of sandwich, swallowed, and placed it down on the paper wrapping.

"But I'm scared," I admitted softly. "Last fall, I got this silly idea in my head that Dunn had romantic feelings for me, and he *didn't*. At all. In fact, the reason he'd been acting all squirrelly and weird back then was because he was going to offer to set me up with someone else so *he* could be free to keep doing whatever half-assed dating thing he's been doing with Jenn. It... it killed me."

Even now, my stomach felt weirdly hollow and achy in a way that had nothing to do with the sugar I'd eaten.

"Right. So you'd rather sabotage your friendship yourself now by avoiding him than take a chance you might get hurt again. *And* you're justifying this decision by convincing yourself that, first, you know what Dunn's thinking without talking to him and, second, you know what's best for Dunn better than Dunn himself does." Carter took a big bite of sandwich. "Makes total sense."

"Hey!" I gaped at this unflattering interpretation of events. "No. That is *not* what's happening here, okay? I'm being careful. I'm being... *cautious*. For both our sakes."

"You're being ridiculous."

"Am I? Whereas you only do thoughtful, reasonable things? Then explain that little move back at the coffee shop earlier. We're dating now?"

Carter grinned as he chewed. "I mean, at the time I hadn't realized that things were changing with you and your little Dunn-bun. I thought I might get to simultaneously rescue myself from her matchmaking *and* make Dunn jealous if he heard about it. In that sense, it worked delightfully well. Ten out of ten, really."

"You're a menace." I picked up my sandwich again.

"*Moi*? And to think, I was planning to call you today to fill you in on a job offer before you stumbled upon me at the cafe. That's ingratitude, Wright."

I snorted. "I already have a job, thank you."

"Mmm, not like this one. Remember Dr. Petersmith?"

"Uh, yeah. Obviously. He's head of the division of internal medicine and a living legend. What about him?"

"He's got a research position open. Genetic epidemiology."

Genetic epidemiology research? At Vanderbilt?

Chicken salad fell out of my sandwich to splatter on the wrapper as I stared at Carter, who smiled smugly.

"He was at my parents' house for cocktails a week ago, and we chatted about it," Carter said breezily. "I mentioned your name, and how I'd reconnected with you, and I reminded him of that research paper you wrote—"

"You did not."

"Did too. I wasn't going to say anything in case it didn't lead anywhere, but then he emailed this morning to ask for your contact information, so I gave it to him. You could head back to Nashville and leave the Thicket for good."

The possibility of doing groundbreaking research was freakin' thrilling... but my gut rejected the idea instantly because leaving the Thicket meant leaving Dunn.

"Uh-huh," Carter said, seeing the look on my face. "I figured that's where the wind was blowing. Maybe agree to meet him for lunch anyway, though, if he emails you. Can't hurt. You don't have to tell him about your are-they-or-aren't-they relationship with Dunny-boy."

I shook my head. "And why is it that you absolutely don't want a relationship, Carter? What's got you so commitment phobic? Why not let Cindy Ann set you up? Tell me all your secrets." I fluttered my eyelashes. "I'm not a heart doctor, but I can pinch hit."

"Nah nah nah. I am not your patient. And I am *not* getting involved in any love-based shenanigans here in Licking Thicket." He looked almost horrified at the idea. "Y'all exchange dead vines as a symbol of affection."

"Excuse you, you're talking about the *Entwinin'*." I grinned. "That's a very important day. It's all about what the vines represent, you understand. The symbolism! Making something new out of something old. Constancy in the midst of change. Taking what *is* and making it something better."

"That is some Kool-Aid drinking right there." He shook his head. "Cindy Ann told me she always gets a daisy vine, and Jenn was thinking this year she might get a—uhm." Carter's eyes darted to mine, and he coughed. "Nothing."

My face fell, but I forced myself to speak lightly. "Dunn best be careful. One year, Victor Proud gave his girl a vine of a Ferris wheel—kind of a circle with a triangle underneath—to symbolize their visit to the county fair... only he handed it to her upside down." I sketched a diagram in the air. "Everyone thought it was an engagement ring."

"Oh my God! So what did he do?"

"He married her, of course. He and Emmaline were together forty-six years before he passed."

"What do you mean, he married her?" This time Carter definitely looked horrified. "What do you mean *of course*? Why not just explain the mistake?"

I shrugged. "'Cause there are some things you just can't come back from."

Carter rolled his eyes to the ceiling. "And there are some things you don't *have* to come back from if you'd just talk about them openly."

"I will! Jesus. I told you I was gonna, and I definitely will. Just not today while everything's still..." I cleared my throat. "Fresh in my mind, so to speak."

"So, tomorrow morning, then."

"Yes." I hesitated. "Though, you know, tomorrow morning we're fishing. Might be better to wait for a time when you and Brooks and whoever else aren't there."

Carter braced his elbows on the table and gave me a no-nonsense look. "Immediately after fishing."

"Sure. Except I have patients." This was a half lie. I didn't generally schedule patients on Monday mornings, but invariably there were a bunch of folks who'd taken ill over the weekend and needed to be seen. "But I'll do it as soon as I can after that."

"Great. And in the meantime, until you find the time to chat with him, I'll just let the town assume you and I are together, pookie." Carter stood and dusted his hands, then grabbed his plate to put it in the sink.

"Wait, what?" I scowled as he walked toward the hall. "No way. That's… that's blackmail."

"Tucker, baby doll, you wound me with your rejection, you really do." Carter stretched his arms to the ceiling. "Now, how would a couple hot young boyfriends spend the afternoon?" He wiggled his eyebrows.

"Ew. Absolutely not… whatever you're thinking. Pick something else."

"Good call!" Carter made finger guns at me and winked as he pulled the trigger. "More crossword puzzle deface-ment it is."

"I hate you!"

"You love me," Carter called from down the hall. "Or at least you're gonna pretend to, until you're ready to cowboy up and talk to your best friend."

Well, shit.

12

DUNN

6-DOWN: Behave as though trying to attract someone (5 letters)

FISHING WASN'T SUPPOSED to be a party. The more people, the more trouble. And by my count, we were in for a whole lot of trouble and not very many fish.

"Why is it so cold?" Mal grumbled as we walked down the path to the dock behind the cabin.

"How can you be cold when you're wearing my parka, long underwear, a fleece hat, and three pairs of socks?" Brooks asked.

Diesel chuckled under his breath. I had to admit, I was glad we had the big guy along. He was good at carrying the heavy cooler that Tucker had insisted on bringing. Apparently Tuck's "friend" Carter was some kind of kitchen savant. He'd spent hours the night before cooking a gourmet breakfast for us to eat on the dock.

If he thought I was eating a single morsel of his food, he was crazy. I wouldn't put it past him to sneak some kind of fancy sleeping pharmaceutical into my share so he could monopolize Tucker's attention all morning.

I'd rather starve.

Parrish muttered under his breath—something about this cold-ass morning being not worth the babysitting exchange they'd had to do with Ava. Paul must have heard, because he shot him a look. Parrish held up his hands in surrender. "Fine. But you don't want to be here any more than I do. Admit it."

Paul opened his mouth—probably to agree—but Brooks stopped him. "Trust me. You want to be here for this." Then he turned to me with a smarmy smirk on his face. "Oh look. It's all couples. Me and Mal, Diesel and Parrish, Tucker and Carter, and you and my little Paul."

I squinted at him. "I wouldn't want to take your little Paul from you, dear brother. Maybe you and Mal could have a third and I'll take Tuck."

Brooks's eyes twinkled. "Oh, but that would leave Carter all by his lonesome. No, I think Tuck and Carter are good. But I went ahead and called Jenn so you'd have someone to share your *shad* with."

I got the feeling he wasn't talking about my fishing lures. "Now I know you're lying. Jenn doesn't get up before the sun. Ever."

"And you would know that, how?" Tuck asked sharply, turning to pierce me with those familiar brown eyes.

"Because I asked her once to do the morning feed at the farm and she politely declined," I snapped. "And I'll have you know it was when I was at your house cleaning up cotton candy and apple pie vomit when you went overboard at Thanksgiving, thank you very much."

Unsurprisingly, Carter looked confused. "Who has cotton candy at Thanksgiving?"

Brooks and Diesel answered at the same time. "Licking Thicket tradition."

"Sorry," Tucker muttered.

"Whatever," I responded. Because my maturity level was about the same as whoever the hell invented cranberry-flavored cotton candy and made it a Thicket tradition.

"Don't whatever me," Tucker said, lifting up his finger to shake it at me.

"Ladies," Brooks interrupted, reaching out to lower Tuck's finger as if calming a gunman. "We're here to have a nice, relaxing morning of fish murder, so I'd appreciate everyone taking a deep breath and retracting the claws. Capisce? Thank you."

I closed my eyes and sucked in a deep drag of early morning air. He was right. I didn't want to fight with Tucker. I loved him. I wanted him to be happy. And I knew being here on this dock by the water made him happy.

The sound of warblers tweeting from the trees reminded me of how much I loved it out here too. This old wooden dock on the edge of Bull Lake was my favorite place on earth. When Gracie, Brooks, and I were little, our great-uncle used to bring us out to his old fishing cabin on Sunday afternoons. Gracie pretended to be a teenager by laying a towel out in the scrubby grass to get a suntan while Brooks and I begged Uncle Waylon to let us fish with him. He taught us everything he knew, but I was the only one who really took to it like he did.

Eventually, Gracie stopped coming with us, and Brooks fell more in love with Ava than with fish. Then it was just me for a long time. Long, quiet afternoons on the dock with Uncle Waylon and the sound of the birds, the lake water lapping against the shore, and the gentle hush of the wind in the trees. When Uncle Waylon passed on, he left the cabin to me. By then, I'd already started the farm, so I didn't think I needed a place to myself.

But every time I came out here to get the place ready to put on the market, I fell back in love with it all over again. And when I started bringing Tucker here, I stopped thinking about selling it altogether.

It was part of me… of *us*, and I wasn't going to let one cocky heart doctor ruin it.

I opened my eyes to see Brooks and Carter already unfolding the camp chairs at the wide end of the long dock. Diesel was placing the cooler at Parrish's direction, and Mal was already sitting in one of the chairs with a giant fleece blanket wrapped around him. Tucker stood halfway down the dock looking back at me. A little line of worry creased his forehead.

"Sorry," I mouthed.

He rolled his eyes but with a soft expression that made me let out a breath and drop my shoulders. It was going to be fine.

We all got set up and sorted with various rods, baits, and lures. Parrish asked a lot of questions of his husband but didn't seem to actually care one way or the other. It was awfully sweet of him to pretend for Diesel's sake because the man looked happy as a clam if clams liked teaching people how to kill their friends.

I took the seat next to Tucker without thinking, and we moved through the motions of preparing without even thinking about it. I tied on his Panther-Martin Teardrop lure because it was one of his favorite lures but the damned thing was hella fiddly. My clinch knots were more likely to hold than his, so he always handed over his line and lure for me to fix up for him. When I was done with his, I moved to my own lure before turning to grab an insulated mug of coffee with a thanks from Brooks.

That's when I saw Carter moving his chair to the other side of Tucker. Which made sense since he was the only person here Carter knew.

"Stop sighing," Brooks said under his breath from my other side.

I sighed again.

"So!" Carter said, all big perfect teeth and hands. "What do we usually do while we're waiting for the fish to bite? Sing campfire songs? Exchange gossip? You wouldn't believe this story about a nurse and surgical tech at the hospital where I work. It's like a season of *Grey's Anatomy*."

He launched into a robust tale of love gone wrong between two people I didn't give a shit about, but Tucker seemed to love it. He laughed and asked questions, so much so that his fishing pole was all over the damned place.

I reached over and placed my hand over his to hold it still. Tuck's entire body stilled under my touch, and I realized it was the first time we'd really touched since that morning in his bedroom.

His hand was cold, so I reached into my tackle bag and pulled out a hand warmer pouch. After tearing it open and shaking it up to activate it, I slipped it between his palm and the rod handle.

"Better," I murmured before turning back to Brooks. "Is Mama getting on your case about the wedding? She said to tell you she'd sorted out the flowers but to ask you if you wanted tools too. I said I didn't think you wanted tools, but I'd ask."

I heard Tucker's chuckle over my shoulder, but I ignored it. I didn't need to see him loving Dr. Smooth-talker any more than I already had.

Mal peered around Brooks's body. "Tulle. She wants to cover the place with tulle."

"Isn't that what I said?" I asked.

Brooks chuckled. "No. You said tools. Like hammers and saws."

"Isn't that what we're talking about?" I asked, annoyed at them making me feel stupid.

Tuck's hand landed on my arm. "Tulle. That netting stuff you found at the thrift store that one time. Remember? You thought you might be able to use it to strain the bugs out of… something. I can't remember."

"Oh. Shit. Yeah. Bridal stuff." I looked over at my brother. "She wants you to wear a veil? Are you going to do that?"

Now it was Carter who was laughing. My face suddenly took on the temperature of the hand warmer I'd given Tucker. "Never mind," I muttered, going back to watching my line. That was the reason we were all here, after all.

Carter said, "That reminds me of the time I had to crack open the chest of a groom on his wedding day. Poor guy was so nervous, he put himself into cardiac arrest."

"You're kidding?" Tucker asked. "How old was the patient? Any comorbidities?"

They launched into doctor talk that sounded both exciting and clinical. The gist of the story seemed to be what a hero Carter was. I bit back another sigh. Maybe I needed to sign up for a class at the community college.

Brooks elbowed me. "Tell them about the time you had to give Bernie an enema."

I shot him a look and then doubled down on it when I looked over at his snarky husband.

"I thought you were a cardiologist and not a surgeon?" Parrish asked politely from his own nest of blankets.

"I am," Carter said. "This was during a rotation with an orthopedic trauma surgeon. It was an incredible learning experience, but I'm happier outside of the operating room."

Parrish nodded. "And someone told me you're only in the Thicket temporarily? You live in Nashville?"

Carter gave Tucker some kind of look. An affectionate, *knowing* look. I didn't like it. Thankfully, I felt a little pull on my line that required my attention.

"That depends on Dr. Symmons. If he doesn't come back, I might make the move permanent."

I fumbled my pole until it went sailing across the water while all of us stared after it in stunned silence.

Tuck blinked at me for a beat before turning back to Carter. "You'd really leave Vanderbilt?"

"Unless you decide to take the job there," he said.

I twisted around in my seat to stare at Tucker while my pole began sinking in the clear lake water, and Brooks stood up to get a better view.

"You're thinking of moving?" I asked, trying not to screech.

"Dunn," Brooks said. "The pole! That's Uncle Waylon's pole."

I flapped my hand at him in the universal sign for shut the fuck up. "To Nashville?"

Tucker's eyes held a familiar warning. A "let's talk later" warning. "Dunn…"

I gnashed my teeth together and began pulling off my clothes. "Fine. *Fine.*"

When I got down to my boxer briefs, I heard at least six men whistle at me in the split second before I took a swan dive off the end of the dock. When I came up from the frigid water, I sucked in a desperate breath. *"Holy fuck,"* I shouted.

Tucker's voice was frantic and bossy at the same time, giving orders to the other guys about something or other. I didn't pay much attention since I was trying like hell to grab the pole and get back to the dock before dying of hypothermia. If I had to have Carter fucking Rogers revive me, things weren't going to end well.

I found the pole and turned back, kicking as hard as I could before reaching the dock. I handed the pole up to Mal and then reached for Diesel's outstretched paw. He yanked me up like a rag doll and plunked my shivery ass on the wooden boards. The air felt even colder than the water, and I was an instant ball of chattering teeth.

"Fuck!" Tucker snapped. "Are you fucking crazy? Why the fuck did you get in that water when there's a rowboat right fucking there!"

My eyes got wider with each subsequent f-word. That wasn't like him.

"It wasn't very far away. Woulda taken me longer to sort out the boat."

Tucker threw several blankets around me right as a low rumble of thunder sounded off in the distance.

"It storms a lot here," Carter observed. "Thought it was supposed to be sunny today."

Brooks shoved a mug of hot coffee in my hands, and I took a grateful sip. "That's the thing about springtime in the South. Unexpected storms pop up all the time. We should pack up before the rain starts."

Tucker tried to rub my arms over the thick layers of blankets, but I pulled away from him. "You should go. I wouldn't want your boyfriend getting his hair messed up."

Apparently that was a bridge too far. I knew it as soon as the words were out of my mouth. The storm on Tucker's face was ten times more dangerous than whatever was headed our way in the sky.

"Get your ass in the fucking cabin," he said in a low voice. "*Now.*"

I opened my mouth to argue with him, but his eyes narrowed just enough to scare me.

"Fine," I said, as if I didn't give a crap. I did. I gave lots of craps.

Brooks looked over at Mal. "See? Told you it was worth the early morning alarm."

Mal grinned maniacally. "I should never have doubted you."

The two of them helped me stumble to the cabin while Tucker stayed to help Diesel, Parrish, Carter, and Paul pack up all of our things. By the time my brain stopped shorting out from the cold, Brooks had started a fire in the stone fireplace, forced another hot drink down my throat, replaced my sodden blankets with dry towels, and skedaddled.

The only person left was Tucker. And he was no more pleased with me now than he'd been back on the dock.

I picked at a hangnail as I heard the first plinks of rain on the tin roof.

"You're mad," I said. Might as well start with the obvious.

"Mm."

I stood up from the hearth and took a tentative step toward him. His skin looked honey gold in the warm light from the fire. I wondered if it was appropriate for me to think he looked sexy right now even though he was mad as spit.

"I'm... sorry?" I said, taking another step. I wanted to touch him so badly. My hands itched to grab him and hold him tight. But I had no idea where we stood after everything that had happened between us.

"What for?"

Ugh. It was a test. I hated these tests. I never did great on tests.

"Jumping in the water?"

His arms crossed in front of his chest. He was wearing a

brown, black, and cream plaid shirt with a puffy down vest over top of it. I loved it when he dressed like a fancy huntsman. "Try again," he said.

I winced. "Being snarky and unpleasant to Carter?"

He nodded. "Being snarky and unpleasant to Carter. And what for? Hm? Why the hell would you be so rude to a friend of mine when he has done nothing to you?"

"Pretty sure you know why," I muttered at the floor.

"Because you're jealous."

I looked up at him and held his eyes. "Because I'm jealous."

"Because you want me all to yourself."

Finally. He got it.

"Yes."

He pointed to the floor at his feet. "Get over here."

Tuck still sounded angry, but I approached him anyway. The towels had fallen off at some point, and I was still in my underwear. The warmth of the fire spread around the room, and the pops of the wood were the only sound except the crackle of the tension between us and my harsh breaths.

When we were almost nose to nose, his voice was sweet as sugar and soft as cotton.

"Get on your knees," he said.

So that's what I did.

13

TUCKER

8-Down: Unhinged, unwell, positively shook (10 letters)

Look, in my defense, I was really, really tired.

I'd spent the better part of the previous afternoon preventing my ex-boyfriend—who, for all his degrees and utter competence in the medical field, had the self-control of a mischievous toddler when it came to my love life or my belongings—from destroying all my crosswords and texting a "couple selfie" of us to my best friend.

And then I'd spent the entire evening after Carter went home trying not to remember all the very insightful things he'd said… like that I was sabotaging my friendship with Dunn by thinking I knew what Dunn wanted better than he did himself. I'd just about convinced myself that Carter had a point.

Except *then* my best best friend had gone and stripped nearly naked and jumped off the dock, not sparing a single thought for how dangerous it was until that first shock of icy water hit him, and proving once again that leaping before he looked was one of Dunn's most charming and exasperating qualities.

Now he wanted me to believe that he'd come to a thoughtful, rational decision about what he wanted from our relationship? No way.

So I did what any super-exhausted, completely frustrated man might do.

I told him to get on his knees.

I was ready for him to balk, but he didn't. Not even a little. In fact, he looked downright eager as he sank down at my feet and looked up at me expectantly.

Well, damn.

I inhaled sharply. My fingers ached to sift through his hair and trace the scruff on his jaw, but I reminded myself that Dunn had gotten on his knees for me because he trusted me *as his friend*. One of us had to put a stop to this, and if Dunn insisted on leaping into things…

Then I was going to have to be the cold water.

"Come on, then," I goaded softly. A log hissed and popped in the fireplace. "You want me? You wanna be the *only* one who has me? Then take me. Open my pants. Suck me off." I curled my hands into fists against the images that leapt to my brain of Dunn doing just that, and my cock went half-hard. *Fuck.*

"Oh, damn." Dunn swallowed hard, and his eyes flared wide. "Tucker, I…I—"

I closed my eyes. "Yeah, no, I figured. It's okay," I soothed in a strangled voice. "You don't have to—"

Dunn leaned forward and nuzzled his nose against my groin. His palms coasted up my thighs, then around to my hips, holding me in place. He mouthed my dick through my jeans, and the two of us groaned at the same time.

"I want to," Dunn whispered. "It's crazy how bad I want it."

Before I could make myself form words, Dunn's big hands were at my waistband, opening my fly and pushing my jeans down to my knees.

"Dunn—"

"Hush. This is another one of your tests, Tucker Wright, and I'm going to pass it."

"Wait! I—"

I had no idea what I'd been planning to say. The second Dunn Johnson—*my* Dunn Johnson—pushed down my underwear and wrapped his calloused fingers around the base of my cock, I couldn't have told you my name.

Then he tightened his grip and stroked me experimentally, watching my face the whole time.

Dunn Johnson was touching my dick.

Dunn Johnson was going to *suck* my dick.

I couldn't believe this was happening, even after all that had happened two nights before. It simply did not compute or map to any previous experience I'd ever had. That tip-tilted smile and those warm eyes staring up at me were like a fantasy come to life.

He leaned in and set his tongue near the base, then moved his mouth carefully up the side and around to the head like he was savoring the taste of me, and I changed my mind. Even in my fantasies, it hadn't been this good.

"You might wanna take that vest off, Dr. Wright," Dunn teased. His hot breath on my skin made my cock jump. "It's about to get warm in here."

Oh, shit.

I stripped my vest off and practically threw it the short distance to the foot of the bed, then tried to do the same with my shirt.

"Whoa, hey!" Dunn frowned as I pulled the button-down over my head. "Careful! I love that shirt. You look fucking hot in it."

"I do?" I stared down at the plaid flannel that had somehow gotten stuck to my wrists like I was a little kid.

"You really do." Dunn reached inside the swath of fabric and unbuttoned the cuffs to free me. "I've always thought so."

"You have?"

Dunn threw my shirt toward the bed to join my vest. "Yeah, Tuck." He grinned up at me, and I swear, it nearly stopped my heart. "I have. Now stop interrupting me when your dick and I were about to get friendly."

He wrapped his hand around me again and lapped at the head of my cock, and I threw my head back to the ceiling. "Hooooly shit."

Then Dunn snickered, and I quickly looked back down because I did not want to miss a single second of this.

Dunn's golden-brown hair glinted in the firelight, while shadows danced along the muscles of his spine. I'd known this man for years and years, but seeing him like this felt like seeing him for the first time. And as he opened his mouth around me with zero hesitation, the way Dunn did most things, a tiny piece of the wall I'd built around myself last November cracked.

No one watching this could doubt that Dunn was seriously, seriously into it. His cheeks were flushed and his eyes watered, just a little, but he managed to find a rhythm using his hand and mouth that made my knees literally spasm for a moment there, which would have been mortifying if I'd been with anyone else.

He popped off for a second, his mouth shiny and wet, and pushed me back a pace, and then another, until the backs of my knees hit the edge of the bed and I sat down.

"Easier this way anyway," he said hoarsely, crawling after me. His voice was wrecked from arousal and—good fucking gravy, there was a thought—blowing me.

He looked so darn pleased with himself, kneeling between my legs, that I couldn't help kissing his smile and tasting myself on his tongue. He let the kiss go on for several beats, but then he pushed me back. "Busy now," he said, stroking me lightly with his fist. "More kissing later."

"Ah, fuck," I groaned as his mouth stretched around me again and he sucked me down. I pushed my head against the bed and arched my back, then reached out a hand to touch Dunn's hair because despite how intimate we already were, I wanted even more connection. Always. "So good, Dunn, baby… Shit. Don't stop."

He didn't. His gorgeous face looked set and determined, and his eyes sparked like this was some kind of competition —which, knowing Dunn, was exactly what he was thinking —and he licked and sucked and stroked me off with increased fervor, like making me come right then was the reason for his existence.

I'd never felt anything so good in my life, and that was a fact, but when the fingers of his free hand tangled with mine like he couldn't get enough connection with me either, *that* was what finally made me lose my mind.

"Dunn!" I cried, clenching his fingers tighter, and my mind fragmented into a billion pieces as my orgasm barreled through me.

It felt like a hundred years before I could do more than blink up at the ceiling, though it was probably only a couple minutes. I was dimly aware of Dunn shucking his underwear, then taking off my boots and socks and jeans, before crawling into the double bed beside me and folding the quilt over the both of us.

"Wait!" I argued. "You…"

"Came in my undies like I was thirteen?" Dunn said ruefully, stroking his big hand up my back. "Yes, I did. Thanks for bringing it up."

Thunder boomed outside the cabin, and rain lashed down against the windows like a gray curtain, making the cabin feel like our own peaceful cocoon.

I snickered and shivered closer to him. "I was almost the same the other night. I couldn't stop myself."

"At least you came on *me*. That would've been way hotter." Dunn pressed a kiss to my forehead. "Oh, shit. Next time, I'm totally coming all over you. Brace yourself."

Next time. Huh.

"Y'okay?" Dunn asked. He pulled back a little so he could see my face.

"Me?" I snorted. "Yeah. I just came so hard it probably registered on the Richter scale. And I'm not the one who just blew a guy for the first time either." I propped myself up on my elbow so I could look down at him. "That's kind of a big deal."

He squinted up at me. "Is it, though? I just did to you what I've liked other people to do to me and hoped it worked." He shrugged. "I mean, it *is* kind of a big deal, 'cause it's you and me, and it's special. But it's also not a big deal, 'cause it's you and me, and you always make me feel confident, even though we both know I can be kind of an idiot."

Ah, damn. Tears sprang to my eyes, and I had to lean down and kiss him. "You're *not* an idiot," I said fiercely. "I will fight anyone who treats you like you are."

Dunn settled his head into the pillow and watched me closely, a little smile quirking his lips. "Even if it's you?"

"Me?" I demanded. "What? I would *never* treat you like that! I couldn't, because I know how smart you are. Who overhauled his whole operation so he could get that Organic Dairy Certification, huh? Who had the vision to make himself the exclusive supplier for Glastonbury Creamery's ice cream *and* those Summer Honey bath products, when *nobody* else would've thought of marketing milk to a soap company? Who figured out how to haul a cast-iron tub up the stairs at the farmhouse with pulleys? It was not *my* fancy-degreed-self, that's for damn sure. And…"

Dunn pushed me over and reversed our positions so I had my head to the pillow while his smiling face loomed over me.

"Then why are you treating me like I don't know what I want when it comes to you?"

"What?" I whispered.

"This test right now. And you avoided me all day yesterday."

Oh.

Well, damn.

I sucked in a breath, ready to deny it… but I couldn't, because that would've been a total lie, and Dunn deserved better. Instead, I settled for, "I don't know exactly. I'm just scared of the change, I guess."

"I love you, Tuck," Dunn continued seriously. "I mean, you know I've loved you since forever, right? And you know I like you better than anyone. I always want to be with you. So why is it hard to believe I want to *be with you*?" He bit his lip. "I didn't expect it, a-and I know it's sudden, and I get maybe you're not a hundred percent feeling what I'm feeling, but I want you to be mine and no one else's. I'd like us to be together."

Serious as his words were, I had to chuckle just a little. His *and no one else's*. That would never not kill me.

"I want that too." I lifted my hand to touch his scruffy cheek. "I… have wanted you for a really long time, Dunn Johnson."

"Wait, really? You have?" He looked stunned but really pleased too.

"I have," I confirmed.

"You don't sound too thrilled about it."

He had no idea. "The thing is…" I hesitated. "I've had to push those feelings down because I knew you couldn't return them. I prayed that I could transfer those feelings to one of those horrible blind dates you sent me on so I could love you as a friend the way you needed. It wasn't always easy, feeling so much and knowing I was the only one."

Sometimes it had killed me.

"Ah, Tuck." Dunn's eyes went soft. "And there I was, trying to find you someone who could love you in the way I thought I couldn't." He shook his head ruefully. "I just didn't know I wanted this then. Maybe I wasn't ready to." He sank down onto the mattress beside me and took my hand, twining our fingers together. "But I'm all in now. I am. I want us to be together."

Was it possible for it to be that easy? I wanted to think so. God, I really, really did.

"I want that too. You can't even imagine how much. But, I…" I took a deep breath and blurted, "I need us to move forward slowly, okay? I want to make sure you're a hundred percent on board and that we're not rushing anything. Our friendship is too important to mess up."

Dunn stared at me for a second, and then he nodded once. "Okay."

"Okay?" Really?

"Yeah, I get it. Whatever you need to feel comfortable. We can move slow, just as long as we're moving forward. *Together*." He leaned in and pressed a kiss to my lips. "I'll wait for you," he assured me solemnly.

I pressed my lips together so I wouldn't laugh. Dunn was so damn cute, and he loved me. I knew that with my whole heart.

But as much as Dunn wanted me to believe he knew what he was doing—and as badly as I wanted to believe that too—I couldn't quite get there. There was so much about being with a guy that he'd never experienced or thought of, and sex was the least of it. Had he thought about kids with two dads? Or having a husband instead of a wife? Had he thought about introducing me as his partner?

Anywhere else in the world, or maybe for any two other people, those were long-term problems that would sort themselves out in time. But here in Licking Thicket, where folks had long memories—and even longer noses they loved to poke into other people's business—these were things we'd have to start talking about the second our relationship became public knowledge. And if he decided this —*us*—wasn't what he wanted romantically in the long term... Well. It was best not to think about what might happen.

I wanted to save Dunn from doing something he couldn't come back from, like Victor Proud with his Entwinin' wreath. I wanted to save our friendship from the consequences of that too.

It had nothing to do with thinking Dunn wasn't smart.

Obviously.

It had to do with thinking he wasn't *experienced* and wanting to protect him from it.

There was a difference.

"This might seem a little crazy," I began, "but what do you think about keeping this between us?"

"As opposed to threesomes?" Dunn frowned. "Not sure what you've heard, but I'm not really into that, Tuck."

"No, doofus." I smacked his arm. Hard. "I know you're not, and neither am I. I meant... What do you think about not telling anyone that you and I are... you know?"

"Together?"

I hesitated, then nodded.

"You're saying you want to keep us a secret?" Dunn wrinkled his nose.

"No! Not a *secret*! More like a… well, actually, yeah, kind of a secret," I admitted. "Only because this is a big change in our relationship, and it's sure to cause gossip. The last thing we need is the stress of your mama asking us our wedding colors, like she is with Mal and Brooks, or Amos Nutter giving us relationship advice, or hell, Carter teasing me every two minutes, right?"

"Carter," he scoffed darkly.

"Hey." I smacked his arm again, even harder this time, but Dunn didn't so much as flinch. "Carter and I are friends and colleagues. That's *all*."

Dunn flopped to his back and rolled his eyes. "And former boyfriends, don't forget."

"Yes, but *former*. As in, very former. As in, I stopped thinking of him the second I started thinking of you." Which was way longer ago than I cared to admit.

Dunn ran both hands through his hair. "Yeah, okay. I just hate thinking he had any part of you that I haven't had." His lips twisted up. "Crazy, huh?"

"No," I said vehemently. "Not even a little. And, baby, he hasn't, I *promise*." I had never felt about anyone in my life the way I felt about Dunn Johnson, and I knew in the way I knew my eyes were brown that I never, ever would.

"He wants you to go back to Nashville with him." Dunn glanced at me sideways. "And I could see in your eyes you were really tempted by that fancy Vanderbilt position."

I snorted. "For someone who claims to know me so well, you're batting zero today. I was hardly tempted at all by the position." Maybe slightly tempted by the idea of returning to the less complicated life I'd had there… but then, that would mean returning to a life without Dunn, which was unacceptable. "Carter mentioned the job to me yesterday out of nowhere, and he only brought it up today to poke at you. Heck, he told you he's thinking about sticking around here himself, didn't he?"

"I guess." Dunn rolled toward me. "Do that thing where you call me baby again and maybe I'll agree to be your secret lover."

I laughed out loud so hard the bed shook. "My secret lover? Really."

"Really." He wiggled his eyebrows and climbed on top of me. The warm weight of his naked body was a thrill unlike any I'd ever known. "It's a promotion," he informed me. "A step up from *best* best friend."

"No way." I cradled his bristly jaw in both hands. "You are still my best best friend. And whatever else you are, *baby*, you'll always be that."

I would make damn sure of it.

14

DUNN

16-Down: Enjoyment, amusement, or lighthearted pleasure (3 letters)

THE FOLLOWING week was kinda fun. At first I'd been a little miffed at Tuck's insistence we keep things on the down-low. But then we'd started sneaking around.

I'd discovered I liked sneaking around. It was an adrenaline rush.

Like the time I rode my bike to his house so no one would see my truck in his driveway overnight. I'd kinda felt like Dorothy in *The Wizard of Oz*, outrunning the black cloud of Thicket gossipmongers.

But biking back at 4:00 a.m. for the morning milking had not been nearly as fun.

Also, the time we went to Sunday lunch at my parents' house and we'd had to act casual. Mama had pulled me aside and snuck some laxatives in my hand. "This'll fix you right up, dear. You look real constipated. Are you in pain?"

Then there was the time we'd run into each other at the

grocery store, and I'd snuck a box of condoms into his basket when he wasn't looking. The time Ava asked me for Tucker's address for some Beautification Corps event she was chairing. I'd looked at her and flat out told her I had no idea where he lived. The time Jordan Brock asked me what the mark was on my jaw and I'd said I'd accidentally popped a champagne cork at my face. It was a lie. Tucker had sucked on that spot until a deep purple bruise had blossomed.

And, honestly, I'd wanted to shout it to the heavens. I wanted everyone in the Thicket to know he was mine, that I'd finally gotten my head out of my ass and locked him down the way things were meant to be.

There was only one teeny-tiny problem.

"Hey, Jenn," I said, standing at the reception counter in Tuck's waiting room. I held my gym bag behind my back in case she started asking questions. "Doc Wright here?"

Jenn's frown turned upside down when she saw me. "Hey, handsome. What are you doing here? Did you come to surprise me for lunch?"

The secret sandwiches in my gym bag were suddenly guilt sandwiches. "Um, no? I needed to ask Tuck something. He around?"

Her eyes narrowed infinitesimally. "If not lunch, then what about dinner? I could cook."

"Er…" I tried not to remember the other time she offered to cook for me. I'd had to order pizza the minute she left just so I could make it through the night.

"Speaking of dinner, we haven't made plans for the Entwinin'." She pouted. "I bet you haven't even made a reservation, and I'll be *super* disappointed."

Crap. "Um, no. I haven't." I licked my lips. "About that…"

Jenn laughed. "Don't look so worried, Dunn. I'm just kidding!"

"You are?" I shook my head, relieved. "Oh, good. You sure fooled me."

The last thing I wanted was to make plans with Jenn. But that reminded me that I really should start thinking about plans with Tuck. I'd already made his wreath, but I hadn't thought any further than that.

"I know you're a busy man, and I'm not a high-maintenance sort of person at all."

"Y-you're not?"

"'Course not! I'm an independent woman. I don't expect you to always be making me reservations."

"No? Oh, that's... that's good. Independence is really... good."

"I'll sort myself out for the whole Entwinin' thing, don't you worry. And, FYI, they're doing a special pasta dinner over at the Italian place." She winked. "I might just make a reservation in your name. Let's say... six?"

Well, dang. That was friendly of her. And Tuck loved Italian food.

"Thanks, Jenn! I really appreciate it." I gave her a genuine smile. "But, um... now that I have you here, I did need to tell you something." How could I tell her I didn't want her free trial anymore if I couldn't tell her the reason why?

She rested her chin on her folded hands and batted her eyelashes up at me. "Shoot. What's on your mind? Hey, wait. Did you... did you hear back from Abilene about my job at the boutique? It's only that Dr. Wright's receptionist is going to come back, and I need to have another job lined up."

"Oh. Uh... no? But, I mean. I didn't ask her, so..." I tried to focus on what I needed to say. "You know how when you sign up for a free trial of something... like, let's say a television channel. Yeah. So then you realize you don't really have *time* to watch any of the shows? So it makes more sense to just... I mean, even if it's still *free*, sometimes you still need to cancel it on account of it's going to start costing you money. You see?"

"Did you sign up for that new sports streaming service? Because my brother said they start charging you before the free trial is over and it's impossible to reverse the charges."

I blinked at her, trying to figure out if we were good now. Vienna stood several feet behind her doing something with a filing cabinet, but she didn't look like she was paying any attention. "No. I don't... no. Okay, so like... we're good to cancel the free trial?"

She shrugged. "If that's what you want. There's no sense in keeping something you're not going to enjoy."

I let out a relieved breath and opened my mouth to thank her for understanding when I heard Tuck's voice.

"Dunn?"

I glanced over and saw Tucker with a little wrinkle of concern on his face. "Yeah, hey. Can I talk to you for a minute? In your office?"

His eyes darted between Jenn and me while he nodded his head. I shot Jenn a combination smile and nod before hotfooting it down the hall after my *boyfriend*.

As soon as we were in his office with the door closed, I grabbed a handful of the back of his doctor's coat and yanked him backward. His arms windmilled, and I barely kept him from stumbling back into me. I quickly yanked him around to face me and kissed his mouth off.

"Thank freak," I mumbled into his mouth. "Been dying to do this for *hours*."

"I talked to you on the phone not twenty minutes ago,"

he griped. But I could see the pink tint to his cheeks and the warmth in his eyes.

"Yeah? Well, that wasn't kissing. Gimme more." We kissed for several minutes until he encountered the shoulder strap of my gym bag.

"You going to work out after this?"

I stepped back and pulled the bag off my shoulder before plunking it down on his desk and removing my jacket. "Nah. This is my incognito bag."

After unzipping it, I pulled out a bunch of daffodils and purple hyacinth. "Here," I said, shoving the newspaper-wrapped bundle at Tuck. I turned back to rummage around in the bag for the jelly jar I'd grabbed from my kitchen. "Hang on and I'll get water."

I went over to the little half bath attached to his office and filled up the jar with water before turning back to his office. Tucker stood there frozen in place, staring at the flowers. I wasn't surprised. They *did* look a little mangled from the bag.

"Sorry they're kinda squished. I've got lunch in here too, so the flowers probably got steamrolled by the bottled water." I reached the desk and set down the jar before reaching over to take the flowers from him so I could arrange them in the jar. "I had to sneak them in, you know? Otherwise I woulda just put the whole kit and caboodle in my truck's cup holder."

Tuck's eyes followed the spring blooms. "You… brought me flowers?"

"Well, yeah. I know you're not a woman. I know that. It's not… I didn't do this because I don't know how to date a guy."

"You *don't* know how to date a guy," he said.

"Correct. But I do know how to date *you*. And you love early spring flowers. You hate flowers from the florist or grocery refrigerator, and you especially hate flower delivery because, and I quote, 'If you're going to make a personal gesture, you darned well better make it in person.'"

Once I was satisfied they looked okay and they were in a spot on his desk where he'd be able to lean over and smell them whenever he wanted, I turned back to him. "And just tell anyone who asks that Vienna brought them in. She has a big garden."

I brushed off my hands and reached into my gym bag for the sandwiches. Tucker's arms suddenly came around me from behind, and I felt the long, firm length of his body against my back. He was trembling the tiniest bit. "Thank you," he whispered.

I clasped one of his hands and slid it up to the center of my chest for a minute before pulling it up and pressing a kiss to the middle of his big palm. Suddenly, my throat felt weird. "Yeah, uh. You're welcome." For the millionth time this week, I wanted to ask him if we could stop this hiding business, but then I reminded myself he was trying to protect himself. And I had to let it happen.

"So." I turned around and ran my hands up the sleeves of his white coat before deciding to peel it off him. No one wanted doctor germs with their lunch. "I thought maybe we could go fishing on Saturday morning, just the two of us."

Once I got the coat off, I nudged him into a visitor chair and handed him a sandwich.

Tucker looked at me with a confused expression. "We always go fishing just the two of us on Saturday mornings."

I grabbed my own sandwich and took the other visitor chair in front of his desk. "Yeah, but this would be like... different."

"Different, how?"

I felt my face heat up. "You're my boyfriend. It'd be

fishing as boyfriends. That's different than fishing as friends."

His soft grin edged around the big sandwich. "Is it? How?"

"When I tie your clinch knot—"

"You make it sound dirty," he said with a chuckle, nudging my boot with the tip of his fancy leather dress shoe.

I bounced my eyebrows at him. "*When I tie your clinch knot*, it'll mean something. You know?"

"It'll mean my lure might stay on?" he teased.

Someone banged on the door. Before I stopped to think what I was doing, I bolted to Tucker's secret cubbyhole and slammed the door behind me.

When I remembered the half sandwich in my hand, I took another bite. Might as well fuel up while I was in here.

"Hey there, darling," Carter's familiar fake-as-hell voice purred. What the heck was he doing here in the middle of a danged workday? Smarmy asshole.

"C-Carter," Tuck stammered. "What are you doing here?"

I mentally fist-bumped my best friend… *boyfriend*… for his question.

Loud footsteps moved across the old creaky wooden floor. "Thought I'd swing by and offer to take you to lunch, but I see there you have… one and a half sandwiches."

"Ha!" Tucker said too loudly. "Ha, *ha*! No that's… I mean, yes. Obviously. But I'm simply ravenous today."

"Ravenous enough to eat a Carhartt jacket even though it smells like hay and manure?"

"Give me that," Tucker hissed. "Now tell me the real reason you're here."

"I thought maybe I could provide you some sexual pleasure, Doctor," he said in a sultry voice. Tuck made a little squeaking sound of distress, and I'd had enough.

I clambered out of the cubby and strode across the office to poke that jerk in the center of his silk tie. "Hands off."

A few seconds too late, I remembered Tucker's complaints about my possessive, jealous act. "I mean," I hedged. "He's... Hands off because he's..." I glanced at Tuck, who had an eyebrow raised and a curl of amusement at the edge of his lips. Still, I'd promised not to tell anyone about us. "He's a strong, independent man who can make decisions for himself," I finished lamely. "And who deserves respect," I added peevishly for good measure.

Carter's nostrils flared with suppressed laughter as he looked between me and the hidey-hole. "'Bout time you came busting out of the closet."

Okay, now that was funny. But I didn't give him the satisfaction of a laugh.

"State your business," I said, crossing my arms in front of my chest while forgetting the partial sandwich in my hand. I went ahead and shoved it into my shirt pocket.

"I came to tell Tucker the head of internal medicine at Vanderbilt is coming through town tomorrow on his way to visit family somewhere, and he wants to have lunch with us."

"With me?" I asked, only because it took my brain a hot second to catch up.

Tucker's eyes dropped to the floor.

"Never mind," I muttered.

"Not quite," Carter said with a smirk. "Pretty sure Dr. Petersmith isn't interested in a quick sub at a stand-up deli with a farmhand."

Tucker's eyes narrowed in anger, but I jumped in before he could defend me. "Yeah, fine. Sorry I asked. I'll leave you to it, then. The dairy nutritionist is coming to consult with me about feed. Don't wanna be late."

I turned to grab my duffle bag when I heard Tuck ask Carter to wait outside for a minute. When the door closed behind him, Tucker eyeballed me. "You just can't help yourself, can you? I've never seen you act so possessive about anything in your life as you do about me."

I walked over and wrapped my arms around him. "I'm sorry. Except... I'm not really. But I'm sorry you're upset. I don't like that."

His arms wrapped around my back. "Why did you hide? Everyone knows we're friends. Friends have lunch together."

I pulled back and kissed him. "I panicked. But I'm good now. See you tonight? But can we stay at the farm because... just because."

His palm cupped my cheek. "Because Bernie misses you?"

"What? No. Bernie? Pfft. She's fine outside in the pen." As if she'd spent more than two nights outside in her whole life. I stepped back, looked around, and gathered up my things. "It's... the paint colors. I still want to get your help on that."

Tuck gave me a knowing smile. "See you tonight, then. But if it's okay with you, maybe we can let Bernadette stay in the house tonight. Just this one time?"

He had such pretty eyes, even when they were giving me a hard time. I kissed him again for good measure. "Well, I mean, if you want to spoil the livestock, that's on you."

I left his office in such a daze, I forgot Jenn was out there.

"Dunn! What were you doing back there all this time?"

I could have sworn I caught Vienna's brain gears turning at warp speed. "Who, me? I was just... having lunch with a friend. Like friends do. Friends have lunch together."

Vienna snorted which wasn't very ladylike. And then Jenn acted like we were still dating. Which also wasn't very ladylike.

"We going out on Friday night?" she asked with a big smile.

My eyes flashed to Vienna for help, but I could see that was a wasted effort. "But... remember about the free trial? We *just* had the conversation."

Jenn studied a deep red fingernail. "I remember us talking about plans for the Entwinin', but we didn't say anything firm about this weekend. I've been real bored and lonely lately. We haven't hung out in *forever.*"

Did she mean... hanging out as friends?

I kinda felt bad for her. Being lonely was never fun.

I swallowed. "Can't this weekend, but I hear Jaybird Proud could use some company. He's a real dab hand at makin' Entwinin' wreaths too. He practices all year on account of his grandpa."

Who said my mama was the only matchmaker in the family?

She pursed her lips and tapped the fingernail against her chin. "Jaybird washes cars for a living down at the Suds Barn."

"Ain't nothing wrong with physical work," I said, a little too quick. Out of the corner of my eye, I caught a giant brown streak of something awful on my work pants. Maybe I should have changed after morning chores.

She was all smiles and cleavage. "Of course not, Dunn. I just meant... he can hardly afford to take me to the new place out on the highway for dinner, and you can."

That was probably true. The Suds Barn paid for shit.

"Especially now that you own part of the Summer Honey store," she added.

"I *don't* own part of the Summer Honey store," I said, lowering my voice so no one could hear us. "And please don't say that again, or I'm going to have every damned woman coming up asking me for free samples."

"That's not what I heard, Dunn Johnson," she said in a singsong voice. "I heard you were a regular beauty baron around these parts. They paid you in stock when they first started buying your milk, and now it's worth a mint. That's why I think you should hire that interior decorator guy to do up your farmhouse for you. Colin, I think his name is. He mostly does restaurants, but I heard he used to be the designer to the stars. And he lives right here in the Thicket!"

She looked around to make sure no one was listening. "And he's… *gay.*"

I stared at her. "What's that got to do with anything?"

"You know. Interior decorator? Gay? You know they're better than anyone at colors and such. He'll make your farm a showplace. The Beautification Corps *would. Just. Die.* They would keel over in their hot pink garden clogs when they took a tour of our… *your* farmhouse."

Her stereotyping was not attractive. "Gay men are no more qualified to decorate my house than straight men!" I may not have been gay… or whatever… very long, but I did know that much.

Just then Tucker came walking around the corner with Carter. Carter, being his same old annoying self, jumped into my private conversation. "Beg to differ, big guy," he said lightly. "Name me one straight male interior decorator around here."

I glanced at Tucker for help, but he just shrugged. "I know Colin Richards—used to be Colin Kearns—but he's gay," he admitted. "He's married to that contractor who did Gracie's extension. Ryder."

"Ohhhh, Ryder Richards," Jenn added with a longing sigh. "He's superhot. And rides a motorcycle."

I remembered my sister and Tucker swooning over the big, muscled man last year when she had the work done on her house. I couldn't help but let out a frustrated growl. "I'm leaving. Gotta meet with a guy about a cow."

"Toodles!" Carter called with a wave.

Jenn called after me. "Pick me up Friday at seven!"

I raced home and got back to work. And if I spent a little extra time with a certain pig, it wasn't anyone's business but mine.

HOURS LATER, I was rode hard and put away wet. Bottle-feeding the calves had been like trying to capture slippery walruses with a tiny pair of tongs. Every time I got a hold of one, another one distracted it until they were all wiggling out of my hold.

Some days were like that. It meant my body was aching, and I had a giant bruise blooming on my shin from where one of the little bastards had kicked me but good. I spent extra time in the shower trying to work out the kinks. The hot water slammed against my tight muscles until I groaned.

"Someone started without me," I heard from outside the shower stall. I glanced over and saw Tucker's blurry form through the steam.

"Get in here. I got cracks and crevices that need scrubbing."

His low chuckle made me smile. I smeared away the steam on the glass door with my hand and watched him undress. As soon as he caught me looking, he turned it into an incredibly frustrating slow striptease.

"Cut that shit out," I muttered. "Get your ass in here before the hot water runs out."

His body was amazing. The man worked out religiously and used running as a stress reliever. The curves of his quads and calves had always drawn my eyes. Lots of times he'd run to my farm and arrive sweating and panting, shirtless in tiny running shorts. He'd double over with his hands on his knees to catch his breath, and I'd sneak glances at his defined shoulders and arms, his slender muscled back and the shallow ridge of his spine leading down into the back of his shorts.

He was beautiful. I'd always thought of him as healthy and attractive, but I'd never really let myself think of him as sexy. But he was. I think I'd always noticed without really realizing it. Two years ago, there'd been a particularly hot weekend in August where we'd practically lived in our swimsuits at the fishing cabin. We spent most of the day floating in giant tubes tied to the dock with a third tube holding a cooler of beer. One of the suits he wore was a teeny-weenie bikini one that I'd made fun of, but… I'd also kinda… felt that hot, weird way you feel when you accidentally see the pale, creamy skin of a woman's inner thigh when she moves just so in a skirt. Like… a dangerous, exciting, illicit little perk had just been granted to you anonymously from the universe. His butt had looked amazing in that suit, and I'd snuck a few peeks at the bulge in the front too.

Looking at his body had always made my skin jitter a little bit, and now I could finally start to admit why.

"You're staring at me like you're measuring me for either a burial plot or a sex collar. I can't decide which one," he said, sliding the door open and stepping in.

"You're sexy as fuck," I said, reaching for him and yanking his naked self against me. I was already hard, waiting for him because I knew whatever we got up to together would result in an incredible orgasm for both of us. Just the thought of giving him that kind of pleasure made me feel less sore and tired.

Tucker wrapped his arms around me and leaned his head on my shoulder as we stood together under the hot spray. "God, this feels good," he murmured.

"Hot shower after a long, hard day is always good for what ails ya," I said in agreement.

"No," he said, looking up at me. "Holding you is what feels good. The shower part is just a bonus."

I clasped his face to kiss him silly as I turned us so he was fully under the water. We kissed and kissed and *kissed* until our dicks were pressing insistently into each other's skin.

"I want…" I wasn't quite sure how to say it. "I want…"

Tucker smoothed his hands over my chest. "You want? Babe, you're not usually reluctant to speak your mind."

"I… what about sex? Like… is that something you… want? Because I'm up for… that."

He bit his upper lip with his bottom teeth and looked at me through his lashes. "You talking about anal sex, D?"

I nodded rapidly in case that helped give support to my verbal, "Yes, please."

Tuck's brow climbed up. "And when you say you'd be up for that, do you mean on the giving side of the equation or the receiving end?"

"I know you're versified," I said, taking this seriously. "Because I overheard you and my brother talking about how you didn't understand why—"

Tuck held up a hand. "Can we… not talk about your brother while we both have boners, please?"

I nodded. "Good point."

"And the term is versatile. Or vers. It means I'm happy giving and receiving. So if it would make you feel comfortable to start out with you—"

I knew I was really bad at interrupting, but I couldn't help it. "Whatever you want! Whichever you like best. I mean… I'm happy to do either. I don't want you to think I'm chickenshit because I am not. And if you can handle a… dick in your ass… then I probably can too." I blinked rapidly at him now that the nerves were catching up to me a little. "But maybe just… just give me some pointers and be patient with me till I get the hang of it. You have a big schlong, and I mean that sincerely."

He looked like he wanted to laugh, but he also looked like his pig had just won best in show at the State Fair. "I love you, Dunn Johnson, more than you could ever know."

I let out a breath and smiled back. "'Cause I have a big one too?"

He shook his head and laughed. "Yeah. That's exactly it. How did you know?"

I pressed the dick in question into his belly. "'Cause I have eyes, Dr. Wright. I'm a medical marvel, probably."

Tuck's laughter in my shower was the best sound ever. I moved my hands down to grab his ass and shake it. "This is mine. Got me?"

He nodded and leaned in to kiss me. "Let's start the easy way. You want this ass to be yours?"

"Mmhm," I murmured against his sweet lips.

"Then take it."

I barely stuck around in the shower long enough to slam the taps closed and grab a towel. I scooped the good doctor off his feet and swung his slippery ass over my shoulder while simultaneously trying to pat him dry with the towel.

"Lube," I muttered, making a mental list. "Condoms."

"No condoms," he said. Tuck's sneaky fingers were taking advantage of their position near my ass with little pinches and squeezes. "I know both of our statuses. Unless... I mean... if you've had sex since..."

I threw him down on my bed and climbed on top of him, noticing the very real worry in his eyes. "Dani?"

His eyes widened. "You haven't had sex since Danyelle? Jesus, that was like..."

"A year and a half ago?" I said, noticing the water droplets caught in his dark chest hair. "Why do you think I was desperate enough to consider your skinny ass?" I teased.

He wiggled around until I was lying over his back and he was arching his perfectly rounded, tight ass against my hard cock. "Skinny ass? This? I'll have you know I squat for hours to have an ass like this. And it's going to be tight as hell around your dick."

I let out an animalistic groan. "Fuck. Let me in. Tell me what to do. Where's the stuff? What do we need? Fuck! I forgot how to work sex."

He laughed into the soft bedspread as I smacked his ass and reached for the pump bottle of lube on my nightstand. I came back to him with enough to get us started. I kissed his shoulder blade and began to kiss a line down his spine as I reached between his cheeks.

"I'm such a fucking lucky bastard," I whispered between kisses. His hole clenched when he felt the cool slick on my fingers, so I shushed him and murmured more words of gratitude and affection. I truly didn't know why he was even giving me a chance. He deserved better than a hick dairy farmer from middle Tennessee. He deserved a smart, polished, successful guy like Carter Rogers. But how could someone like Carter possibly love Tucker Wright more than I did?

I used my fingers to tease him while moving my body up to whisper dirty shit in his ear. God, I wanted to make him lose his mind with lust. "So tight for me, aren't you, sweetheart, mmhm. Squeeze my finger. Like that. Fuck, what you do to me. I want inside your body, to be closer to you. Please."

"Dunn." His voice shook and his eyes stayed closed. One fist was tightly clutching the comforter while the other had grabbed my wrist. He couldn't seem to decide if he wanted me to push deeper in or pull out.

"You okay, baby?" I asked before kissing the edge of his ear. "Am I doing it right?"

He huffed out a laugh which made me smile. After a few minutes of my teasing him with my fingers, circling around, dipping deep inside, he spoke again, so softly I almost didn't hear him. "Are you sure?"

I reached for the lube and got another pump before returning to my task. As I slid more fingers inside, I moved my lips back to his ear. "One night at the cabin last summer, you fell asleep on the sofa. It was hot as hell, and we were both in our underwear."

"I remember," he said in a drugged-out voice. "I couldn't stop staring at your bubble butt. You slept on your stomach in tight boxer briefs, and I thanked God for that. Several times. Pretty sure I slept with my hand in my pants."

"Mm. Pretty sure you didn't. I was watching you too. You stretched out your leg at one point, and I could see the head of your dick. I stared at it." The hot clench of his body was making me crazy with need, and the memory of watching him—worried he was going to catch me perving on him—made my dick even harder. "I thought about the guy you'd gone on a date with… Winn? Pinn? Something like that. The rude fucker from Knoxville. Anyway—"

"Gen," he corrected with a laugh. "Short for Genesis. He was raised super religious I think."

I didn't care what the guy's name was. "I pictured him licking the head of your cock, the smooth purple head I could see in the early morning light through the window. I don't even know why I was imagining it. Maybe I wanted you then and was too stupid to realize it. But, God, the thought of him sucking your dick made me feel so funny. *Angry.* At least I thought so at the time."

His breath was coming faster and faster as my fingers stretched his hole.

"D, baby, you're... I can't... please."

I moved over on top of him and slicked up my cock. Just the quick, utilitarian strokes were almost enough to shoot me off. "Fuck," I hissed. "Want you so much. I've fucking dreamed about this since that kiss in the orchard last fall."

Tucker spun around so fast, he knocked me onto my back on the bed. "What?"

He climbed on top of me, his chest heaving with breath and his cheeks flushed apple red. I ran a hand up his chest and used the other to jack his dick because I knew how good it felt. "You're so fucking sexy. I'm trying really hard not to think about wasted time."

His face softened. "You're making me crazy. For real. What do you mean you dreamed about this?"

"That kiss. Jesus, Tuck. That kiss changed everything. Ever since then, I just... I can't... nothing sits right. Nothing feels right. Nothing makes sense. It's why I kept trying to get you settled with someone so I could stop fucking thinking about it."

"And now?"

I took in a deep breath, held it for a beat, and then blew

it out. "Now I think I finally understand what people mean when they call it making love."

Had he been any other person in the world, I would have been embarrassed to use that phrase. But he wasn't. He was Tucker.

"I love you," he said, eyes shining and hands smoothing over my skin like he was trying to calm a restless horse. "No matter what happens. I love you so much."

"I love you too. And I want you to know I'm not always the smartest guy or the smoothest guy, but…" I firmed my jaw. "I'm the best one for you. You got me?"

Tucker lifted his hips up and reached down to grab me by the dick. I sucked in a breath.

"I've got you," he said softly, so softly, as if still gentling that nervous horse. "I've got you," he murmured again as the tip of my cock pushed against his tight entrance. "I've got you."

When he finally sank all the way down and his fiery-hot body was squeezing the life out of me, I thought maybe I'd died and gone to heaven for real. My arms tightened around him like barrel bands, and I wondered, if only for a split second, why the hell no one had told me how good this was before.

"Tuck," I whimpered, reaching up to pull his face down for a kiss. "This is for real, right? You and me?"

I expected him to say hell yes. I expected assurances. Hell, I was even looking for long-term promises, if I were being honest. But that wasn't exactly what I got.

"Don't let go," he begged as his hips began moving faster.

So I held on to him for dear life and promised him I never would.

15

TUCKER

3-Down: Settling up, calculating, (over)thinking (9 letters)

"DUNN JOHNSON, if you don't stop pushing me up against every vertical surface, we will not have time to meet your family for coffee before my first... uh... *fuck*... my first patient."

I meant this to come out as a very severe warning, but since Dunn had pushed me up against the wall in the hall outside the kitchen and was right then rubbing his jean-covered cock against my chino-covered ass while his hot mouth sucked lightly at the side of my neck and my lungs struggled to take in adequate oxygen, it's possible that this didn't come out quite as severely as I'd intended.

Or severely at all.

"Tucker Wright," Dunn growled as he kneaded my ass cheeks, "if you don't stop being so goddamn irresistible, and this tight little ass of yours doesn't stop begging me to rub against it, I will *have* to push you against every flat surface between here and the Wisteria Cafe just to remind you who owns it."

Holy. Hot. Damn.

Was my boyfriend a jealous, possessive caveman throwback?

Why, yes. Yes, he was.

Was I *here for it*?

My hard cock and the sudden dampness at the front of my boxer briefs suggested I really fucking was, especially after our night last night.

True fact: orgasms with Dunn Johnson were *always* enjoyable.

Truer fact: orgasms where Dunn Johnson whispered filthy words about all the times he'd noticed my dick over the years, followed by him telling me we were "making love," followed by him railing me into the mattress so hard I could still feel it this morning, were by far the *most* enjoyable.

"Emergency wedding party meeting," I reminded him breathlessly. "Brooks will come looking for us if we don't show up."

Honestly, at that moment, I didn't care. I was more than willing to let Dunn drag me back to bed and let the whole world come knocking on the door. But Dunn groaned and took a tiny step away.

"Yeah, okay," he said, blowing out a breath. "Gotta do my best-man duties and find out exactly what kind of tools my mom's torturing Mal and Brooks with."

I grinned, only a tiny bit disappointed to have gotten my way. Dunn was as proud as three peacocks that Brooks had chosen him, rather than Paul or any of his other friends, to be his best man, and it was adorable.

Like everything Dunn did.

I was *so* gone for him.

"I keep telling you, it's *tulle*." I turned around and fixed the collar of Dunn's jacket, patting it into place.

Dunn's hands covered mine. "You sure?" His voice was low, and his eyes glinted in a way that suggested he knew very well that it was.

"Yeah. Pretty sure," I said, and then I leaned up to kiss him, just because I could. "Now come on."

"Just to say," Dunn said, taking my hand as we headed down the stairs, "when I get married there won't be any tools *or* any tulle. Vegas or bust, baby."

My stomach flipped like I'd missed a step. "Is that so?"

"Yep. I mean..." He darted a glance at me that I couldn't quite interpret. "Not that I'm in any hurry, of course."

"No, of course," I echoed. I grabbed my coat from the rack in the mudroom and pulled it on as we went down the back steps, grateful for the excuse to turn away from him for a second.

Was Dunn trying to tell me not to get my hopes up? Or was he worried that I didn't want him to get *his* hopes up?

I wasn't sure when I stopped being able to predict and understand every thought that ran through Dunn's head, but I was pretty sure it was around the time his tongue first entered my mouth. And while I didn't want things to go back to the way they had been—*heck, no*—I also did not enjoy the way things currently were. It felt like the place we communicated best these days was in bed—or the shower, or the couch, or against the desk in my office—where words weren't necessary.

We strolled down Walnut Street toward the cafe. I wanted really badly to hold his hand again, but I couldn't, so I took out my phone and looked over my calendar for the day.

"So, whatcha got planned after coffee, Dr. Wright?"

"Pretty full docket today," I informed him. "Lots of patients."

"You maybe free for lunch? I feel like I might have a sore throat you should look at." Dunn made a hacking whistle, like Bernadette when she had a cold.

"That sounds… frankly terrifying—"

Dunn laughed.

"But I can't. Today's my lunch with Dr. Petersmith."

"And Carter."

I snickered. Was it petty that I loved how he said Carter's name like the man was the antichrist and not an insanely wealthy twentieth-generation doctor from Belle Mead? Maybe so, but I didn't care. "Yes, and Carter. We're just catching up."

"Hmm."

I narrowed my eyes and looked over at him. "What's *hmm* mean? It's just a lunch."

"A lunch about you taking a job." Dunn hunched and put his hands in his pockets.

"About me *not* taking a job."

Dunn hesitated. "Thought Carter said it'd be more money. And, like… *prestige* and whatnot."

I shrugged. "Eh. I suppose it would." Prestige among a certain set, anyway. Like the Belle Mead Rogers. Not so much here in the Thicket.

Another hesitation. "And you're really not even gonna consider it? Why?"

I blinked. "At the risk of stating the obvious… because the job is at Vanderbilt, which is located in Nashville, while my boyfriend owns a dairy farm, which is located in Licking Thicket."

I waited a second for Dunn to agree that this was a nonstarter.

He did not.

Instead, his mouth twisted to one side like he was thinking about something awfully hard.

"I mean…" I chuckled lightly. "You don't *want* me to take the job, do you?" He couldn't possibly. Hell, even before we'd become lovers, the separation had been a nonstarter. Dunn was my person. But now?

"Not exactly. I mean…" Dunn licked his lips and gave me another one of those looks I couldn't read, damn it. "I mean, unless you wanted to? I'd definitely want you to do it, Tuck, if you wanted to."

My fingertips felt weirdly tingly.

"But… you live *here*," I said yet again, certain there was some disconnect happening, but unsure where.

"Yeah, I know," he said in a really resigned way.

I shook my head quickly to clear it. Was I crazy? Was he? Were we speaking different dialects of the same language? "Well, to be perfectly clear, I'm *not* flipping taking it, okay?"

"Yeesh. Okay." Dunn held up his hands. "Fine."

"Good Lord. What the heck are we even—" *fighting about*, I started to say.

But Dunn interrupted. "Oh my stars and garters. Is today the fourth?"

"Ah…" I glanced down at my phone screen. "Yep."

"April fourth?" he asked, with that adorable little wrinkle he got over his eyebrows.

"Yes. Why?"

Dunn stared at me. "Why? *Because it's April fourth*, Tucker!"

I threw both hands up in the air, convinced we'd have understood each other better if we started playing charades. "So?"

"So? It's the Entwinin'! *Today*. And I've been so distracted, I haven't even made plans!"

"*Oh.*" I took a deep breath and let it out slowly, unable to stop my relieved grin. "I forgot that was today. Probably since I never actually, um… did the whole wreath-making thing before."

"I know." Dunn's mouth twitched up in a little smile that made me light-headed in the best possible way. "I've seen your attempts at tying clinch knots, Tuck, it's fine. You stick to the crosswords and the doctoring. I'll do the wreathing."

"Hey!" I grinned and smacked his arm lightly. "I'll have you know I totally *could* make a wreath. Probably."

Dunn laughed out loud.

"I just haven't had any reason to try in the past." And, honestly, I'd always worried my heart would be in my eyes while I gave Dunn his wreath, or that maybe I'd be unable to stop at "Happy Entwinin'" and would accidentally blurt out, "Please have babies with me." Now, though? "In the future, I guess I will," I added.

Dunn smiled warmly, clearly pleased, and my stomach settled because we were back on track. Finally.

And then Dunn threw his arm over my shoulder.

"We can head over to the Italian place tonight. I heard they're doing a special Entwinin' dinn—" he began.

"Whoa-ho-ho!" I exclaimed, ducking away. My eyes darted up and down the street to see if anyone might have noticed. "Hold your horses, buster. We're moving slow, remember?"

Dunn frowned. "What, still? Even after last night?"

I peered at him. "We had sex, Dunn. That doesn't solve all our issues." Especially when Dunn was intent on overlooking all of them.

"We *made love*, Tucker," Dunn corrected hotly. "And yeah, it kinda does. Or at least I hoped it would. I mean—"

"Hey, hey, Dr. Wright! You still hanging around with

this doofus?" Brooks Johnson called with a wide, friendly smile for his brother and me.

Mal looked up from his phone screen and slapped Brooks gently in the stomach. "What my better half means is, 'Good morning, Dunn and Tucker. Happy Entwinin'.'"

"Yeah," Dunn muttered. "Whatever."

"Hey." Brooks frowned. "Who peed in your cornfl—"

Mal slapped him again, more firmly this time. "Brooks means to say, 'I'm sorry you're having a bad day, Dunn. Come have a look at this picture of the wreath Paul made Ava and get cheered up.'" Mal handed over his phone and snorted. "Poor Paul's been taking lessons from Jay Proud in wreath weaving for a month now, and neither Brooks nor I can figure out what the heck he's made."

"Is it a cherry?" I looked at the wreath, which was a circle surrounding a pair of smaller circles on sticks. "Is Ava fond of cherries?"

"I said a lollipop," Brooks volunteered with a shrug. "Your idea sounds better."

"I think flowers. Two of 'em, 'cause there's Paul and Ava." Mal shrugged.

Dunn peered at the phone over my shoulder, then leaned back and crossed his arms. "I think it means Ava's pregnant," he said. "I took a class from the county extension office on genotyping livestock, and that's a symbol they use to mean—"

Brooks hooted. "Uh, no. Anyone within a ten-mile radius of Ava when she was in labor with Beau knows she's not going back to *that* well. None of us would survive it."

"And for your sake, I'm not gonna tell Ava you compared her to livestock either." Mal grinned and held open the cafe door. "Anyway, I guess Ava appreciated Paul's effort. Her text says she cried and cried, so I'm guessing the wreath was really symbolic, whatever it was."

I shot Dunn a look. My money was on Dunn's interpretation, but I'd keep my mouth shut until she came into my office.

"Whose wreath was symbolic?" Cindy Ann said, standing up to give each of us a kiss as we filed around the three tables she'd smooshed together for our meeting. She glanced at Brooks. "Yours?"

"Ava's one from Paul. He took lessons from Jay Proud," Brooks explained.

"Ah, poor Jay. Making wreaths for everyone this year, but no special someone to give one to. I heard he even helped old Amos make one for Emmaline." Cindy Ann sighed as she sat back down between Red and Brooks and set her hands atop a massive binder bulging with fabric samples.

"It's true." Red winked as he nodded for me to take the chair beside him. "In the shape of an apple, to commemorate them fallin' in love after their first date at the Bobbin'."

"Well, I got *my* wreath this morning." Cindy Ann glanced coyly at her husband. "To commemorate *my* first date." Red laid a hand over hers with a loving look that made Cindy Ann blush. "You know, when you boys and Gracie were little, I used to imagine the special folks you'd find to exchange wreaths with, and now y'all *have*. It's a great satisfaction as a parent, I don't mind telling you."

I sat up a little straighter and squirmed in my chair. There was no way she was talking about *me* when she said that.

Brooks snorted. "If you're telling me you imagined the person I'd be exchanging wreaths with"—he laid an arm over Mal's chair—"we need to be having a conversation about tonight's Lotto numbers, 'cause you were way more in the know than I was back then."

Cindy Ann rolled her blue eyes again. "You hush with

that sass, mister. It's true that while I've had my eye on Dunn's special someone for a few years now, I was *possibly* a bit shortsighted about yours until he came on the scene." She gave Mal a loving smile. "But now I wouldn't change him for the world either."

I held my breath and forced a smile in Mal's direction that I absolutely did not feel. Cindy Ann was talking about Jenn as Dunn's special someone. She had to be. And I felt sick.

This was exactly the sort of thing Dunn wasn't prepared for. Cindy Ann and Red were really good people, and I knew they'd come around to the idea of Dunn and me dating… *eventually*. But first they'd have to give up the dreams they'd had for their son, just like they'd done with Brooks.

Maybe that wouldn't be so easy the second time around.

This was why it was best for Dunn to be sure about him and me.

Like, *sure* sure.

Surer than a person could be after a week of nookie and a half dozen unenlightening conversations.

"Hey," Dunn said gruffly. His boot kicked my loafer gently under the table. "Y'okay? You look kinda peaky all of a sudden."

"Oh, yeah. I'm great," I said faintly. "I maybe need a coffee." Or maybe some of that Jameson that Dunn ordered every once in a while.

Dunn frowned and moved so his thigh was pressed tightly against mine. "I'll go get you one."

"Nonsense." Red pushed up from the table. "I'll go. My treat."

I breathed in through my nose and gave Dunn what I hoped was a reassuring smile.

The look in his eyes, which said he wasn't sure if he wanted to kiss me or shake me, indicated it hadn't worked.

"Hey, grab one for me and Mal too, please?" Brooks asked.

Red nodded. "You got it."

"See how I take care of you, baby?" Brooks wiggled his eyebrows at Mal.

"Oh, I see." Mal snorted but leaned into Brooks's side just the same. "I got my wreath this morning," he volunteered to the table. "Though, to be fair, it wasn't so much a wreath as a hook."

"A *hook*?" Cindy Ann shook her head, bewildered. "But I didn't think you liked fishing, Malachi."

"Oh, I don't particularly." Mal grinned wickedly. "This was to symbolize that he'd hooked me." He held up his left hand and wiggled his ring finger.

"That is *not* true!" Brooks poked Mal's ribs and made him laugh. "I told you, it was to symbolize that *you* had hooked *me*. And you know very well I was limited by what I was capable of constructing, unless you wanted me to buy you one from the flower shop!" Brooks sounded incredibly put out. "Not all of us are *artists*."

Mal laughed out loud again, and Brooks pulled him closer.

"I'll love you forever, Malachi Forrester, but if you're marrying me for my weaving skills, prepare yourself for disappointment until death do us part."

Mal's laughter settled into a grin. "Fortunately, you have other gifts, baby."

Beside me, Dunn shuddered. "I do *not* want to hear about Brooks having *gifts*. Not with our mama at the table."

Cindy Ann shook her head at Dunn with fond exasperation. "So what about you, Mal? What sort of wreath did you construct for Brooks?"

"Oh. Um." Mal licked his lips. "Well. Funny thing about that—"

"He forgot!" Brooks crowed.

"No! Pfft. *No.* I told you it was *special* and it was *coming.* Later." He waved a hand vaguely. "When the muse visits."

Cindy Ann pressed her lips together. Brooks pulled Mal closer to press a kiss to his head.

"I'll love you forever, Brooks Johnson, but if you're marrying me for my ability to remember dates, *you're* doomed to disappointment for the rest of *your* life."

Brooks grinned down at Mal. "Can't wait," he said softly.

"Yeah," Mal said just as softly. "Me neither."

"Ah, my boys." Cindy Ann sniffled, watching them.

Meanwhile, I pressed a hand to my stomach because I wanted that so badly, and it seemed so out of reach.

"Dunn, honey." Cindy Ann tilted her head. "What about you? What's your wreath like?"

"Oh, well actually, Tuck is…"

"Thinking of going fishing tomorrow!" I blurted, kicking Dunn under the table. "Y'all are welcome to come."

Red came back and set down my coffee. "That'd be nice! Been a while since I went fishing."

Cindy Ann's lips pursed. "That's not really news, is it?"

I laughed, uncomfortable. "Guess not, now that I think on it."

Dunn sat forward and braced his elbows on the table. "Actually, what I was gonna say was…"

"You're dying for coffee too?" I cut in loudly. I pushed my paper cup in his direction. "That's alright! Have some of mine, friend!"

Dunn stared at me like I'd lost my mind.

I was pretty sure he was right.

Unfortunately, everyone else was staring at me too.

"Tucker, honey," Cindy Ann began worriedly. "Are you okay? I'd offer to get you a doctor, but..."

"Ha! Yes! Good one. No, I'm fine. Just... fine." I waved slightly. "I'll maybe... have some coffee myself."

"You do that." She leaned over to pat my hand.

"What I'm trying to say," Dunn insisted, "is that—"

I stood up from the table and pushed my chair back with a squeal. "Actually, I changed my mind. I'm *not* okay. I need air. Outside air. Dunn, could you, um... help me find some?"

Dunn's jaw worked and his nostrils flared. "Yeah, Tuck. I'll find it for ya."

He stalked outside right behind me.

When we reached the sidewalk, I whirled around to face him. "What does *slow* mean to you, Dunn? *Dear God.*"

"It doesn't mean *standing still*, that's for sure!" Dunn looked as angry as I'd ever seen him. "What's the problem?"

"The problem is, it's only been a week!"

"I think you mean it's *already been an entire week*," Dunn shot back. "And especially after last night—and don't you dare say it was just sex, Tuck, don't you lie—"

I bit my tongue.

"I don't want to hide this anymore." He ran a hand through his brown-gold hair. "I get you're reluctant 'cause I didn't know what I wanted from you before, but I couldn't help that. And hiding our relationship now is only going to make that worse."

I blinked, because the man had a good point...

A very good point.

But so did I, damn it.

"If you tell your parents, everyone will know, Dunn. Everyone in town. Your old baseball coach, and Mrs. Ferguson at the bank, a-a-and some of them might side-eye you and some of them might do worse, like threaten your business. The kids I've volunteered with, they—"

"They're not *me*, Tuck. I'm a grown man. I have choices. And I halfway wanna rent a billboard on Highway 50 that says Dunn Johnson finally wised up and Tucker Wright is off the market."

I shook my head vehemently, my heart in my throat. "You *think* you want that—"

"I know I do."

"—because you've never come out before."

"Because you won't let me!"

"Gahhh." I grabbed two handfuls of my hair and tugged. "Why must you be so unreasonable? I'm not *saying* not to come out. Of course I'm not! I just want you to think, Dunn. Please. For once, just think before you act. Cindy Ann's had your future Entwinin' person picked out for years." I waved a hand toward the cafe. "What if... what if you decide being with me is too hard and you regret your decision? You cannot unring this bell."

"Why would I want to? And... being with you, Tuck? I *couldn't* regret that. Shit, do you even hear yourself?"

I swallowed hard. "What if you hate me?" I whispered. "What if it ends our friendship forever? What if I lose you for good?"

"What if the sky falls? What if the world ends?" Dunn mocked. "You're doing it again, you know."

"Doing what?" I pressed my fingers to my eyes. "Worrying? I do that."

"You're thinking for me. You're treating me like I can't think for myself."

"I'm not, Dunn. I promise. I just... I love you. I want you to be happy. I swear, that's *all* I want."

Dunn shook his head slowly and came closer. Close enough to take me in his arms, but he didn't.

"When I was inside you last night, Tucker, and you were calling my name, I thought, 'Shit, Dunn, this is what it's all about. This is what it's *always* been about.' I felt like someone finally let me in on a secret." His warm breath tickled my ear. "And meanwhile, *you* were thinking I was, what? Gonna run back to Jenn any minute so I could please my mom? Like you and me were the ones on a ninety-day free trial and I might decide to exchange you for some steak knives?"

"No!" I protested weakly. "Not exactly."

Dunn snorted disgustedly. "You did. You actually did." He stepped away from me and inhaled sharply, his green eyes filled with hurt. "You know, maybe I should've stuck with Jenn. At least I knew where I stood with her. At least I knew how *she* really felt about me."

I gasped. "What? Jenn wants you to marry her because she thinks you're somehow gonna steal Summer Honey from Abilene and Jenn'll run it like some *Devil Wears Prada* wannabe! She wants your mom to give her a spot on the Beautification Corps! She doesn't love you the way you deserve."

"I know Jenn doesn't love me," Dunn said sadly. "But I'm starting to wonder if you really do either, Tuck."

My jaw dropped. "Are you… are you kidding me right now? You think Jenn might be better for you than me? Ha. Well, then… well, then… if you can't tell the difference, maybe you *should* be with Jenn!" I set my hands on my hips. "Maybe you two deserve each other."

Dunn snorted. "When you're over your freak-out and ready to stop hedging your bets, call me." He stared through the window of the cafe and gave a brief salute at his mama… which was the point when I realized most of his family and a solid percentage of the town gossips had been watching us. And then he walked off.

Fuck.

Part of me wanted to race after him, but the rest of me was rooted to the spot while my body flashed hot and cold. I stared down at the sidewalk, but it was weirdly foggy and I couldn't see it.

Cindy Ann appeared suddenly and wrapped an arm around my waist. "Come on in, honey. Your coffee's getting cold."

I shook my head. "I can't. I need to... I have... patients." I waved in the direction of my office.

"It's still early, and you're no good to them at *all* like this anyway. Come on now," she said firmly, pulling me back inside.

She pushed me down into my seat and took Dunn's empty one. "Now, then. What's going on?"

"Dunn and I..." Broke up? No. *Shit.* We did *not.* "We had a fight."

Cindy Ann nodded. "A lovers' quarrel."

"Those are the worst," Red piped up sympathetically. "Especially when you're at the beginning like you two are. Thank goodness we grew out of that. Remember, Cindy Ann?"

"I remember two weeks ago when I wouldn't let you eat a third helping of Lurleen's bread-and-butter custard for *breakfast,* and you didn't speak to me for the whole day," she said wryly. "I don't know if we've grown out of it, Red. We're just too old and settled to storm off when we know we're gonna end up back where we belong in the end anyway."

Red chuckled. "True enough."

"Now, you and Dunn on the other hand, Tucker—"

"Wait." I sniffed and looked around the table from Cindy Ann, to Red, to Brooks, and then Mal. "You... Y'all know? About me and Dunn?"

"Was it supposed to be a secret?" Brooks winced. "'Cause honestly, anyone who's seen you together in the last half year knows the score." He tucked Mal more closely against him. "Truth is, when you're in love, it's not as easy to hide as you think."

"Ugh." I buried my head in my hands. "So the hiding was all for nothing? I let the cat out of the bag anyway?"

"Not *you*, honey. *Both* of you," Cindy Ann said. "Dunn looks at you with so much love it just... pours right off him."

I lifted my head. "It does?"

"Yep. It's kinda gross," Mal said happily, cuddling closer to Brooks.

"It's so severe that a concerned citizen might've figured it was his duty to google whether high levels of human pheromones were harmful to cattle, just in case." Red shrugged sheepishly. "And they're *not*," he added, glancing around the table. "If anyone else was curious."

"But... this only started a week ago. For Dunn, I mean. He just jumped in, and... and you know how Dunn looks before he leaps..." I broke off with a sigh.

Cindy Ann and Brooks burst into laughter, and Mal quickly followed. Red just watched me patiently.

"Tuck," he said, "you two might've only noticed it a week ago, but you've been it for each other since..." He shook his head. "Months ago, I guess."

"Years," Cindy Ann corrected matter-of-factly. "That's how I knew you'd be the one my boy ended up entwined with."

"Wait, me?" I blurted.

"Who else, honey?" She shook her head. "Dunn's not the quickest mind on the planet, but that boy is *steadfast*. You must know that."

I nodded, because I did. He was dependable as the day was long.

"He recognized how special you were long before he recognized what y'all could be to each other, but I'd swear he was in love with you even then. And I couldn't be more pleased."

"But... it might be hard—harder—for him, being with me. *You* know." I nodded at Mal and then Brooks.

Mal frowned and nodded. "Maybe. Maybe not. But I wouldn't change who I love, even if I could, Tuck. Would *you*?"

I blinked. No. No, I wouldn't.

"And his life would be an awful lot harder without you," Brooks pointed out. "Nobody else in their right mind would understand why he lets his pig sleep in the dining room."

"One day when Dunn was eight," Cindy Ann said, holding my hand tightly, "Dunn asked me where ice cream came from. So I explained how farmers like Ava's daddy, our next-door neighbor, raised cows for milk, and the milk was turned into ice cream and other dairy products. And that was that. Dunn never said another word about it. I figured he'd forgotten. Then, a year and a bit later, he came to me out of a clear blue sky and said he wanted to buy Mac Riner's farm when Mac retired, but he was gonna turn the cow-calf operation into a dairy farm, and he'd raise cows that made ice cream and only ice cream."

Mal snorted. "That's so Dunn."

"It surely is." Cindy Ann lifted an eyebrow at me significantly. "And that's just what he did, Tucker. Even though there were lots of other, easier, *less messy* choices. And he's never regretted it."

I pressed a hand to my stomach.

God, that was true.

So, so true.

And not only did Dunn never complain about the mess or the physical strain or the occasional heartbreak of the life he'd chosen, he reveled in it. All of it. Even the hard bits.

Shit. *Shit.* What had I done?

Dunn Johnson was the person I loved best in the whole wide world... and I'd practically shooed him away because I was so scared the two of us being together wouldn't be enough for him, when the truth was, life was all about choices. Loving Dunn meant living in the Thicket and turning down the fellowship with Dr. Petersmith, and I hadn't hesitated for a minute to do that, right? Why couldn't I imagine Dunn would do the same?

"For what it's worth, Dunn didn't leap into things with you, Tuck." Red set his hand on my shoulder and shook it a little. "Might seem that way on the surface, but the boy fell kinda slow and gentle. Only question in my mind was whether you'd still be around once he finished falling."

"Laws, don't get me started." Cindy Ann groaned. "You have no idea how hard it's been to keep a handsome, lovable doctor from meeting a decent man all these years. I thought the gig was up when you dated sweet Parrish Partridge last fall." She shook her head. "That was a close call."

"I think I've made a huge mistake," I admitted.

"Ah, cheer up, son. Most of my quarrels with Cindy Ann end with me saying that too." Red patted me on the back. "Whatcha gonna do about it?"

"I'm gonna show him how much I want him," I whispered, my mind whirling with plans. "And then I'm gonna ask him what he wants... and I'm gonna believe him."

"Excellent," Brooks said, rubbing his hands together. "How can we help?"

"Well, first," I said slowly, "I'm gonna need to see a man about some vines."

16

DUNN

7-Down: A person with whom one is friendly despite a fundamental dislike or rivalry (7 letters)

I RARELY GOT MAD. Honestly, it took a lot to get me there, and everyone knew it. Tucker, especially, knew it. But he also knew that when I finally hit my limit, I was *done*.

I slammed the truck door closed and peeled out of my driveway. My morning chores had gotten the shit end of the stick, and even Luisa, who was ornery on a good day, had stopped to ask me what the hell.

"You got a bug up your butt?" she'd hollered across the milking parlor where I was cleaning some equipment. "Because I already told you I cleaned those. You know, when you were sleeping late with your girlfriend like some kind of prima donna? Well, some of us were actually working for a living."

"I don't have a girlfriend," I'd snapped back.

"Fine, your boyfriend, then. Whatever. Just stop

cleaning shit I already finished. You want to help, then clean out the troughs."

I don't have a boyfriend either, I'd almost said. But I'd bitten my tongue against even putting that negativity out there in the world. Instead, I'd kept quiet and thrown myself into work.

Now that the work was done, I had too much time to think. And none of my thoughts were good. My brain was like a spinning top that wouldn't fall down. It kept going round and round with all of my arguments for why Tucker should listen to me and why he needed to stop treating me like I didn't know my own damned heart. And then there was the fear, the gutshot pain of thinking he might actually want to leave here and go to Nashville. Maybe he had greater career ambitions he kept bottled up and hidden deep down.

I'd always thought he was meant for greater things than being a small-town family doc. He was smart as hell, and any big-city hospital would be lucky to have him. Tucker Wright was the kind of man who could do groundbreaking research and be known around the world for advancements in medicine. So why was he sticking around a little hick town instead? Maybe he just needed a little push. Was he waiting for me to encourage him to reach for his own stars?

If so, I was in big trouble because I wasn't quite that selfless. It would take a stronger man than I was to fall on that sword.

Before I even knew where I was going, I was pulling into the nearby town of Great Nuthatch which had invested heavily in a brand-new welcome sign after Licking Thicket had gotten the custom one Mal had made a year and a half ago.

Their sign had been poorly designed, and the "hatch" part kept getting removed and carted away in the dead of night, which I commiserated with. My dad had spent many a sleepless night dealing with the same issues in the Thicket before our sign was made out of metal and cemented dozens of feet underground.

I pulled into an empty parking spot in a very full lot outside of the cardiologist's office. Maybe I hadn't thought it through, but now that I was here, I knew exactly what I needed to do.

Interrogate the douchebag Dr. McFlirt and find out exactly what the hell was going on with Tucker and this job interview thing. If Tucker moved to Nashville, I was going to have to prepare myself for the utter agony of trying to support him in that decision.

I slammed my way out of the truck and strode through the glass doors into the reception area. The waiting room was full of patients, but I was here on an important mission.

"Dunn Johnson to see Dr. Rogers, please," I said to the receptionist in my most assertive voice.

The young woman nodded, typed my name into the computer, and then blinked up at me. "And what time is your appointment for, sir?"

"I don't have an appointment. It's an emergency visit. It'll just take a few minutes."

She frowned and glanced at my chest where I hadn't realized I was rubbing. It hurt. Ever since Tucker had denied me in public, it hurt like a sonuvabitch. How dare he? How could he possibly think I wasn't all in after everything that had transpired between us? After I'd been *inside of him*.

"Sir, do you need an ambulance?"

I shook off the memory of the two of us in bed together. "I mean... maybe. It does kinda hurt. But first I want to talk to Carter. Can you get him for me, please? Just... it'll just be a second, I promise."

She shot a worried glance at me as she stood up and scurried back into the office behind her. A minute later, Carter appeared, all professional and shit in his white coat.

Asshole.

"Dunn? What are you doing here? Is everything okay? Is it your dad?"

Okay, now that... that was nice. I didn't want him to be a nice guy. I was hopped up on anger and annoyance, and he was going to make the perfect target. If he could just stop caring about my dad's heart, that'd be great. "No. It's Tuck. Can we talk? It'll just be a minute. It's important."

He hesitated for a minute before sighing. "Sure, come on back."

I followed him to an office and closed the door behind me. Carter took the chair behind the desk, and I sat opposite him in one of the visitor chairs. I perched on the edge of the seat and clasped my hands together between my knees. "So, like... give it to me straight here, Doc. What's the deal with Tuck going to Nashville? Is this what he wants? Is this..." I swallowed. "Is this what's best for him? Is that why he's being weird with me?"

I hated asking him for advice regarding Tucker. I despised the very idea that he could know anything about Tucker better than I did. But we were past the point of protecting my pride. I needed answers.

"What happened?" he asked.

I threw up my hands and stood so I could move around. I felt caged and antsy, like my entire life was wobbling on a cliff's edge.

"We were together, right? I mean, *really* together. And I thought... I thought... this is it. It's finally... it's finally right. And it was good. *So* good. But then he..." My voice broke a little, so I swallowed and tried to calm down. "He keeps putting the brakes on, and now this lunch with this doctor about a job, and I can't... I can't handle not knowing what he really wants."

"Did you ask him?"

I glared at him. "You are incredibly smarmy."

He laughed which of course only made him more attractive in an assholey way. "How dare I ask you to communicate clearly and maturely with your life partner," he said calmly. "I must be a monster."

I nodded aggressively. "You are. You really are." I had to admit, I did kind of like hearing him call Tuck my life partner. That was exactly what he was, and he'd been my life partner for a while now. I just hadn't realized it. "But that option's off the table now since I... got a little upset at him earlier. So now I'm here. Desperate times and all that."

His office wasn't very good for pacing, but I did my best.

Carter steepled his hands together in front of his smirk. "Ah, I see. You've come to the subject-matter expert on all things Tucker Wright, is that it?"

I lunged toward him, but he rolled the chair out of my reach with another laugh. "Never mind," I snapped. "I can see you don't give a shit about him if you're not willing to help out his *best friend in the world*."

"Calm down, Farmer Johnson. He's not going anywhere. If you're so oblivious that you can't see how goofy in love that man is with you, maybe he deserves better."

I knew he was messing with me, but I snapped at him anyway. "No one is better than me for Tucker Wright. No one."

Carter's wide, easy grin surprised me because it was 100 percent sincere. "Good. As long as you realize that, I can help."

I was surprised by his quick agreement. "What's the catch?"

"No catch. I genuinely like Tucker and want what's best for him. I believe that's you. So let's figure out how to get you two fools out of your own way."

I side-eyed him. "Still waiting for the catch."

He pointed to the office door. "I have three more patients, and then we're going out for a very boozy lunch. I'm going to need a little medicinal help if I'm going to strategize love shit with you. Go wait for me out there in the waiting room."

I did as he asked. It took all of my self-control not to text Tucker with a thousand different thoughts. Things like "please God take me back" and "I'm sorry, I'll do anything you want" were top of the list, but there were also gems like "what's the name of that song I like to listen to when I'm mad" and "can you meet me and Carter for boozy lunch to talk about my shitty non-boyfriend?" Thankfully, my phone was dead anyway after I forgot to charge it overnight at Tucker's.

When Carter finally came out of the patient area, I'd had just about enough perky HGTV episodes in my eyeballs to make me want to flip a house. "Finally," I muttered, standing up and following him outside like a puppy. When the lights blinked on a nearby douchey sports car, I rolled my eyes. But then I did a little internal dance because I was getting ready to ride in a Ferrari SF90 Spider. *Please, baby Jesus, let him put the top down.*

I touched it reverently. "This one of them new Priuses?"

He chuckled. "You enjoy playing the cowpoke, don't you?"

I slid into the racing seat and bit back an appreciative groan at the way it hugged my back and hips. "Don't know what you mean."

"You have an app on your phone called ParlorBoss. I asked Tucker what it was. He said your milking business is fully automated with mobile parlor management software, and you've done all the work to transition your herd to fully organic certified. You're also the exclusive supplier to the fastest-growing creamery in the southeast, and you've diversified into bath products as well. You're not stupid."

"Mpfh," I said, reaching out and running my fingers across the smooth control panel on the dash. I would never admit to the warm feeling I got in my chest from hearing those words spoken by someone as educated and successful as Carter Rogers.

The low rumble of the engine turning over almost made me hard. I made a noise in my throat.

Carter laughed. "I dream of someone sucking me off in this car, so you might want to stop making sounds like that."

I shot him a look. "Keep dreaming." I almost, *almost* told him out of habit I wasn't into guys. But then the image of me sucking Tucker's dick flashed through my mind, and I choked the words back.

He drove the short distance to a pub I recognized. Private Lewellyn's Bar and Grill had been shortened over the years to just plain Private's. It was the perfect place for two guys to get drunk and awkward for an afternoon.

"They have killer burgers," I said. "The mushroom and swiss is good. Fish and chips is decent too. Oh, and the macaroni bites are…"

I saw his lip turn up in judgment. "Or they have big salads too," I added. "If that's the way you wanna be."

The woman at the door sat us in a deep booth near the back. I asked her for whatever draft special they had going on, and Carter asked for one of their fancier beers. "You sure you don't want champagne?" I asked.

He lifted a sculpted eyebrow. "You buying?"

I muttered under my breath and perused the menu even though I already knew what I was getting. When the server returned with our beers and took our order, I sat back with a deep gulp of my beer and a relieved sigh.

I wasn't quite ready to start in on myself. I needed more time for the effects of the beer to kick in. "What about you, Doc? You looking for someone special? I mean, besides my Tuck?"

He studied me over his glass. "I love Tucker." Before I could get good and mad, he added, "But he's not the one for me. Even if he wasn't already head over heels in love with you, he and I don't suit. If it had been meant to be between us, it would have worked out better in school."

"Do you date? In Nashville, I mean?"

He shrugged. "A little. My job is hectic, and I work extra shifts at the hospital. It's one of the reasons I volunteered to stand in for Dr. Symmons here for a little while. I needed a break. I was getting burned out, and it was beginning to affect my health."

"I'm sorry 'bout that," I said, taking another sip. "It's one of the reasons I'm not sure I could handle living in a big city. The pace is too much. Too much noise and too many people."

Carter sat back and nodded like he was thinking things through. "I can see why you like it in the Thicket. It's nice to run into people you know everywhere. Hell, even your mom sat with me at the coffee shop the other day when she spotted me in line. I also enjoyed going fishing with the guys. I mean… I know it didn't turn out like we'd all hoped, but I envy you that group of friends. I don't have that."

Well, fuck. I didn't want to feel bad for Carter Rogers. Just the barest niggle of a pity party started in my gut, so I tried to drown that crap out with another beer.

It took several.

"So, um... my mom, you know?" My voice was kind of slurry when we got back around to the topic of Carter's love life. We'd been interrupted by a gaggle of my old girlfriends from high school who'd been on a ladies' lunch at a nearby table. Those girls used to flirt with me like crazy, but apparently Carter being fresh meat made me chopped liver.

Good riddance. I didn't need them anyway. I was gay now, or whatever.

"Anyway," I continued. "She says there are eighty-two guys in Licking-Nuthatch... or, wait. It's Pecker Lurch. Thicket-Lurch PFLAG we can set you up with." I punctuated my thought with a soft burp. The onion rings had done me so right. "Except Tucker, of course."

"Mm." He nodded and took a sip of something that looked suspiciously like sweet tea. "I can only handle one at a time. Maybe two. Then there was that time I did four, but Tucker did most of the work."

Beer dribbled down my chin when my hand froze on its way to delivering the glass to my lips. "Huh?" The words continued to soak into my already beer-soaked brain. "Say what? You and Tucker—"

The built-in wooden booth table stopped me from standing up like I'd wanted. The damned thing nearly cut me in half. Carter just laughed. "God, you're so easy to rile. Sit back down. I can't believe you thought Tucker was the kind of guy to have an orgy."

"I don't know what gay guys do!" I barked. Several tables around us turned to stare. "Never mind! Mind your business," I snapped at one table in particular where I recognized some faces from a neighboring farm. "Clyde, especially you. Don't think I didn't see you ducking out of

Quick Snips the other day without tipping Railene. That shit's not okay. She's got dogs to feed."

I sat back down and pointed a finger at Carter. "And stop messing with me. I've got problems." I rubbed my chest. "Heart problems. It hurts right here."

"That's the bar food. Your heart's fine."

"What if he doesn't want to live on a farm?" I couldn't imagine giving up my herd for him, but I'd probably do it if that's what he wanted. "Where would I put Bernadette?"

"Who's Bernadette?" he asked, waving the server down for another refill. I looked at his long, elegant fingers and the expensive watch on his wrist.

"My cat," I mumbled into the last dregs of beer.

"That's right. I'd heard you liked pussy," he said matter-of-factly.

I tried not to spit my beer all over the table. "Not true! You take that back! I like *dick*."

Several gasps came from nearby tables, but I ignored them and stared into my empty glass. Small towns weren't always great, despite Carter's earlier claims. People gossiped like crazy since everyone knew everyone.

Carter lowered his voice. "That right there is a prime example. You don't stop to think about the reality of being a gay or bi man in the world, and that's one of the things that scares Tucker."

I blinked up at him. "What do you mean?"

"It makes you a target. You have to constantly be aware of your surroundings, your safety. It might be easy for you since you pass as straight, but the minute you say shit about liking dick, you make yourself a potential target. It's always something that Tucker is aware of, that men like me are aware of."

"What do you mean men like you?"

He hesitated as if looking for the right words. "Pretty

boys. The kind of man who plucks his eyebrows and wears floral ties and pink dress socks. We don't exactly fit in here in small-town Tennessee, and men like that..." He flicked his eyes toward Clyde's table where the guys were dressed in dusty boots and Carhartt work pants. "Sometimes hassle men like me and Tucker when given the opportunity."

Carter's soft voice broke through my tipsy haze enough to make me pause. "But... but Tucker's never been hassled by anyone." I spoke with a confidence I suddenly didn't feel.

He sighed. "Dunn. Tucker and I walked out of a movie theater one night after a bunch of kids threw popcorn at us and called us names. I know for a fact he had slurs yelled at him in high school, and when I put my arm around a guy at a concert one night in college, two guys shoved us until we stopped touching each other."

My stomach fell. "But that... that..." I clamped my back teeth together. Of course there was prejudice against gay people. I wasn't stupid. I just hadn't really stopped to think it through since we lived in the Thicket where everyone knew us. Brooks and Mal didn't get hassled. Did they?

And people like that wouldn't hassle me, would they? I was big enough and strong enough to handle myself in most situations. Would it be different if Tucker and I were holding hands together in public?

I shot a glance at Clyde's table as my head began to process things differently. I was just one person. Even though I'd known many of these guys for a long time, was it possible they'd feel differently about me if they knew I was in love with another man? Why hadn't I realized how naive I'd been about this?

Carter reached a hand over and placed it over mine on the table. I started to pull away, feeling sudden, self-conscious nerves I'd never experienced before, but he tightened his grip. "Just stay still for a minute," he said through a fake smile. "Humor me." His thumb brushed intimately over the back of my hand, and he toyed with my fingers while he started flirting with me.

Sure enough, it only took a minute before two of the five guys sitting with Clyde eyeballed us with a noticeably peeved expression on their faces.

My entire body tightened.

"Shit," I said, pulling my hand back and taking the shot of Jameson that had magically appeared in front of me. I was pretty sure if a doctor ordered it for me, it was considered medicinal. "You made your point."

He reached for my hand again, and I let him take it. This time he squeezed it. "This is too new for you to really know how you're going to handle things long term. It's not about you and Tucker, Dunn. It's about *you*. He's scared you're going to have regrets. That it's going to be too hard. Hell, lots of gay guys worry when they date someone who's bi. Maybe it's not rational, but we think they'd have an easier life if they left us to find a good woman instead."

He studied me and squeezed my hand again before letting go. "He's scared, Dunn. That's all."

Chuck Grimball stood up from the table of guys and wandered over to us with a frown on his face. "What in the hell are you doing?" It was clear they'd had almost as much beer as I had. Lord only knew why they weren't at work. "Holding hands with this guy? Are you crazy? What's gotten into you, Dunn?"

By then, I was fired up and ready to take no shit from anyone. I scrambled my way out of the booth and stood face-to-face with him. "What's it to you, huh? You got a problem with me?"

He poked me in the chest. "Yeah, I got a problem with you. My mama has spent three weeks talking about getting you together with Doc Wright, and now you're here with this guy? What the hell, man? Tucker deserves better."

Two of the guys plus Clyde all nodded their agreement while I stared at him in disbelief. Carter muttered, "Well, of course."

I finally grinned like a loon. "I love you, man. You're looking out for my baby." I slapped Chuck on the shoulder and turned to Carter with a giant grin on my face. "He's looking out for my man. See there? He cares about me and Tuck."

Chuck looked confused. He thumbed over his shoulder at Carter. "So why you cheating on him with this guy?"

I sighed. Why did people have to be assholes? "I'll have you know this guy is a good man," I shouted, shoving Chuck in the chest. "He takes care of people's *hearts*. Do you know how incredible that is? How smart you have to be to do that? He takes care of my daddy's broken heart!" I shoved him again and wobbled a little bit myself. What was in that shot?

Carter stood up and threw some cash down on the table. "I think maybe it's time to go, big guy."

"There is nothing wrong with being a pretty boy!" I added. "Also? Until you've had your dick sucked by someone who has a dick, you don't even know how good it can be. You don't even *know*, do you hear me? You..." I pointed in a circle in the general direction of all the guys sitting with Clyde. It made me a little dizzy, if I was being honest. "All of you don't. Even. Know."

I was riled up, my adrenaline spiking because I was very aware now that things could have ended very differently and probably would have anywhere but Licking Thicket where these guys had known me half my life.

Carter mumbled some polite crap at them and grabbed me by the elbow. "Time to go, hot stuff," he muttered as we made our way through Private's and out into the fresh air of Great Nuthatch.

"That's right," I said, suddenly remembering something. "You gotta get to your lunch with Dr. Petersmith and Mr. Right."

He chuckled softly. "In case you didn't notice, it's five o'clock in the afternoon. Lunch was a long, long time ago."

He was right. I looked around in surprise and saw the sun was much lower in the sky. "When did that happen? Wait. You let Tuck go alone? What if the Petersmith guy talks him into moving away?"

"Tucker canceled. Texted me to say something had come up."

I stopped in my tracks and stared at him. "Is he okay?"

Carter shrugged as if the answer wasn't important. It was. It was really important.

"Is he okay?" I repeated, this time much louder.

Carter held up a finger and pulled out his phone. After dialing it, he held it up to his ear. "Hi, Jenn, it's Dr. Rogers. Is Dr. Wright available? … Mmhm. Okay. No, it's not urgent. I'll call him later. Thanks."

He put the phone back in his pocket and said, "He's with a patient right now. He's fine. You, however, are not fine. Let's get you home and in bed. You're swaying so badly you're going to fall on your face."

"Am not." I took a step toward the car, missed the curb, and fell on my face.

17

TUCKER

18-Across: Plan, contrive, concoct (6 letters)

"AH, MOTHER*FUCKER*," I hissed as my penknife once again slipped against the wisteria in my hand and sliced into my fingertip. "Welp, there goes the pinkie."

"Y'okay, Doc?" Vienna stuck her head into the open door of my office. She glanced down at my vine-covered desk sympathetically. "Need another Band-Aid?"

"No," I muttered around the finger in my mouth. Then, realizing I was being both petulant *and* unhygienic, I changed my mind. "Okay, maybe."

Vienna winked and ducked back out.

It was absolutely ridiculous that a grown man couldn't twine a vine without needing five — *now six* — Band-Aids, but nobody had warned me how dangerous this shit was.

As it turned out, wisteria vines were more like big honking wisteria *branches*, at least when you were the one guy in all of Licking Thicket who hadn't had the foresight to source some cute, whippy little ones weeks ago and didn't have time to soak your branches overnight to ensure what Jay Proud called "maximum twinin' compliance."

The only branches Jay had left were wrist-thick, hardy ones that had grown in their own peculiar patterns over the years. They weren't even what a person could call *minimally* compliant. This morning, high on love and optimism, that had seemed kinda symbolic of me and Dunn—solid, strong, unique. I could totally work with that.

Five Band-Aids later, I'd begun to doubt.

"I just wanna make a heart," I'd told Jay in a quick, panicked phone call around the time I was supposed to have been sitting down to lunch with Dr. Petersmith at the lunch I'd hastily cancelled. "But this vine is all twisted and won't lay flat. I think it's defective!"

"Nah, nah. You gotta work *with* the vine, Doc," Jay the wisteria guru had admonished. "Let it be what it's going to be, and don't stress so much about perfection."

Which, okay, was maybe even more symbolic.

I'd scrapped my original wreath idea and come up with something better. Something more me and Dunn.

And now it was finally, finally done.

"Here we are!" Vienna came bustling back in with a bandage and a tube of antibiotic ointment. "Well, now." She glanced down at the wreath on the desk. "Isn't that a mighty fine, ah… twisty shape… you've got there."

"It's a clinch knot," I informed her. "You know, the kind of knot you use to tie the lure to your fishing pole?"

"Nope." She smiled blankly. "Not a clue."

"Oh. Well…" I took a deep breath and admitted, "It's for Dunn."

"Yeah, honey, I figured. But…" She pursed her lips as she wiped off my cut and dabbed ointment on it. "I sorta wondered if you mightn't be making something a teensy bit more… romantical? Not to say your clutch knot—"

"Clinch knot."

"Right. It's cute, but it doesn't exactly scream, 'Let's stop dillydallyin' and start shackin' up,' if that was what you were going for."

I narrowed my eyes. "Wait, you knew? About me and Dunn being…?"

"An item? Well, sure." Vienna blinked and wrapped the bandage around my finger. "Was it meant to be a secret? Anyone who hasn't known about you two for *months* must be willfully blind."

I didn't bother correcting her about how long Dunn and I had actually been together. I was starting to think the two of us fell in that willfully blind category.

Vienna gasped. "Oh, wait! So does that mean that the other morning when I saw him clomping down the back stairs, and his eyes got all wide and he dropped to the ground and somersaulted himself into the mudroom yelling, 'You haven't seen me, Ms. Vienna!' he was actually trying to be sneaky?" She shook her head. "I thought he was just being Dunn."

I rubbed my bandage-covered hand over my forehead.

This was the man I wanted to entwine myself with for all of eternity.

I probably should have felt something other than bone-deep contentment at the idea.

"To put your mind at ease, I'll tell you that this is *very* 'romantical.'" I tapped my wreath. "You know Dunn and I go fishing a lot? Well, back when we started spending time together, I thought he was the handsomest man I'd ever seen. There was just something about him that made my heart say *this guy right here*, you know?"

"Aww." Vienna's mouth pursed in an exaggerated frown, and she pressed a hand to her heart.

"I got so nervous around him. *So* nervous, Vienna. My

stomach would flutter, and my breath would get caught… and even though I'd been tying clinch knots since my pawpaw taught me to fish when I was *four*, I could not for the life of me make my fingers cooperate. I'd end up tangling the line every single time. So Dunn started doing it for me."

He'd slide over next to me, whether we were sitting up on the bridge or down on the dock at his cabin, frown down at what I'd attempted, and then give me a sweet smile. "Don't you worry, Tuck," he'd say. "You can't be good at everything."

"And I kept letting him." I laughed lightly. "All this time, I've let him. All these months and years. And now… well, now it's time to tell him why."

"Is he coming over to get you, then?" Vienna asked excitedly. "Now?"

"Er. Not exactly." I stared down at my phone, which had remained stubbornly silent all day, despite me leaving Dunn half a dozen messages and texting at least a few more. It wasn't like him not to answer me.

Then again, he'd never been quite as mad at me as he'd gotten this morning, and I didn't totally blame him. That was why, as the day went on and he still hadn't returned my calls, I'd thrown myself further into making my wreath, snatching pockets of time between patients and during lunch, when I should've been talking to Dr. Petersmith.

If Dunn needed me to make a big apology, I would. He deserved at least that much from me.

"I'm heading out to his farm to see him," I decided on the spot, standing up and dusting off my pants.

"Good idea. Maybe bring him some of that cake you've got in the kitchen freezer under the asparagus spears. Or the chocolate pie you're hiding out in the garage."

I paused and blinked up at her. Clearly *none* of my secrets were as secret as I'd thought.

"You go on," she said, shooing me out the door. "I'll clean up the mess."

I grabbed my wreath... er, wreath-esque creation... off the desk and pressed a quick kiss to Vienna's cheek. I called Dunn's number one more time as I headed for the front stairs, but it just kept ringing.

"Oh, hey, Jenn?" I called as I passed the reception desk, tucking the phone against my chin and my wreath under my arm. "Do me a favor and reschedule my first couple morning appointments tomorrow, please?" If everything went as well as I expected, I'd be spending the evening at Dunn's place, and I didn't want to rush back.

"Oooh, sorry. Can't," Jenn said. She finished applying lip gloss and made kissy-faces in her little mirror before shutting the mirror with a snap. "I'm heading out any minute."

"Out?" I frowned as I glanced down at my phone and disconnected the call. It was just about five thirty, and even though my last scheduled appointments were done, she was supposed to be here booking appointments and taking messages until six. "Did you clear that with Vienna?"

"I didn't think I had to," she said, sounding bored. "*You* might not be aware, Doc, but today's the Entwinin.' Those of us who have sweethearts have plans. It's an expected thing. You don't ask for the day off on Thanksgiving."

I blinked. Jenn had a sweetheart? I had no idea. I wondered if she'd gotten back with Monster from the Devoted Dogs, and then wondered uncharitably whether *he* had an "in" on the Beautification Corps, since that seemed to be Jenn's criteria for romantic partners. For all I knew, he did.

"It's not *quite* like Thanksgiving," I said wryly. "But far be it from me to stand in the way of you and your sweet-heart. Just let Vienna know when you're —"

The front door opened with a jingle of bells and Cody Remer from Jackson's Flowers stepped inside, panting and sweating despite his uniform of shorts and a polo shirt. "Uh. Hey, Doc. Hey, Jenn. I, uh." He pressed a hand to his stomach and stood straight, trying to draw oxygen. "*Phew*. Sorry it's so late, but I've got a wreath delivery for you, Jenn. The guys've been working on it all day. They said they've never worked on one so big before. I'll just, ah…" He glanced out at the front yard uncertainly and then seemed to size up the doorframe. "I mean, I guess I could bring it in? But it might be a bear and a half to get it back out. It was all I could do to hustle it down the street. Had to stop for water twice," he added as an aside to me.

Jenn tittered. "Oh. My. Word. A wreath for *me*? How lovely and completely unexpected!" She took a second to bend over and jiggle her boobs into place inside her bra, while Cody and I exchanged a quick look and then studiously glanced at the ceiling. She smoothed her tight sweater dress down and grabbed her purse from the bottom drawer of the reception desk. "I'll be happy to come outside, Cody!"

This I had to see.

So, apparently, did everyone else in the Thicket, because when I stepped outside, it was to find no less than a dozen Thicketeers assembled on the sidewalk looking at the… the… the… *thing* on my tiny front lawn.

The thing was more like an Entwinin' *topiary* than a wreath, nearly as tall as a redwood, and I could not imagine how many wisteria vines had to be sacrificed for this homage to bad taste. On the bottom was a vine-shaped outline that looked vaguely like an SUV, if I had to venture a guess. On top of that was the enormous shape of a house, complete with wisteria windows, a wisteria roof, and a wisteria door. Above the house, thicker vines spelled out the word L-O-V-E, where the *O* was very clearly a diamond ring, and on top of *that* was a heart... made out of the exact whippy kinds of vines I hadn't been able to find.

"What the frickity freak is that?" I demanded of no one in particular.

Jenn gave me a satisfied smile over her shoulder. "*That* is an Entwinin' wreath." She clasped her hands and stared at it with a happy sigh. "The kind I deserve."

"Merciful heavens," Vienna whispered from behind me.

"Jesus, please us." Carter pushed open the little gate by the sidewalk and came up the walkway, taking care to keep a distance from the Entwinin' pillar, lest it should reach out and suck him in. "I thought you said this shit was supposed to be *symbolic*, Tucker," he said as he climbed the steps. "Constancy in the midst of change or whatever. What is *this* fuckery? Have I mentioned that this town is a hoot?"

"Who the heck paid for this thing?" Dot Johnson shook her head.

"Who's dreamed it up?" Monette Ivey, Ava's mother, called from the sidewalk. "That's what I'd like to know."

"Oh, yes, Cody!" Jenn said, her eyes positively glowing. "Where's the card? In fact... in fact, why don't you read it out loud?"

Cody patted his pockets, plainly panicked. "Shoot! I don't... I think... I must've left it back at the shop. It, uh... it definitely said 'To Jenn.' And then, uh..." He scrunched up his forehead in confusion. "Thanks for being patient. I'm ready for a commitment to you, my darling. And then... I love you." Cody expelled a breath like he'd passed a test.

Carter looked at me, wide-eyed, and I... well, I couldn't take my eyes off the monstrosity in front of me.

"And?" Birdie Johnson demanded.

"A-and?" Cody looked around, bewildered. "And that was all, I swear."

"But who sent it?" Colin Richards said, shifting his little daughter up on his hip. "Who was the card from?"

"Oh, that." Cody waved a hand. "It said 'Dunn Johnson.'"

"Yes, it did," Jenn breathed.

Uhhh. What?

No way. There was... there was simply no way.

I felt the weight of a dozen gazes—every assembled person *except* Jenn, who studiously avoided looking at me—but I couldn't think of a damn thing to say. There were no words forceful enough.

And then a limousine pulled up to the curb and honked. "Car for Jennifer Shipley?" the driver called through the open window.

"That's me!" Jenn yelled back, waving a hand excitedly. "Dunn and I have a date at the Italian place. I might be a bit late tomorrow morning, Doc." She tossed me a wink. "If he proposes, I might not be in at all! Night!" She skipped lightly down the steps to where the driver was waiting with an open door and a glass of champagne.

I felt like my feet were rooted to the spot.

How? *Why?*

He'd invited *me* to the Italian place, damn it.

Jenn was stealing the date that should have been mine!

The second the car pulled away, I sucked in a breath and whirled for the door, then ran back to the mudroom to grab my car keys. I let myself out the back door without even closing it and headed for my car.

Carter stepped in my path.

I huffed out a breath and clenched my fists by my sides. "Carter, get out of my way. I have a date to crash and possibly a man to hog-tie, kidnap, and stow in my basement. Unless you're willing to go down for a felony with me, let me go."

"Tucker Wright, I care about you. I'm not letting you go off half-cocked," Carter said in a warning tone. "You've gotta know Dunn Johnson was not responsible for that... thing on the lawn." He waved a hand toward the Entwinin' Pole.

"Of course I know that!" I scoffed. "Jenn ordered it herself. She had to have. Couldn't have been any more clear if she'd spelled out the word DESPERATE instead of LOVE."

"Okay," Carter said with a relieved breath. "Okay, then. So you've gotta know Dunn's not on any hot date with Jenn right now either—"

"Oh, no." I shook my head. "No, that I do *not* know. That is exactly the sort of wrongheaded thing he *would* do, because for an intelligent, capable, loving man, he's an utter *fool* when it comes to relationships just like I am, and..." I was mortified to find myself on the verge of tears. "And I hurt him very badly earlier, and I may have pushed him past the point of no return. I *told* him to go be with Jenn, and for the first time in our friendship, it seems the man took me at my word. Now for fuck's sake, Carter, stand aside so I can catch that limo!"

"Or. *Orrrr.*" Carter spun me around, laid an arm over my shoulder, and forcibly walked me toward the sidewalk. "You could stick with me, and we could chat about this, and you could remember that you are a reasonable, rational individual, in possession of a big brain and good sense. Then you could go and talk to Dunn *calmly,* laying out all your fears and hopes for the future, and—"

"Carter, I know you mean well, but that sounds stupid." I shook my head miserably. "It was my big, overthinking brain that got me into this mess! I called Dunn all day long, and he didn't answer his phone. He's obviously been stewing in anger all day—"

"Oh, he's been stewing in something," Carter muttered.

"What?"

"Nothing," Carter said hurriedly. "What were you saying?"

"I was saying Dunn's clearly pissed, and—" I moved my arm in a sweeping circle… and my silly Entwinin' wreath fell out. I'd forgotten it was even there.

Well. Looked like I wouldn't be needing it this year, didn't it?

"You know what? Never mind." I dropped the silly thing on the ground and kicked it over to the fence.

Miss Sara, who made the best frosting in town, was the most senior member of the Beautification Corps, and was also a local judge—thus making her three times more powerful than any human had a right to be—met me on the sidewalk with a sympathetic smile.

"Tucker, honey, not to, er… add to your troubles, but we have zoning laws against… this sort of thing inside the town limits," she said, blinking at the wreath. "You're gonna have to move that from your property within three days or be fined."

Fucking figured.

"Miss Sara, how does one apply for a burn permit here in the Thicket?"

She blinked. "Oh, I… Er. Over at Town Hall, I suppose."

"Excellent. Bonfire at my place tomorrow," I said with a tight smile. "I'll supply marshmallows. Carter?" I called. "Carter, I thought we were walking here."

"We are!" Carter jumped up from where he'd been kneeling on the ground a couple of paces back and tucked something in his jacket pocket. "Just, ah… tying my shoe."

"I changed my mind." I stalked down the street toward the center of town, not waiting for Carter to catch up. "I spent the whole dangity day constructing a wreath I'll never get to use. If I'm not interrupting their date, I'm going to the Tavern. I'm gonna have a few shots of that whiskey Dunn likes—"

"Jameson," Carter supplied.

"Yeah." I shot him a suspicious glance. "How'd you know?"

"Lucky guess," he said smoothly. Then he sighed. "Come on. I'll buy the first round."

"Isss jess that he's such a *good man*," I explained to Carter, four or seventy minutes later. "The *best* man. I dint *wanna* love him. I couldn't help it."

"Yes, yes, so you've said. Twelve times in the last ten minutes." Carter glanced up from whatever the heck he was typing into his phone and sounded a trifle bored. "You'll note that I'm not arguing. From all my observations, he seems like a very good guy. Very devoted."

I closed my eyes and nodded. Even people who didn't like Dunn thought he was a good man. That said something.

I wasn't sure what, but I'd ponder it later.

"Devoted. Thass exackly it. He loves his mama, and he loves Red, and Gracie and the girls, and Brooks and Mal. And he loves *me*." I sniffed and twirled an empty shot glass on the table. "And Bern'dette."

"His cat."

"Nah, his pet pig," I said happily. "He pretends she's not his pet pig, but I think that's 'cause Dunn's not so great at recognizing the truth of things right away."

"Like… recognizing that his cat is a pig?"

"What? No. Jeez, Carter. Pay attention. He doesn't realize that his pig is a pet, just like he didn't realize that his friend was his true love. But if you're gonna make someone a bed under the dining table near the heating duct to keep them warm, I think that means you care about them more than average, wouldn't you say?" I snorted and shook my head.

Carter's jaw dropped. "Dunn makes you sleep under his dining table?"

I blinked. "Carter, I think you might be a li'l bit drunk."

"After this day?" He nodded. "It's entirely possible that I'm drunk off fumes."

"Bern'dette. The pig. Sleeps under the dining table. Obviously."

Carter hesitated. "I just want to be sure I'm getting this finally. Bernadette—who is definitely a pig—sleeps under Dunn's dining room table. Inside the house."

I nodded. "Bern'dette was a runt, you know? Dunn had to keep her really warm and bottle-feed her every few hours for seven weeks 'cause her mama wouldn't." I held up seven fingers in demonstration. "An' he heard that talking to piglets helps 'em thrive, so he took to watching sitcom reruns with her, as you do, all night, every night, and singing songs with her. She still squeals when she hears the theme song to *Golden Girls*. Then he'd wake up and do all his regular farm chores with just Lu for help during the day. But he didn't complain, 'cause that's just what Dunn does."

Carter nodded and pushed my water glass in front of me. I drank without thinking.

"You know," I whispered. "When I was a kid, I wanted to be a doctor 'cause I thought it was the coolest thing ever to fix people, but what Dunn does… it's even better." I lifted my eyes to Carter's. "He takes care of living things.

He nurtures them. He keeps them safe and lets them grow. I respect him so much for that."

"Wow." Carter blinked, then blinked some more. "Shit. Okay, he really *is* the best man. I *wish* someone would say something that profound about me. Ever." He huffed out a laugh. "Have you told him that?"

I shook my head. "I never, never did. At first, it seemed too sappy, you know? Not the sort of shit one friend tells another friend while fishing. And then, now that we're not just friends… it never occurred to me it was something he needed to hear." I blinked. "I think maybe that's the problem, Carter. Me and Dunn are just *too* close friends."

"Oh, good Lord," Carter said softly, rolling his eyes. His fingers punched his phone keys faster.

"No, no! Hear me out! Iss like… there are all these things we think we know about each other, right? 'Cause we've known each other so long and so well? But everything's changed now. And we can't go around making ass… ass…"

"Assumptions?"

"Assussshuns," I agreed. "I shoulda told him days ago that I was scared. But I dint. I got all the wis… the wis…" I frowned. "The *branches* to make a wreath, and I… I… I… *entwined* them in a knot that was all symbolical. And I was gonna give it to him tonight in a big perfect speech and explain the symbolicalness, and then our fight was gonna be over and Dunn would love me again. I got all these Band-Aids for nothing." I held up my bandaged fingers sadly. "I shouldna waited for perfection, 'cause that's silly. I shoulda just said the things. Because if you can't be all the way honest with the person you love, Carter, then what even good is the love?" I banged the table gently. "What. Even. Good. Is. The. Love?"

"Uh-huh. *Uh-huh*! There's that crossword-solving vocabulary I've come to expect!" Carter encouraged.

"I do love him!" I insisted... possibly loudly, given the number of people who turned toward me. "I love Dunn Johnson. And I will never leave him and go to Nashville because I don't want a life that he's not in. And I want him with me no matter what, even if he's right now eating tater tots with Jenn at the Italian place."

I frowned. Did they serve tots at the Italian place?

No matter. I would forgive him his betrayal.

Then I would tie him to my bed and make him eat tater tots with *me* until the end of time.

"I will fight for him, Carter. An' I will care for him. An' I will nurture him too. An' I will not give up, even if he is a fool." I belched delicately. "Or even if we both are."

Carter glanced up from his phone again. "Praise Jesus, we've had a breakthrough." He lifted a hand to call Ethan over. "Ethan, buddy, can you get Doc Wright here a burger and the strongest coffee you can manage? We've got places to be in exactly... forty-six minutes."

I narrowed my eyes, but I couldn't quite get Carter to focus. "Whass happening in forty-six minutes? Are we goin' to get Dunn? Who do you keep texting, anyway?"

"You'll find out in forty-six minutes, buddy. And for the sake of my liver, let's hope it sticks this time."

FORTY-THREE MINUTES later I was significantly more sober and exponentially more pissed off as Carter's fancy-assed Porsche-a-rarri—whatever the heck you called it—hit every rut and bump on the road to Dunn's fishing cabin, making my stomach slosh uncomfortably.

"I keep telling you, this is not where he *is*, Carter. This is our speshul—ahem, *special*—spot. Dunn wouldn't take Jenn here, even if he was mad at me."

Carter was not listening to me.

"I've got an ETA of two minutes, Daisy Duke," he said into his phone. "And on a five-point drunkenness scale, we're at..." He glanced at me consideringly, and the car hit another nasty bump. "Eh. I'd say a 4.0? Mostly sober, but I had to help him into his seat belt, and he's ornery as hell."

"Ornery! Yeah, I'm ornery! You'd be ornery too if you were basically being kidnapped and taken in the wrong direction—" I began.

I heard a voice answer back that sounded suspiciously like Cindy Ann's. "We'll be there in three, Doctor Strange. And we're at a 4.8 on the drunkenness scale: massively hungover and snarling like a black bear."

Carter glanced at me again and hesitated. "Daisy, are you sure this is... wise, all things considered?"

"Meh. Wise went out the window a while ago. It's *necessary*," the possibly-Cindy Ann-person said firmly.

"And it's fucking *fun*," a voice that was almost definitely Brooks's added.

"Carter. Rogers. What is going on?" I folded my arms over my chest.

"You'll find out in 1.5 minutes," he said.

When we reached the front of the cabin, the driveway was empty in the twilight.

"See? I told you." I unfolded myself from Carter's little sports car and spun in a circle. "No Dunn. No Jenn. No cars. No—hey!" I exclaimed as Carter reached over and slammed my door, then locked it. "Carter, what the hell are you... Where are you going?"

Carter drove twenty feet away, then stopped and rolled down his window. He threw something onto the driveway at my feet. "You'll thank me for this, Tucker Wright! At least… I really, really hope you will."

"Get back here!"

But it was too late. Carter's car was nothing more than brake lights on the driveway.

"I am going to *kill* him. I am going to tell Cindy Ann to set him up on three dates a day. I am going to make him a hundred dating app profiles. But first I am calling for a ride."

I patted my pocket for my phone, which I knew for *sure* had been there when I got in the car, because Carter made me show it to him before he helped me with my…

"Oh my God, you stole my phone, you fucker?" I screamed to the night. "This is betrayalllll!"

I kicked the ground and found that I'd actually kicked… "My wreath?"

I bent down and picked it up. How the hell had Carter gotten it? And what the actual fuck was going on?

The sound of an engine roaring up the driveway made me straighten.

Thank *fuck*.

I'd gotten as far as yelling, "This is the most irresponsible excuse for a practical joke I have ever—" before the car made it into the clearing… which was when I noticed it wasn't Carter's sports car—it was a plain, white van, and it barely slowed down before the side door slid open and a very large *something* hopped out and hit the dirt with a squeal.

"*Deesus Cwist!*" the something said, and I'd know that pissed-off voice anywhere.

"Dunn? Oh, holy shit. Dunn, baby, what's happened?" I dropped to my knees beside him in the dirt. In the dim light, I saw that he was kneeling with a bandana tied loosely around his mouth and another around his wrists in front of his body.

"Love you, boys!" Cindy Ann Johnson called from inside the van. "Be back tomorrow!"

"Haul ass, Mama," Gracie called from the passenger seat. "Before either one of them sobers up."

"Mama, you are the worst kidnapper ever," Brooks muttered. "Now hurry up and close the door so we can get the van back to the Devoted Dogs. They've gotta prep for their Meals on Wheels delivery tomorrow."

The door slammed shut, and the van disappeared down the driveway.

"I'm seriously, *seriously* gonna kill everyone involved," I muttered, fighting to loosen the ties around Dunn's wrists. "I'm pretty sure I could make it look like an accident."

"Gwet in wiine," Dunn muttered from behind the gag. He shot me a baleful look that said I was definitely on the list of "people involved."

"Excuse you!" I said, immediately going from concerned to annoyed. "This is *not* my fault. I was dropped here, same as you."

"Yoo don ha a gag."

"Yeah, well, maybe because I wasn't being as loud as you."

The ties on his hands came free, and he reached up to pull the gag over his head, then threw it on the ground, gave me another disgruntled look, and headed for the cabin door.

I pushed out a breath and turned to follow him, half expecting him to close the door on me.

He didn't.

Instead, he stopped just inside the doorway and stared down at the cabin's hardwood floors, which had somehow been covered in... rose petals?

"Jesus. We've been Ava'd," Dunn said sourly. "I'd know that woman's handiwork anywhere."

But I couldn't say anything. I was too busy staring at the walls, where thousands of fairy lights hung like bunting, casting a warm glow on the pictures that had been hanging there so long I'd ceased to notice them.

There were pictures of gap-toothed little Dunn holding a fishing rod bigger than he was while his great-uncle Waylon stood beside him helping. Pictures of all three school-aged Johnson kids holding fish up for size comparison—Gracie's the biggest by a mile. Pictures of Waylon and Red, sunburnt on the dock, beer koozies in hand. Pictures of Dunn and Waylon when Waylon was older, frailer, and Dunn was the one propping *him* up. And there were pictures of Dunn and me too. Pictures from a fishing tournament three summers ago and one from last spring. Pictures from last Christmas when we weren't even here at the cabin, but sitting side by side at Cindy Ann's dinner table...

All the most important times in Dunn's twenty-eight years of life were commemorated on this wall.

I was in more than half of them.

I drew a shaky breath, and tears stung my eyes like I was maybe still a little tipsy.

Just tipsy enough to recognize some essential truths — like the fact that Dunn Johnson had really, truly loved me beyond measure for a long, long time, and I'd be the world's biggest fool if I didn't trust him with my heart.

Just tipsy enough to tell him so.

"Dunn," I said in a low voice, clutching my wreath in my hand. "I'm sorry."

18

DUNN

5-Down: The final part of a narrative in which matters are explained or resolved (10 letters)

I was going to kill my brother. Even though I'd made the threat hundreds of billions of times before, this time I meant it.

"Ass-face numbskull pesty little shits," I muttered, rubbing at the red marks on my wrist from where my own brother and sister had basically hog-tied me.

I also needed to add Carter effin' Rogers to the murder list. If he hadn't gotten me so drunk, I would have never been such an easy target.

Needless to say, my day had gone to hell in a wisteria-woven handbasket, and I was beyond over it.

I pulled my Entwinin' vine out of my pocket—the one I'd made weeks ago for my *best* best friend—and threw it at him. "There. Don't say I never gave you nothin'," I hollered. The little twist of vines, soft and warm from being in my pocket all day, hit him in the chest and fell to the floor with a soft tap. "Last time I'll ever be stupid enough to do that."

Tucker stared down at the little clinch knot I'd made him. I'd even attached a hand-tied bucktail jig to the end of it. The little sparkly lure looked pathetic on the cold wood floor. "The whole town thinks you gave a vine to Jenn," he whispered. "And you were gonna take her out to dinner."

Now, that just made me madder. "Like hell. And for you to even suggest such a thing makes me see red like... like I can't even tell you how much. Have you lost your mind? Who do you think I am?" My voice was getting progressively louder as I went on which reminded me I was hungover despite still being half-drunk. "Do you actually think I give one iota of a shit about Jenn pain-in-my-ass Shipley? For real?"

As I shouted, Tuck's eyes grew wider. He finally snapped and joined the fray. "That girl is in love with you, and you treat her like dog shit."

Well, that just took the cake. "That girl wants my bath bomb business and my mama's sponsorship on the Beautification Corps. She's been using me all along thinking I'd give her status or something. I don't know. But I do know she doesn't know beans about me as a man." I ran my fingers through my hair and sighed. "And also? That accusation is really rich coming from you. Because *I* am in love with *you*, and you treat *me* like dog shit!"

The harsh words filled the room like poison gas. Tuck's face fell and his eyes filled with tears. I rushed forward and took him in my arms. "Shit, shit. I'm sorry, baby. I'm so sorry." I would have said anything to get him to stop crying. I hated seeing him upset. It made the whole world wobble on its axis.

"No, I'm the one who's sorry," he said in a broken voice. "I didn't trust you. I didn't listen. I... I..."

I pulled back and tipped his chin up before swiping at the wet streaks on his cheeks. "You were scared," I said gently. "I know."

"I love you so much," Tuck said hesitantly. "And I'm terrified that this isn't going to last. What do I do if this doesn't last?"

I held his face in my hands. "You come back to me and *make* it last." I glared at him. He was the best thing that ever happened to me, but I couldn't take much more of his hesitation. It was killing me. "Because I'm not letting you go. This—what we're trying to have between us right now —has to last because that's the only way I can picture my life anymore. Do you get what I'm saying?"

"I love you," he said again. Tears spilled some more, but this time I leaned in and kissed them away.

"'Course you do," I said roughly. "I'm a delight."

I took his mouth with mine, starting off as gently as I could stand before stepping closer and bringing the rest of our bodies together. As soon as I felt his hard-on brush against the front of my leg, I couldn't hold back anymore.

"Need you," I growled. "Need you so badly. Want you to fuck me. I need you to know I'm all in."

Tuck looked kiss-drunk and dazed. "You don't need to prove yourself to me."

I shook my head and let out a low laugh. "You don't get it. I want it all with you. I want to try everything. I did some online searches and… I may have made a list. But I want to start with that—you inside me. I want to know how it feels and how it makes you feel. It feels so fucking good when I'm inside you, when I look at your face. God, Tuck. I want you to feel that too."

After picturing all that, my dick was hard as nails. I groaned and pressed it into his stomach. "Please," I added. "I'm not trying to brush off your concerns. I know we need to talk about lots of things, and I made a list of those too. But first... first I want to get naked and put my hands all over you, kiss your face off, and make you come. I can't think straight until then, okay?"

Tucker smiled at me, his expression so full of affection it made my throat tight. "Okay." He leaned in and nuzzled into my neck, pressing tiny kisses against my skin and teasing me with the tip of his tongue.

Some kind of faint instrumental music played in the background, no doubt my sister's influence on the romantic scene. Candles were lit everywhere, and a fire crackled in the fireplace. I gently extracted myself from Tuck's embrace and led him over to the bed. There were rose petals everywhere which made me blush for some reason.

I couldn't imagine my family preparing this love nest for me and Tucker, but at the same time, their shenanigans tonight were such an obvious sign of their approval of our relationship, it made me feel seen and loved.

"Your family did this," he said, reading my mind. "It means..."

"I know."

"It means *everything*." His voice was rough with emotion as he turned me to face him. "Dunn, I'm so sorry I hurt you. I never want to hurt you. Ever."

I stepped closer and began to peel his clothes off. "I know. And I'm sorry I blew up at you today. You know that's not usually how I roll. I just felt so frustrated and helpless. I couldn't figure out how to convince you my feelings were real. This isn't a phase or an experiment. It's like..." I tried to put it into words he could understand. "It's like coming out of anesthesia. Yes, it's a little rough and you're not yourself at first, but it keeps getting better and you become more and more of yourself after a while. Only now... whatever was broken is fixed. Ultimately, you feel better. You wouldn't want to go back to being broken again or... or sedated even."

Tuck bit his top lip to keep from laughing, so I pinched him. "Shut up," I muttered. "I'm a farmer, not a fancy wordsmith."

"I don't know. You seem to do pretty well with words most of the time." He was shirtless now, and my eyes were locked on his dark pink nipples hardening in the chill of the room. I reached out and ran my thumb across one. Tucker sucked in a breath. "You going to miss having big breasts to fondle?"

I met his eyes and held them as I moved in and took the tight bud between my teeth and ran my tongue over it. My hands grasped his sides and held him still while I tortured the sensitive spot. "Do I look deprived?" I asked slowly while moving over to assault his other nipple. I unbuttoned my pants as I sucked and nibbled and shoved both jeans and boxer briefs down to show him how rock hard I was for him. My dick looked like the Washington Monument shooting straight into the sky.

"Flaccid," he teased breathlessly. "Poor guy. There's pills for that, you know."

"Mm." I sank to my knees and moved my teeth and tongue in little seeking nibbles down to his belly button. "Maybe I need to see a medical professional."

He let out a soft chuckle. "You're going to make me play naughty doctor one day, aren't you?"

I grinned up at him and nodded. "Proctologist, probably. And it's going to be my first internal exam. Go easy on me, Doc. Gentle fingers."

He rolled his eyes. "I'm never going to be able to give another prostate exam again without thinking of this moment. You owe me."

I took his hot dick in my mouth and ran my tongue

around it aggressively, enjoying every single gasp and groan that came out of Tucker's mouth. "Fuck, D. You're killing me. Please tell me someone left some lube here. Want you to *fuckkkk*!"

After a few good sucks, I pulled off and stood up to finish getting my clothes off. "Nope. You're doing the fucking. Lube is in the drawer. Always prepared. It's actually the kind you have at your house in case there's something special about it you like. I also keep an extra set of your clothes here, a set of your toiletries in the bathroom, and your favorite snacks in the cupboard. And if you didn't know that already—"

He shoved me off-balance, and I fell backward onto the bed. "Stop talking, Dunn Johnson," Tucker growled, climbing on top of me and attacking my skin with kisses and bites. I grabbed his bare ass with my hands and squeezed. He was so fucking sexy, it made me wonder exactly what kind of alternative universe I'd been living in before that I hadn't noticed. How had I not gotten hard every time we'd touched or every time I saw him without his shirt on? Hell, even smelling his armpits turned me on now, and that was supposed to be disgusting.

It wasn't. Not one single bit. I'd watched a video online about people who identified as straight until well into adulthood before falling in love with someone unexpected. One of the stories was about a woman who, like me, had gotten closer and closer to her best friend until it turned into sexual attraction. During the interview, she'd talked about becoming so close to her friend, she wanted to share everything with her, even her sexual pleasure and exploration.

That's exactly how I felt. To me, this was an extension of the closeness we'd already been building for so long. Knowing no one else was ever going to come between us was both a relief and also thrilling. I'd always felt uninhibited around Tuck anyway, so now I got to be uninhibited with my sexual partner.

I'd never been afraid to tell Tucker my biggest fears or my scariest hopes and dreams. And now... now the person I got to spend my life with was the person I could be myself around. Completely and utterly.

It was like falling in love with myself, only a version way hotter and smarter and sweeter.

"I just want to say one more thing," I managed to say while he assaulted me with his kisses. "I love you. I love you so much, Tucker, and I'll do anything to make you happy."

He opened his mouth to challenge me, I could tell. So, I cut him off. "Except fuck you right now. Because it's seriously my turn at receiving, and I'm not taking no for an answer. But other than that, anything."

I loved looking up at him while he was propped above me. He was so hot and familiar and *mine*, it made my heart thunk and my dick jump. "Hurry, though," I urged. "Because my balls are starting to hurt, and it's pretty awesome I can tell you that since you're a guy and you know what I'm talking about. Also, you're a doctor, so you have to know it's not good for me to have blue balls."

His cheeks turned pink as he laughed. "You're still you, aren't you? Even while we're having a moment declaring our love for each other, you're talking about your nuts."

I gave him my best pitiful look. "I think I need a doctor. My nuts are desperate."

He steamrolled across my body on purpose, squishing me into the mattress on his way to grab the lube.

"Argh!" I cried. "Suffocation isn't good for your resume, Doc Wright."

Tuck came back with the bottle of lube. "There is a very easy fix for epididymal hypertension."

"Ass fucking? Please say it's ass fucking."

He yanked off the remaining grasp my jeans still had on my ankles, then crawled back up my body, spreading my legs apart and encouraging one of my knees to bend. I was nervous, not gonna lie. But I trusted him.

"I'll need to…" He shook his head and laughed "No. You're not luring me into playing naughty doctor right now. In fact, I think it would be best if you stopped talking altogether."

I clamped my lips shut as his lubed finger found my hole. The resulting intake of breath caused me to bite my lip. "Fuck, that hurts!"

Tucker's face fell, and he yanked his hand away. "Sorry!"

"No, baby," I said, tonguing my lip. "I bit my lip. You're good. Really good. I love it when you touch me. Anywhere."

His face relaxed and he leaned against me again, reaching down to play with me. He ran a thumb across the tight skin of my balls. Watching his big, masculine fingers playing with me made my heart thunder. No one had ever made me feel so good in bed. He knew *exactly* how to touch me to make my body shake with need.

Tucker took his time, teasing me with slick fingers, and then his mouth on my dick. I changed my mind about who needed to fuck who about a thousand times, but no matter how much whimpering and begging I did, that mesmerizing man stayed the course.

Finally, fucking finally, he decided we were ready for the next step.

"I thought you already fucked me," I teased breathlessly when he pulled his fingers out of me to lube up his cock. "Skinny little thing wiggling around in there. That was you, right?"

He glared at me. "I'm going to remind you you said that in about three minutes."

When he put the fat head of his cock against my hole, I clenched and grunted. My body wasn't so sure about all of this after twenty-eight years of no-thank-you, sir.

Tucker leaned over me and put his lips to my ear. "I never told you this," he began to murmur. "But I came to Fossie Creek that day because I knew you were going to be there."

My heart seemed to stop thunking around so I could hear him. His dick pressed against me in gentle in-and-out motions. As soon as I let out a breath, I felt it stretch me open. His low voice continued.

"I overheard you telling someone at the cafe that you were headed to the bridge over Fossie Creek for some fishing. You were so good-looking, so hot and muscled and... capable. You stood there in your work clothes, dusty from the farm, and you smelled like sunshine and sweat mixed with hay and animals. You were like a walking sex poster to me, but it was more than that. I'd heard so much about you from my brother years before—stories about you looking out for people, helping people, always ducking recognition for it. And when I saw you then... as a grown man... god, D. It was like a strike to the chest with a fist."

I closed my eyes and let his words wash over me.

"I wanted you even then. Hell, I knew you were straight. You were even dating some girl at the time. But I thought... if I can just get to know him as a person, have him in my life somehow, even as a fishing buddy, that would be enough."

He was thrusting gently in and out of me as his words relaxed me, going slowly enough to let my body adjust to him. All I could do was hold on tightly and let myself drink in his voice.

"It wasn't enough," he whispered, almost to himself. "Feels like it'll never be enough."

"Shh," I said, running my fingers through his hair. "I'm here. Not going anywhere. I love you. *Fuck*, you're hung like a bull."

"Breathe, sweetheart," he murmured through a laugh. Then he pushed in again and groaned. "You feel so fucking good. So good. I never thought I'd get to feel you this way. No way am I going to last."

My hands wandered all over his arms where he held my legs up and then back into his hair. "Want you to feel good," I said. "Don't need to last."

He moved one hand until it was hot and tight around my dick. Just thinking about his dick inside me and him holding me down had made me hard again.

Tuck's teeth clenched with the effort to hold back his orgasm. "Gonna come inside you. Then I want to flip you over and pound your tight ass again. Never stop. Stay inside you all night, then roll over and let you do it to me."

His hips had picked up speed to match the pace of his hand shuttling along my dick. As soon as I imagined pounding into him, it was over.

"*Fuck! Aggh!*" I cried, shocked that I was able to come this way after being so nervous before. I threw my head back as warmth splattered against my stomach. My entire body contracted around him, and a strangled sound escaped his throat. Two more slams of his hips against my ass, and he pushed in as deep as he could to hold himself there as he groaned out his own release.

We lay in a sweaty pile of heavy breathing for a few minutes before he pulled out. It was a horrible feeling. "Never thought I'd wish your dick was still in my ass," I muttered, clenching around nothing.

He rolled to the side and ran a hand down the side of

my cheek. "That's what all the men say," he said with a wink.

Sex was a messy business. For once in my life, I didn't have to worry about being sweaty, stinky, slimy, or gross. Tucker was all those things too, and we'd never cared about that kind of stuff between us. He'd seen me covered in worse than spunk and had never blinked an eye.

I rolled over on top of him and mashed my sticky gut against him.

"Ew," he said. "You're covered in cold jizz."

My jaw dropped open in surprise.

"I'm kidding," he said, smacking my ass. "It'll turn to glue in a few minutes, and then you'll never be rid of me. That was my plan all along."

I nestled into the side of his neck, suddenly feeling a little unsure. "That was okay?"

Tucker's arms came around me and held me tightly. "You could have accidentally elbowed me in the balls and I still would have enjoyed having sex with you," he said with a low chuckle. "There's no world in which it would ever not be okay. The worst sex with you is above the best sex with anyone else."

"You think you're complimenting me, but you're kinda saying it was bad," I said into his collarbone.

The rumble of his laughter shook my chest. "There's fishing and then there's *fishing*, Dunn. You're good at the first kind, but you suck at the other."

I propped myself up so I could meet his eyes. "I'm being serious. Give me a ten scale and especially note any areas that need improvement. I'm not opposed to practicing over and over until I get it right."

"Mm, let's see. A ten scale… well, I don't have any of those nice placards to hold up, so I'm just winging it here."

"Needs must," I offered.

"Ten out of ten for willing to hang in there even when the chips were down," he said, putting a fingertip to his chin.

I nodded. "High tolerance for pain, and I ain't no coward. What else?"

"Ten out of ten for midcoital love declaration," he said, tapping his chin with the fingertip.

"Always a surefire move. The judges love it," I agreed.

"I'm going to go with an eight out of ten for the little bit of early jitters, but you ended on a high note."

I leaned in to kiss his grin. "I'll say."

His face was flushed a delicious pink, and the edges of his dark hairline were damp with sweat. His smile was infectious. "Not bad for a rookie."

I reached under his arm to tickle the one spot that always drove him crazy, and we ended up wrestling across the bed until we fell to the floor in a heap of tangled limbs.

"Shower," he demanded through heaving breaths. I was way bulkier than he was, so he never stood a chance when we wrestled. It was one of the things I loved about doing it.

I stood up and reached for him, yanking him up and smacking his ass. "Good game, son."

"I'm concerned about the various role-playing situations you've alluded to just tonight," he muttered as he marched his sexy ass in front of me to the bathroom.

"Your butt is so fucking tight," I said. "And pale as shit. It's so white, every time I catch a glimpse of it, I'm reminded no one else gets to see it but me. And that makes me wanna fuck it. Ooh! We could play cabana boy and rich tourist at a nudie resort."

"We might not be sexually compatible," he said with a frown of polite dismissal. "All this work just to discover your kinks were the deal breaker. Who would have expected such a turn of events? Shame."

I leaned past him to turn on the water in the shower. "Not true. You actually like role-playing too. You know how I know?"

Tucker narrowed his eyes at me. "I don't think I want to hear this."

But he did. He really, really did. "Because I came over to your house to fix your garbage disposal the other day and deliberately wore my lowest-riding jeans and my tightest undershirt. Then I leaned over and watched you out of the corner of my eye, Dr. Pervert. And do you know what I saw?"

He let out a nervous chuckle. "Stop. You're embarrassing yourself."

"Mm, don't think so. I saw a geeky little homeowner all a-flutter over his big strong handyman. He stared at that handyman's ass crack until a little puddle of drool formed at the edge of his mouth." I stepped into the shower and pulled Tuck with me, wrapping him up in my arms despite his struggle to evade my grasp. "And I decided right there and then that naughty little homeowners who imagine dicking down their handyman needed to be bent over the kitchen table and taught a lesson about manners. With my mouth. On your asshole."

The state of his dick proved me the winner of this little debate. I crowed in triumph until he pinched my nipple.

"Ow. Geeky homeowners are mean," I muttered, rubbing the sore spot.

"You owe me a thorough rim job," he said. "Now that we've agreed you're all fine with the gay stuff." He used finger quotes, but it wasn't a joke.

I reached for his hands and pulled them against my chest. "Okay, I'm being serious now. I had a long talk with Carter today."

Tucker stared at me in surprise. "My Carter? Carter Rogers?"

I must have made a face because he shook his head quickly and backpedaled. "I don't mean *my* Carter. I mean, oh, Carter?"

"Mmpfh. Anyway, he pointed out some things I hadn't really thought through well enough. And not because I didn't know or care, but because I've never experienced them. I don't know what it's like being judged for being with another man or being perceived as gay by someone who has a problem with it. He helped me understand better. And... all I can say is, I'm willing to learn. I'm willing to go through hard times if that's part of what happens when you and I are together. Because I can't think of something that could happen that would possibly make me think you weren't worth it."

Tucker took a deep breath and let it out. "You're a smooth-talker for a big strong handyman."

"Don't stereotype," I said with mock offense. "I expected better from a learned man such as yourself."

He searched my eyes for a beat. "You know you're smart, right? You always have an insecurity around your education, but that has nothing to do with how smart someone is. You run a large, well-respected business, and even if you didn't, even if your full-time job was scratching pigs behind their ears, I'd still love you and think you were one of the best men I'd ever met."

I puffed out my chest. "It takes a strong man to love a pig, Tuck."

He nodded solemnly. "So true."

"Not that I would know," I said with a sniff. I prepared to remind him that all of my pigs were stock animals, not pets, but he beat me to the punch.

"Since your pig is a cat," he said with a twinkle in his eye.

"You talked to Carter too," I said, lifting an eyebrow. "Since I saw you last."

"He took me out drinking," Tucker admitted.

I sighed and reached for the shampoo. "Apparently he likes to do that. Meddling bastard."

"Says the man whose family performed felony kidnapping to get us together tonight."

I began scrubbing his hair. "Crime is their love language."

He closed his eyes and preened like a cat in the sun. "I love them. You know that's the best part of dating you, right? I get them too."

I rinsed his hair off and forced him to open his eyes. "We're not dating," I said, using his finger quotes against him. "We're together. Like… the m-word."

His inky-dark lashes dripped as he blinked at me. "If you think for one minute, Dunn Johnson, that's how you're going to *propose marriage* to me —"

"What?" I squeaked, faking outrage and confusion. "Marriage? Who said anything about marriage? I was talking about moving in together. You know, the m-word… *moving.*"

He froze for a beat while his brain slowly caught up and reminded him I was a jokester asshole. "You suck," he muttered. "And that's still not a proposal. It's doubly not a proposal now."

"Don't worry," I assured him. "I have it all planned out. It goes with the rim job I owe you. You're never gonna believe where I'm planning to hide the ring."

He laughed again which was all I needed. As long as Tucker Wright was happy, I was happy and all was right with the world.

"Why did you ditch me on Entwinin' night to go out with Carter?" I asked after I got his body good and slicked up with the bar of soap.

"It's a long story, but you should know Carter was looking out for you. He likes you, and he pushed me to give you another chance. He even saved my wreath from the trash so I could give it to you."

That stopped me in my tracks. "You made me something for the Entwinin'?" I'd waited my whole life for the person I loved to make me a wreath, and Tucker had finally been the one to do it.

He nodded and his face softened. "It's a clinch knot."

"The one you don't know how to make."

"Except I do," Tuck admitted.

"I know."

"You do? Then why do you always tie it for me? And why did you make me one for my vine?"

After rinsing him off, I pulled him back into my arms and stood with him under the steady stream of hot water. "Because I always want to do the hard things for you, and I want you to know you can always count on me to try and make your life a little easier. I don't want you to ever think you have to go it alone, even if it's something as simple as tying a knot."

"You're saying tying the knot is easy?" he asked in a voice laced with love, teasing, and promise.

"With you? Easiest thing I'll ever do."

And it was.

9-Across: A particular state of bliss (8 letters)

"Friends, family, neighbors: I'd like to introduce you… for the very first time… to Mr. and Mr. Johnson!"

Red Johnson's voice boomed out over the PA system, and the group of assembled Thicketeers packed into the show barn at the town fairgrounds—which was to say *every* living resident of Licking Thicket and even a couple of honorary Thicketeers Mal and Brooks had invited from out of town—exploded into cheers and whistles.

Meanwhile Brooks and his husband had eyes only for each other. Their gazes locked, and the pure, stunned joy on their faces as their lips met in their first married kiss spread across the whole room, blanketing us with its warmth and making everyone, from the fussy babies to the crotchety old-timers, stop and smile for a moment.

Cindy Ann gave a happy little sob before running up from the front row to throw herself on Malachi's corn-flower-blue tuxedoed back and hug the stuffing out of him.

Meanwhile, Red, whose eyes had been leaking unashamedly since halfway through the service, clasped an arm around Brooks's periwinkle-clad shoulders and shook him heartily.

"Best day," he said brokenly, and it wasn't clear whether he realized he was still holding the microphone. "*Proudest* day."

Meanwhile, the other Johnson—*my* Johnson—turned around to search for me in the crowd, as he always did. When he found me standing against a pillar in the back, where I'd ended up after giving my seat to old Muriel Cribbs, he gave me a look that was half-amused and half-sentimental, as if to say, "Are you seeing this craziness?"

Oh, I was totally seeing it. Just like I saw how Brooks reached out and yanked Dunn into the group hug, and how Dunn hugged his family back, harder than anyone.

"This town," Carter said from beside me. "Is…"

"A hoot?"

"Special," he whispered.

I turned my head to look at him and did a double take. "Holy crap. Dr. Carter Rogers, are you crying right now?"

"No!" He sniffled. "Fuck, no. It's June, Wright. It's hay fever season." He sniffed again. "But if I *were*, who could blame me? It's just so *beautiful*. Almost makes a man wanna reconsider playing the name-hyphenation game someday. A distant someday. Maybe."

I blinked in shock, but before I could respond…

"Name hyphenating ain't no game, son," Amos Nutter said, catching Carter's comment as he and Emmaline Proud strode past. "Joinin' your name with another person's is a serious undertaking, whether you end up hyphenating or changing your name entirely."

Emmaline nodded, and her pink pillbox hat swayed precariously atop her gray curls. "When Amos, here, asked me to marry him last month, I was all of a dither! I've been a Proud more than half my life. My children are Prouds. My grandchildren are Prouds. I'd be giving up the proud Proud legacy and becoming a Nutter in my old age."

"And then there's me," Amos said, jabbing a thumb at himself. "I been a Nutter since the day I was born. At this point, I couldn't stop being a Nutter anymore'n I could stop breathing," he said solemnly. "I'm a Nutter to the core."

"But we love each other," Emmaline said, giving Amos an adoring look. "And whatever he is, I want to be."

"Same goes, honey." Amos patted her hand fondly. "Which was how we decided, in the end..." He shot Carter a dark look. "After *thoughtful consideration*, as it should be."

I was going to regret asking, I just knew it. "So, um... What did you decide?"

"We'll be Proud Nutters, of course," Amos said, lifting his chin regally, daring anyone to comment. "We felt the hyphen wasn't necessary."

I nodded. "Of course you will be. And I couldn't agree more."

"Now, Carter," Emmaline said, threading her arm through his. "You seem like a sweet boy. Have you met my grandson, Jaybird?"

"Your... I... That is to say... Jaybird Proud? The man who makes those... those vine wreaths?"

"The very one!" Emmaline said, pulling Carter away.

Carter's eyes pleaded at me for rescue, but at the same moment a pair of arms wrapped around my waist from behind, so I wiggled my fingers at Carter in a little goodbye wave and left him to his fate.

Carter's eyes narrowed on my waving hand, then flared wide. "Hey, wait a minute. Is that—"

I snatched my hand down quickly.

"Way to be subtle, baby," a teasing voice said in my ear.

"Well, hey," I said, leaning back against Dunn's solid strength. "If it isn't my *best* best man."

"Missed holding you," he grunted, his nose burrowing into the little hollow behind my earlobe so he could sniff me.

I knew exactly what he meant, 'cause I'd missed being held.

Still…

"It's only been twenty minutes," I teased, turning in his arms. "Surely you can go that long without me."

"Twenty *entire* minutes," he repeated. "While you and Carter were standing over here, getting all teary-eyed."

"Hey! It was a beautiful ceremony, and my man happens to slay in a cornflower-blue bow tie." I lifted my hands to his shoulders and patted his tie fondly.

"You know, it's not too late," he whispered in my ear.

"Not too late for what?" I said blithely, pretending not to know what he meant.

"Not too late for us to have the big Yes at the Steak 'n Bait. To have the ceremony and the tears and the flowers." He gestured around the barn, at the decorations that had taken the Beautification Corps the better part of a week. "And the cute little place cards, and the thousands of fairy lights hanging from the rafters, and the candles in jelly jars on the tables. The fiddle players warming up. The poor twigs that were just livin' their lives until Ava Siegel attacked 'em with a can of spray paint, festooned them with crystals, stuffed 'em in a pitcher, and used them to decorate the gift table. It's not too late for… *the hyphenation*."

"You will recall I specifically chose *no* hyphenation after giving it 'thoughtful consideration.' I do not want us forever known as the Wright-Johnsons, thus implying that there are wrong Johnsons somewhere. And I will *not* answer to

Tuck Johnson-Wright, because you just *know* someone was gonna say they tuck theirs to the left."

Dunn snorted. "And that someone was probably going to be me."

"Precisely. And the other option, where you'd take my name, was ridiculous."

"Oh, I don't know," Dunn said slowly. His big body shook with laughter, but his voice came out as a deep, sexy rumble. "I think Dunn Wright is a pretty appropriate name for me, darlin'. Especially after last night."

He pulled back just far enough to give me a wicked smile.

I shook my head, fighting back my own smile, and trailed my hands down his arms until I could twine our fingers together, then ran my thumb over the black tungsten band I'd placed on him a few days ago in a tiny chapel in Las Vegas.

"We're Mr. and Dr. Johnson," I reminded him. I lifted up on my tiptoes and leaned into him, wrapping my arms around his neck and inhaling the leather and cut-grass scent of him, reveling in the knowledge that we belonged to each other in the eyes of the law now, the way we'd belonged to each other in our hearts for years, even if we'd only gotten out of our own way and admitted it a couple of months ago. "That is the *only* thing I care about."

After the Entwinin' and our night at Dunn's cabin, things had moved at lightning speed... but it hadn't felt like they'd been going too fast, more like we were making up for lost time. We'd gone directly to Cindy Ann and Red's the next day to share the news—though Dunn had waited an entire two hours longer to tell Brooks, on account of the hog-tying—and I'd moved the better part of my Milano stash and most of my belongings into the farmhouse the following weekend.

The weekend after *that*, we'd been cuddled in bed on Sunday morning talking about what to do with my newly empty space in town when our convo had suddenly taken a turn.

"If I want to make the apartment in my house fully separate from my practice downstairs, I'd have to do a ton of construction to block off the staircase, which would be expensive and annoying." I'd trailed a lazy finger down the center of his chest and around his nipple while his hand traced patterns on my upper arm. "But at the same time, if I'm gonna be staying out here at *your* place, it'd be bad for my whole upstairs to not be used, right? I should just sell it and move my practice, I guess, but… well, I love that secret hidey-hole. Especially since my boyfriend likes to push me into it when he brings me lunch so he can kiss me silly."

"I guess it's your call in the end, since you own the place," Dunn had said in this weird, stilted way. His hand had stopped stroking my arm.

I'd snorted and lifted my head from his chest to frown at him. "And since when has that stopped you from giving me your honest opinion about anything, or stopped me from taking it? Just the same way we bought a gallon of Elegant Gray for the spare room 'cause I liked it best, even though you wanted navy blue and it's technically *your* house and *your* farm." I'd flopped back down.

Dunn had hesitated for one second, watching me from the corner of his eye, and then he'd rolled us, fast as lightning, so I was on my back underneath him. "You want my honest opinion, Tuck?"

He'd propped his elbows in the bed on either side of my shoulders, but the full weight of his lower body was resting against mine, and I'd had to spread my legs to make room. Even though he'd fucked me so beautifully and thoroughly I'd seen stars not twenty minutes before, and even though

I'd been reasonably certain I couldn't get an erection at that moment to save my soul, my eyes had still gone half-shut and I'd had to catch my breath at how good and right it all felt, which had made me just a teensy bit slow on the uptake.

"Mmmm. Always want your opinion, baby," I'd said a little breathlessly, like "opinion" was code for "dick," which it maybe kinda was.

"I think we should get married," Dunn had said.

My eyes had popped wide in shock. "We what?"

"No, no, now, just listen." Dunn's jaw had done that sideways tick it did when he was preparing to be stubborn. "You love me, I know that for an absolute fact. And you've gotta know, Tuck, that I love you just as much. I need you the way… the way… crops need rain. And without you, I'd be nothing but a rotting corn cob, waiting for the crows to peck at me."

My eyes had gone even wider. My man was no poet…

Except he also sort of was.

"And I know it's fast," he went on, like he mistakenly thought I needed convincing. "I know maybe you're thinking we haven't settled into things fully. I know we only just went public a couple weeks ago, and people are still getting used to the idea of us being together officially. Heck, Ethan at the Tavern just asked me again how much I spent on Jenn's Entwinin' wreath—"

He'd rolled his eyes.

I'd narrowed mine.

"Do *not* remind me of that woman," I'd bitten out.

There was no love lost between me and Jenn Shipley, and there never would be.

The morning after the Entwinin', she'd informed me with a sniff that she no longer needed employment, since she was going to be Monster's old lady—according to

Vienna, when Jenn and her onetime biker paramour had found themselves alone at the Italian place on Entwinin' night, they'd decided it was fate and had immediately rekindled their relationship—and she'd never really seen much of a future with a "small-time cowhand" like Dunn Johnson, anyway.

It had taken all my self-control to force a smile and give her all my best wishes. Then, on the offhand suggestion from Dunn's sister, I'd rented a wood chipper from the feed store, spent the entire afternoon turning the Entwinin' monstrosity on my lawn into mulch (much to Carter's amusement), hired a guy to dump it in her driveway as a parting gift, and gone home to let that incredibly gorgeous "cowhand" make love to me until my rage turned into passion, then soul-deep satisfaction.

The whole thing had been wildly cathartic.

But that didn't mean I'd wanted the woman's name on Dunn's lips ever again, especially not in our bed.

"But that's exactly why I'm thinking… why do it halfway?" Dunn had continued, not realizing the dark turn my thoughts had taken. "When you and me already know we're forever, Tuck, why not just go all in? Make this *our* farm. *Our* farmhouse. *Our* place in town, with that hidden closet in the office. Make it *our* future that we're building, where we're entwined until the very end."

"Oh." I'd sucked in a shuddering breath, because oxygen had suddenly been in short supply. "Oh, Dunn, I—"

Dunn had quickly pressed a kiss to my mouth to halt my words and breathed against my lips, "Wait, no! There's more. You haven't heard the best part."

"Haven't I?" I'd stared up at his handsome face in wonder. I'd been pretty confident I'd heard the best part. In fact, I'd known for *sure* that was the best thing I'd ever heard *in my life*.

"No, see, I'm not talking about us getting engaged, I'm talking about us getting *married*. And none of this business of 'How many people are you inviting from your side of the family, Tuck?' and googling 'Who gets to pick the flavor of the groom's cake when you've got two grooms?' and 'Do we spend the money on the satin bows or go for the *sateen*, and what does that say about our commitment to one another?'"

He'd shuddered, no doubt remembering Cindy Ann's most recent emergency wedding meeting, and I didn't blame him. I had a much higher tolerance for party planning than Dunn did, and even I'd been traumatized by how many *feelings* she had about the minutiae of it all.

"I don't give a damn about any of that, and I know you don't—"

I'd shaken my head. I didn't.

"And I know Brooks and Mal don't either, not really. Mal just convinced Brooks to let Mama have her fun, and that's fine for them. They don't mind the spectacle, and the Thicket is kinda what brought them together. You and me, though…" He'd stared at the pillow beside my head like he was gathering his thoughts. "We were both raised right here. You didn't leave for long, and I never left at all. All our stories are Thicket stories. And a hundred years from now, Amos Nutter will be telling young whippersnappers about those crazy kids Tucker and Dunn and all the antics we got up to over the years."

I'd snorted. "In a hundred years?"

"Amos Nutter is immortal," Dunn had said solemnly, his green eyes back on mine. "You'll never convince me he's not a vampire."

"Doctor-patient confidentiality precludes me from confirming or denying," I'd said primly.

"Precludes." Dunn's lips had twitched. "Have I mentioned how your vocabulary turns me on?"

I'd shaken my head, and Dunn had poked me in the side.

"Stop being sexy, Tucker. *Shit*. I'm tryna focus here. Where was I?"

"Amos Nutter is a vampire?" I'd blinked innocently.

"Shush. Before that."

"All our stories are Thicket stories?"

"That's right." He'd cleared his throat. "And *this* story — the story of you and me and how we got married — I want that to be *our* story. Just us."

"Okay."

"So I think we should just… just *do* it. Fly to Vegas. You and me. We'll spend the rest of our lives with my family, but this one day I want to be *ours*, eating tater tots and watching the Vegas sunset, side by side."

"Okay."

"And besides which, if we get married, that will provide a more stable home life for Bernadette, which would improve her longevity."

I'd laughed out loud and brought my hands up to frame Dunn's face. "Baby?"

"Yeah?"

"I said *okay*."

"You mean…" He'd frowned. "You mean *okay*-okay? As in, you agree with me? About getting married."

I'd nodded. "I mean, I was on the fence, but now that I know it's for Bernie…"

Dunn had poked me in the side again, and I'd sobered.

"You are all I've ever wanted, Dunn Johnson," I'd told him, pushing his hair back from his face. "Only a fool would say no to you. I can have us packed for Vegas in an hour."

Except, as it turned out, it hadn't quite happened that way.

I mean, first we'd had to spend another hour or so in bed, doing what Dunn called "pregaming the wedding night," and then, before I could even get out my phone to check my schedule or book us a flight, Lu had called from the barn to say Trippy, one of Dunn's heifers, was in labor and it looked like a tricky one.

And then Mossy and Melaina had calved too.

And then one of the Carpenter kids from out on Winter Church went to sleepaway camp and came down with the flu on her first night back... but not before sharing her water bottle with her brother, sisters, and at least three other kids in the neighborhood.

And then, somehow, April had become June, skipping May entirely, and it was time for the monthlong wedding festivities.

Thicketeers tended to get pretty excited about June in general, what with the fields all abloom, and the bass running, and the kids out of school for the summer, and the annual Lickin' on the horizon.

Thicketeers with a June wedding on the calendar were even more excited.

And Thicketeers preparing for the June wedding of their former town golden boy, Brooks, and their favorite adopted son, Malachi? Well, that went beyond excitement. The air had fairly buzzed with electricity for weeks, and they'd lost their minds with the thrill of it all. What had resulted was a jaw-dropping, once-in-a-lifetime, no-holds-barred bovine spectacular.

The celebration had begun with a two-day family-friendly bachelor extravaganza. There'd been a barbecue cookoff with Parrish Partridge judging the meats, Diesel Partridge judging the vegetarian entries, and little Marigold Partridge toddling around presenting the winners with kisses.

There'd also been a dance contest, which Amos and his Emmaline had won hands down both in the technical skill category and the endurance category—although Amos been heard telling Emmaline after the fact that he'd *had* to keep dancing for hours, since his hip had locked that way.

And there'd even been a town-wide tree house raising at the playground across from the elementary school, led by Ryder and Colin Richards and the Richards Renovations crew, to commemorate the tree house over at the Iveys' place where Mal had slept when he'd first come to town.

A week later, Cindy Ann had assembled us for a Bovine Bike Parade, in which we'd all dressed up in cow paraphernalia and ridden from the town square, to Diesel Partridge's salvage yard, to the town sign, to commemorate what Cindy Ann was calling Mal's "historic trek" to find just the right cattle brush to finish his sculpture. It had been such a good time, they were thinking of making that an annual event... which I guess was how most of the Thicket traditions had become traditions, if I stopped to think about it.

And then *last* weekend, there'd been a photo shoot for the wedding party out in Amos Nutter's field by the town sign. Amos had once again painted his herd for the occasion, arranging them to spell out "LOVE LOVE LOVE!" in rainbow letters. It hadn't been his fault the poor cows got startled by Mac Davis riding past on his Harley just before the photographer snapped the pictures and ended up spelling out "EVOL VOLE OLÉ!" (or that Juniper, the other "V," refused to come out of the trees until milking time). Fortunately Malachi hadn't seemed to mind this at all, if the way he threw his arms and legs around Brooks, kissed his face off, and said, "Thank you, Brooks Johnson, for giving me this town," was any indication.

So, what with one thing and another, it had been this past Wednesday before Dunn and I had found ourselves waking up in bed together of a morning, with nothing to worry about but ourselves for nearly forty-eight hours.

"Are you thinking what I'm thinking?" I'd asked softly when my boyfriend had kissed me awake.

Dunn had smiled the smile he only smiled for me, we'd left Lu and Carter in charge of our businesses and our Bernadette, and by the time we'd gone to sleep that night, I'd been kissing my husband.

That simple. That *us*. That perfect.

Well. Perfect… except for one teeny, tiny, honestly *infinitesimal,* little problem.

"Holy heckballs." Colin Richards rushed over, his brown eyes shining like maybe they'd opened the bar and started passing out Fuzzy Thickets already. "What is that hardware on your finger, Tucker Wright?" He pointed at my hand where it rested on Dunn's shoulder.

Shit.

I licked my lips. I cleared my throat. I searched the room for my mother-in-law, who didn't *know* she was my mother-in-law yet, and then I began to stammer.

"This is… it's… we… Funny story, actually." I forced a slightly panicked-sounding laugh. "Dunn, baby, you tell the best stories. You tell it."

See, you might think Dunn and I would have been smart enough to spend some of our time in Vegas, or maybe on the plane ride home yesterday, thinking about how we might break the news of our marriage to Cindy Ann and the rest of the Thicket…

But you'd be wrong.

We both knew the whole situation was going to take some finessing. After all, we'd kinda cheated Cindy Ann out of planning a wedding for Dunn like she'd planned for Brooks, and she was bound to be upset. Still, I was hopeful she'd forgive us in time.

We'd planned to hide it until after Brooks and Mal's wedding, for sure, so we wouldn't steal any part of their thunder, but we'd been so jet-lagged the night before that we'd forgotten to take off our rings before the rehearsal dinner. Cindy Ann had been too distracted to notice, and... well, I think we'd gotten cocky.

This morning, I'd definitely *meant* to take my ring off... but instead, I'd stood in the bathroom after my shower staring down at the metal on my finger until my husband had come up behind me and peered over my shoulder to see what I was doing.

"I like having it there," I'd told him plaintively. "Is that silly? It just seems wrong to take it off or hide it. But I guess it's just for one evening, right?"

Dunn's hand had covered mine. "Leave it," he'd said, all gruff and growly. "I like seeing it there too, baby."

Needless to say, his possessiveness had incited a predictable reaction that had involved both of us getting back in the shower, and... ahem. Here we were, still be-ringed.

And now caught.

"That," Dunn said confidently, "is one of those rings they give out in high school."

I blinked at him. So did Colin.

"You mean a class ring?" Colin's husband, Ryder, came over then, their daughter Sadie perched on his hip. "That's no ring from Licking Thicket High, man. Where's the bovine? Where's the LTH on one side and the MOO on the other?"

"Not a *class* ring," I scoffed. "Gosh, no. The... um... the other kind of high school ring." I rubbed my lips together. "Boy, oh boy! I am *parched*. Dunn, baby, I think we need to go find ourselves a drink. And maybe those little appetizer things with the cheese and the—"

"Wait, d'you mean a purity ring?" Parrish Partridge asked from my other side, leaning in to look at my hand while his husband held their daughter on his shoulders nearby. "I wore one of those back in high school. It was to let people know I wasn't gonna have *you know what*"—he glanced significantly at little Sadie and at his own daughter Marigold—"before marriage." He smirked. "'Course, back then it was easy to abstain since I didn't know how good it could be. Nowadays I could never, um..."

"Keep talking, baby," Diesel called.

Ryder ducked his head to laugh into Colin's shoulder and tried to pretend it was a cough.

Parrish's eyes went round, like his mind had finally caught up to his mouth. He looked back and forth between me and Dunn, then down at our rings, and his gaze took on a pitying cast. "I mean... no, that's... that's really cool. That's, like, a bold choice in this day and age. For both of you to, um, to not... *you know what*."

"They're not purity rings," Dunn bit out, pulling me against his side.

"No," Parrish agreed, clearly humoring him. "No, of course not. But if they *were*—"

"They're *not*," he insisted.

"—that would be so, so fine. And if you needed to talk about anything, either one of you," Parrish said kindly, since he was the world's sweetest human, "especially since you're kinda new to this, Dunn, Diesel and I would be happy to—"

"I'll have you know, we *you know what* like bunnies!" Dunn announced in his outdoor voice. "We *you know what* all the livelong day! I *you know whatted* him first thing in the morning, and Tuck *you know whatted* me before we left the house, and we're gonna *you know what* each other at the same time when we get home! It's *not* a ding-dang *purity ring*!"

Gracie, who'd been walking past with a plate of cake, stopped and blinked at her lunatic brother.

"So, then, what *is* it?" Ava Siegel waddled into the fray like the Don Corleone of the Licking Thicket Beautification Corps in a cornflower-blue, maternity-cut best-woman dress. Her poor ankles were swollen already, but her blonde ponytail, thicker and lusher than ever, swayed behind her. Her husband, Paul, stood at the edge of our rapidly expanding group looking every bit as satisfied as a man who'd gotten Miss Licking Thicket 2010 pregnant with *twins* could possibly look.

"Puff pastries!" I said, snapping my fingers. All eyes came to me, and I felt my face go hot. "Those cheesy appetizers I love so much! They're puff pastries. And Dunn, my darling, I insist that you right now come with me and get one. Or a dozen—"

"Hey! What's going on over here, party people?" Mal said cheerfully. One of his hands held a champagne glass, and the other was twined with Brooks's. "Dancing's about to start, and…"

"Dunn and Tucker are wearing *rings*," Ava pronounced.

My mouth opened and closed like a fish. "I… it… we…"

"Got engaged," Dunn said, shrugging sheepishly. "Tuck and I got engaged, darn it all. And we didn't wanna steal the limelight on your big day, Brooksy, so we were *trying* to keep it hush-hush. We haven't even told Mama yet."

"That was your first mistake," Ava said seriously. "But oh my gosh, give us all the details!"

"No. No, no. Nope. We're celebrating Brooks and Mal today," I said. "We'll talk about us later. We—"

"Tucker Wright," Brooks said in a deep voice that stopped my babbling. "If you think finding out my brother hooked the love of his life is gonna ruin our wedding, you're crazy."

"Nothing could," Mal said, grinning up at Brooks. "Besides, we wanna hear details too. Who asked who?"

I swallowed. "Well. I guess you could say it was, uh…" I motioned at Dunn, who shrugged.

"It was… it was kind of a…" He squinted. "A mutual… asking… situation?"

"More like a decision," I volunteered. "That we wanted to get married."

Everyone's eyes went wide, and I wondered what I'd said wrong.

And then a voice came from behind us, and I knew.

"You… are getting *married*?" Cindy Ann whispered exultantly. "Oh. My. Stars. My boys! I didn't know if this day would ever come!"

We barely had time to turn around before she tackle-hugged us.

"Tell me everything! Dunn, did you get down on one knee? Tucker, honey, are you thinking fall wedding? Did you get it on camera? Unless you were naked. I do *not* wanna see you naked. Oh, Red! Red! Come on, boys, let's find Red and tell him! We can announce the engagement to the whole town from right up on the stage!"

I gave Dunn wide eyes as his mother and Gracie pulled us across the floor and up the stairs to the little platform where the auctioneers stood during livestock auctions, which also happened to be the spot where they crowned Mr. and Ms. Licking Thicket every summer.

The irony was real.

"Do we really have to do this publicly?" I asked. "It's Brooks and Mal's wedding, and —"

"Nonsense. Non. Sense. They don't mind a whit! Now, y'all stay right here!" she whisper-hissed, leaving us behind the curtain. "I'm gonna find Red and get him to turn the mic back on and set everything up."

"Sure thing, Cindy Ann!" I said brightly. "Sounds *great*." But the second she departed, I turned to Dunn and whispered, "Baby, you've got to tell her."

"I *can't*. You tell her. She gave you her sweet tea recipe, just like she did with Mal, and she *still* won't give it to me or Brooks. She clearly likes you best."

"Not possible." I brushed the hair out of his eyes and pulled him toward me to kiss his forehead. "My husband is the sweetest and *most* lovable." I pressed a kiss to his lips. "Who wouldn't love him best? He's also the bravest. And most honest. And the handsomest. And sexiest. And he's totally gonna get mutually *you know whatted* when we get home. And—"

He sighed and wrapped his arms around my waist, tucking his face into my neck. "Fine. *Fine*! But I just don't know *how*. Am I just supposed to flat out say, 'Mama, Tucker and I aren't engaged, we already flew off to Vegas and got—"

The crowd gasped as the curtain flew open, and I tried to make Dunn hush, but it was too late.

"—married three days ago.'?"

I'd be willing to bet the only other time this barn had gotten that silent that fast was nearly twelve years ago, when Brooks Johnson had outed himself on a hot mic in front of the whole town.

It was kind of weirdly fitting that our story ended the same way.

"Uh." I turned to the crowd, held up my left hand, and said, "Surprise?"

Cindy Ann appeared directly below the stage, with Big Red Johnson by her side. "Do you mean to tell me," she yelled up, "that after spending three *years* unable to figure out how to get your acts together, you two've managed to get yourselves hitched in two months?"

I looked at Dunn.

He looked at me.

We wrapped our arms around each other's waists and nodded.

"Ha *ha*! Did I call it, or did I call it? All y'all better pony up!" she yelled triumphantly. "I done *told* you they'd be married by the Fourth of July, and every one of you took that bet! Now the town square's gonna have a new pergola come Lickin' time, thanks to Dunn and Tuck!"

Wait, what?

"Y'all oughta know by now not to bet against a Johnson woman knowing her own son!" Cindy Ann turned back to give us a wink. "And you *really* oughta know by now that here in the Thicket, every fool can find happiness, but only the smartest folks figure out how to keep it. Now, Red, get those fiddlers out here!"

Dunn clasped a hand over his eyes and laughed out loud. "Tucker? I'm not sure if my mama just called me smart or a fool."

"Well, whatever she called you, I guess I'm the same." I shook my head, mystified.

"Smart fools, then?" he teased. "No hyphen needed?"

I looked up at the man I loved, the man I'd married, the man who challenged me and teased me and made me better every single day. "Just plain fools," I told him softly.

Then I pulled him down and kissed the hell out of him, right in front of the whole town, because I would *always* be a fool for Dunn Johnson.

And I didn't mind that one bit.

WANT MORE LICKING THICKET ROMANCE?

Check out *Fakers* (Brooks and Mal's story), *Liars* (Diesel and Parrish's story), and *Flakes* (Ryder and Colin's story) which are available now!

You can also preorder Carter's story ***Hijacked***, part of the new Thicket Security series, coming in September 2021!

To find out the clues in the crossword, visit May's website or Lucy's website to download your own *Fools* Crossword Puzzle. The answers are in the back of the book.

A LETTER FROM LUCY & MAY

Dear Reader,

Thank you so much for reading *Fools*! If this is your first book by one of us and you'd like to read more, we suggest you start with *Fakers*, book one in the Licking Thicket series, or Lucy's *Borrowing Blue* and May's *The Date*.

We would love it if you would take a few minutes to review *Fools* on Amazon, GoodReads, or BookBub. Reader reviews really do make a difference and we appreciate every single one of them.

We've been friends and fans of each other's work for a couple of years, so we weren't surprised when writing our first collaboration went so smoothly. We were surprised, however, that it didn't end up being a standalone novel like we planned. The town of Licking Thicket stole our hearts and now we've turned a standalone into a series! Check out the rest of the Licking Thicket series on Amazon and stay tuned for the upcoming spin-off, Thicket Security.

The first book in Thicket Security is Carter's story, coming in September 2021! Needless to say, our favorite "heart doctor" will *not* be content to just settle down and fall in love in the Thicket. His path to love is going to be one heck of an adventure and we can't wait to bring it to you. Pre-order *Hijacked* today!

Be sure to follow Lucy and May on Amazon to be notified of new releases, and look for us on Facebook for sneak peeks of upcoming stories.

Feel free to sign up for our newsletters, stop by www.LucyLennox.com, www.MayArcher.com, or visit Lucy's Lair and Club May on Facebook to stay in touch.

To see fun inspiration photos for this book, check out the Pinterest page for Fools.

Happy reading!

Lucy & May

ALSO BY MAY ARCHER

Whispering Key Series

Off Plan (Whispering Key #1)

On the Run (Whispering Key #2)

Love in O'Leary Series

The Date (O'Leary #.5)

The Fall (O'Leary #1)

The Gift (O'Leary #2)

The Note (O'Leary 2.5)

The Secret (O'Leary #3)

The World (O'Leary #3.5)

The Fire (O'Leary #4)

The Night (O'Leary #5)

The Castle (O'Leary #5.5)

The Light (O'Leary #5.75)

The Way Home Series

ABOUT MAY ARCHER

May lives outside Boston. She spends her days raising three incredibly sarcastic children, finding inventive ways to drive her husband crazy, planning beach vacations, avoiding the gym, reading M/M romance, and occasionally writing it. She's also published several M/F romance titles as Maisy Archer.

For free content and the latest info on new releases, sign up for her newsletter at: https://www.subscribepage.com/MayArcher_News

Want to know what projects May has coming up? Check out her Facebook reader group Club May for give-aways, first-look cover reveals, and more.

You can also catch her on Bookbub, and check out her recommended reads!

ALSO BY LUCY LENNOX

Made Marian Series

Forever Wilde Series

Aster Valley Series

Virgin Flyer

Say You'll Be Nine

Twist of Fate Series with Sloane Kennedy

After Oscar Series with Molly Maddox

Licking Thicket Series with May Archer

Visit Lucy's website at www.LucyLennox.com for a
comprehensive list of titles, audio samples, freebies, suggested
reading order, and more!

ABOUT LUCY LENNOX

Lucy Lennox is the creator of the bestselling Made Marian, Forever Wilde, and Aster Valley series, and co-creator of the Twist of Fate Series with Sloane Kennedy, the After Oscar series with Molly Maddox, and the Licking Thicket series with May Archer. Born and raised in the southeast USA, she is finally putting good use to that English Lit degree.

Lucy enjoys naps, pizza, and procrastinating. She is married to someone who is better at math than romance but who makes her laugh every single day and is the best dancer in the history of ever.

She stays up way too late each night reading M/M romance because that stuff is impossible to put down.

For more information and to stay updated about future releases, please sign up for Lucy's author newsletter on her website or join her exciting reader group here: https://www.facebook.com/groups/lucyslair.

CROSSWORD PUZZLE ANSWERS

1. DELUSION
2. DOLT
3. VEXED
4. OBLIVIOUS
5. TOOL
6. HYPOCRITE
7. REVELATION
8. FLUMMOXED
9. YOLO
10. AWKWARD
11. CONFOUNDED
12. FLIRT
13. UNBALANCED
14. FUN
15. RECKONING
16. FRENEMY
17. SCHEME
18. DENOUEMENT
19. CONJUGAL